S.I.N: GLUTTONY

S.I.N. Gluttony

ISBN 10: 099122390X

ISBN 13: 978-0-9912239-0-9

Cover art by Makayla Romo

Printed in the United States of America

Dedicated to my Grandfather Walter Avery. He is without a doubt the greatest man I have ever known and I can only hope I can be a fraction of the man he was in life.

PROLOGUE

Jason Jacobs was insane. Stan Freason knew that now.

The two had made a lot of progress in the first few weeks after they met. Jason broke down barrier after barrier with Stan's guidance which, in turn, allowed Jason to accept that the past atrocities of his childhood were not his fault and eventually they worked to the point that Jason forgave his deceased parents for the years of constant abuse.

But one little event, one little bump in the road, was all it took for Jason to lose himself once again.

"Why didn't she forgive me Doctor Freason? Why?" Jason shouted. "You're going to tell me why she didn't forgive me and I am not going to fucking untie you until you do!"

Stan was held hostage in his own home. The single story, one bedroom and one bathroom home had become a prison; the windows in the darkened room looked like prison bars. The living room changed from a place of relaxation and calm to his own personal hell.

"I was getting better Doctor Freason. I was making progress wasn't I? What gives? Why didn't she take me back?" Jason cried again with choked gasps, punctuating his own duress. The kitchen knife trembling in his hand also helped damage Stan's own calm.

Stan would speak if he could. He was not at a loss for words but Jason had sealed his mouth with duct tape as well. *I'd talk if I could, Jason.*

Stan thought since he couldn't outright inform his former patient.

Jason was sweating profusely from his forehead and his armpits. His trembling hand was griping the handle of the kitchen knife for dear life as his words did most of the stabbing for now. "You said I was making progress Doc! You said I was getting better! You lied to me you son-of-a-bitch! This is your fault Stan. Everything happened tonight because you said I was okay!"

In spite of those words the tip of the knife was pressing against the naked flesh of Stan's chest. With every shout the tip of that knife was scraping skin which had Stan balancing between physical and emotional pain.

The harmonic sound of police sirens brought relief for the doctor but also a new set of problems. *Thank God! The neighbors must have heard the screaming.* Stan thought to himself as a fresh tear rolled down his eye.

"Great! Just wonderful! Someone called the fucking pigs on me! I thought you could handle me on your own Stan. I thought I was just a simple bi-polar case!" Jason said as he shifted himself behind Stan. "Don't think I don't know how the fuck this works."

The audible slam of two cop cars did not bring the emotional calm Stan hoped for. They also were not charging through the door like Stan thought they would.

Stan cried out through that duct tape but silenced himself when Jason pressed the knife against his chest enough to actually break the skin between his pectoral muscles. Jason planned for humiliation as well.

"Look at you. You're not even a man.; can't even grow chest hair you fucking pussy." He spat.

His fear was gripping him but the police were now pounding on the door. Stan pried a bit of tape from his mouth, "That's a bold claim from a mousey motherfucker like you!" That earned him a hard slap across his cheek from Jason's free hand.

"Shut the fuck up you worthless excuse for a shrink!"

That outburst of language from Jason was enough for the police to enter with probable cause. The solid wood frame of Stan's front door nearly shattered when the police kicked it in with guns drawn already.

"Police! Put your weapon down and step away!" The officer on the right shouted while they both stood their ground.

"Get the fuck out of here! This doesn't involve you fucking pricks. Me and the good doctor here were just having a civil fucking discussion of why he's so fucking terrible at his job!" It was another puncturing sting to his ego.

It was enough to cause Stan's head to begin swimming. His eyes narrowed on the guns that were in front of him just a yard or two away from him in that chair and the feel of cold steel from the kitchen knife was even closer. He was relieved that the blade was no longer on his chest but that was when he realized it was at his throat as well.

"Just shoot him!" Stan cried.

Instinct took over Stan's consciousness. The moment lasted forever and Stan didn't realize what he had done. For a few moments he felt weightless; like he was floating in space. In a desperate, subconscious bout for survival Stan had kicked his body back into Jason. The blade slid away from his throat as his head bashed into Jason's sternum.

The burning sensation Stan felt didn't register until after he had hit the ground. His arms felt crushed and his ears rang from the series of the gunshots the officers fired when he hit the ground.

1

Ryan McCallister was annoyed. This was nothing new for anyone that was acquainted with the man.

"We spent ten grand for this vacation and now we are going to have some wine country pricks slumming around us." Ryan said. He tossed his recently opened cell phone on the dashboard of his black Tahoe pick-up truck. "Fucking vampires, I knew I should have signed a damn contract or something."

"Would you just calm down Ryan? This trip isn't for you anyway, remember?" Maggie McCallister brushed a few strands of her rich, almost maroon locks of hair from her eyes. She was nearing her thirties like her husband but kept in shape just like he did. Ryan made sure of them.

Ryan rapped his fingers against the top of his steering wheel. "Yeah, I know, but it's the principle of the situation you know? This was supposed to be a nice, large home that overlooked the ocean and was suppose to be all relaxing and peaceful. What if these other people suck? I mean we gotta spend a week with them babe."

"It should be alright Ryan, I'm sure they are good people and if they are a bunch of ruffians I am sure you can set them straight. Unless, of course, they aren't keeping you firefighters in shape back home." A backseat voice of reason chimed out. The exotic tone was feminine and unmistakable from the back of the rumbling truck. "Maggie can help out too if she gets annoyed with them also!"

"Ryan knows about my temper well enough Jasmine. He doesn't need to be reminded of that." Maggie giggled. She turned her blue eyed, freckled gaze back towards the backseat. "You two just worry about enjoying your time out here. I've always had your back sis, even if you're the hotter one between us."

"That's up for debate." Ryan said.

"Well don't you just want to get your brownie points in with the wife?" Jasmine teased. Her green eyes pierced the rearview mirror to distract Ryan but he did not waver. "That is a good idea though Ryan, I remember when I was first adopted by mom and dad Maggie showed off her rough side with any boys that bothered me. Oh my God do you remember Bobby Mannaghan? You made him wet his pants the first day of middle school!"

Maggie cackled at the memory. "Well he did make fun of your scar Jazz. You know that is a trigger for me."

"Yeah but in this day and age it doesn't bother me anymore. I'm a big girl now, I may have lost my birth parents to that drunken asshole but you, mom, and dad were more than I could ever hope for." Jasmine did use that rearview mirror to fix her shoulder length black hair before her well manicured hand laid across the thigh of the fourth passenger.

Ryan peered into the rearview mirror to those in the backseat. "Alright I get what you mean. Family takes care of each other. Doesn't hurt when you've got an Egyptian Goddess for a wife does it Stan?"

Stan wasn't paying attention to Ryan at all. The twisted face of Jason Jacobs haunted Stan for the last three months. He was lucky to be alive but that night ensured he had physical and emotional reminders of the night and the painful hospital visits afterwards. He sometimes had a horrible time even climbing out of bed in the morning despite how many months had passed.

"Thinking hard again baby?" Jasmine squeezed his leg gently and always seemed to know what was going on in his head.

"Not really." Stan's eyes were focused on the rows of trees they were passing by. "The trees tend to get hypnotic after you stare at them for a while," he lied, kind of."

Ryan sighed as he drove down the road. "Oh and apparently these pricks are sending a baby sitter from their company to ensure that everything goes smooth. If you ask me I don't think some fruitcake businessman is going to be much help to us if we are bunking with Charles Manson."

The resounding slap to the back of Ryan's head echoed through the truck. "Ryan McCallister do you even have a filter? How stupid are you?" Maggie roared.

The physical assault generated a tug at the corner of Stan's mouth.

Jasmine's hand found her husband's and gave it a reassuring squeeze. "Did I just see a smile? Maggie, keep abusing Ryan."

"Hey! I'm the one driving here. Keep pushing me woman; I'm dying to turn this car around." Ryan protested.

Maggie gave a proud shake of her head and crossed her arms over her modest chest. "That just means that instead of sitting next to me for the next fifteen minutes or so we'll have to be next to each other for another hour or two." An elbow pegged Ryan's bicep soon after.

Ryan's agitated growling brought another smile to Stan. "We're men Ryan. We can take the punishment. Especially you, you are a brick wall after all."

"I know Stan. I just gotta let her keep beating on me to think she has some sort of control in our relationship. I got to keep my short hair for a few punches to the chest. "

Maggie huffed. "I just thought you'd look good in longer hair, that's all. Nice and thick and brown."

"Maggie . . . I am a firefighter. An actual one, compared to the other guys I'm a freaking Fabio. Count your blessings."

The scuffles between the two seemed to end in her favor more often than not but he had her this time around. "Score one for the short haired males." Stan made a line with his finger.

The massive span of forest road they had traveled for nearly two hours finally broke as the pick-up drifted to a halt.

Stan guessed that the large, black, iron bars of the gate in front of them were as thick as his own leg and the barricade spanned the length of two vehicle lanes. The gate connected to the forest by huge brick walls that stretched forever into the woods around them. Stan figured the wall didn't reach for miles but he also could not see anything past twenty yards of where they sat in the road. "They really didn't skimp on the square miles for this place to sit on."

Past the barrier that separated the group laid a large stretch of smooth, green land with a winding pavement pathway that ended at the luxurious vacation home they were going to stay at for at least a week. The mansion was large even from the football field and a half distance away. "Look at how gigantic that place is. I think there has to be like twenty-four rooms or something like that just from the twelve sets of windows I see in the front." Maggie said while everyone simultaneously gazed at the structure. "Hurry up and buzz us in sweetie, I want to see this place up close." She pestered Ryan.

On their left side a steel pedestal sat. It was a heavy duty column that had been cemented into the ground to prevent most vehicles from knocking it over in the event that they did not see the large reflective panel on the side of the column. At the top of the pedestal sat a plastic, black plate; a tiny red light stared at Ryan while he rolled his window down. He unbuckled his seatbelt and reached his hand into his back pocket. He was grasping at nothing but his own ass at that point.

"Don't tell me that you left your wallet at the last gas station or something." Maggie whined.

Ryan replied by shaking his head, "No, it's in the back. I probably slapped it in a suitcase or something for safe keeping. Hold your horses." He kept the truck running and hopped out. The cramp in his legs from driving all that time began relieving itself when he started stretching right outside of the vehicle. "Christ this feels good. You've drained the youth out of me Maggie. I feel like a cripple." He teased.

"Don't blame me sugar. I don't recall making you sit on your ass and watch Sports Center all weekend long."

Ryan feigned annoyance and left his door wide open. As he rounded the back Stan decided that he needed a stretch as well and popped out of the vehicle moments after Ryan did. When he ventured back Ryan lowered the hatchback.

"Feeling alright?"

"Yeah, I'm doing alright. I guess a vacation for me and Jazz has been overdue. I appreciate the both of you chipping in on this, I mean it. I think I might have needed this more than I thought. I'm already starting to feel more relaxed in the last hour than I have for the past three months."

Ryan cocked a smile. "Don't mention it. You're my brother by marriage after all. Also, and don't mention this to Maggie, but if everything goes well for us here I'm taking her somewhere damn nice next year. I'm talking international incident type of proper getaway you know?" The Irishman said while reaching into the back of his truck. He dug through the dozen suitcases that were piled against one another. With a grunt his fingers curled around a burlap bag that had been tied shut.

When the bag was opened Stan got a glimpse of several toiletries Ryan had packed with them. He was surprised to see that it was mostly comprised of condoms. "Were you thinking something tropical or something like a spiritual journey?"

"Yeah, Maggs and I are converting to Buddhism. Reach nirvana and all that shit!" He said while yanking out his wallet. "Damn things always find their way to the bottom of whatever it's in. Anyway I don't know at this point. If we do tropical we'll have to pack a shit load of sunscreen."

"What about a trip back to the motherland?"

Ryan was confused. "You mean get back to our similar roots? I mean I have Irish ancestry in me but Maggs has never told me if she's Scottish or Irish. Fifty-fifty aren't good enough odds for me to take if it ends up pissing her off." He laughed. He haphazardly tossed the burlap sack into the truck bed. He slammed the hatchback shut without worrying about anything falling out.

A second later there was a rustling sound that emanated from the left side of the forest. Stan shifted and looked over Ryan's shoulder to see if it was anything worth worrying about.

Ryan looked over his own shoulder and offered a shrug. "Well, Stan, if we get too bored maybe they have some BB guns and we can go squirrel hunting."

2

Jasmine was fully wedged between Ryan and Maggie's seat. She finally got a glimpse of the clear blue sky after they managed to scan their way past the bulky gate. She gasped.

"Well son-of-a-bitch," Ryan began, "I guess the brochure wasn't bullshitting us after all."

Calling the timeshare a mansion was a bit of an understatement. In terms of sheer size it was more like a castle. The building itself was two stories high and about as long as any stadium. The windows were well sculpted and had an arch to them at the top of each glass and wood design and the mansion itself sat in a proud brown color which looked recently coated. The roof itself was slopped, forcing the top of the building into an almost church-like, steeple design.

"Damn. This was only a grand for a week? Seems like a bargain to me. Then again this is completely and utterly out of the way so I wonder if that covers food and entertainment." Stan wondered.

There were about a dozen trees peppering the front landscape while the group traveled up the pathway to the large parking lot. "Looks like we will have a good amount of shade if I want to just lie out and read. Jasmine can work on her tan. Not that she needs to of course." Maggie said.

"Just the way I was built sis. You know I'd kill for curls. The red would just not fit well with my own hair." Jasmine pointed out. She knew that Maggie had some insecurity but they were always very close. Almost inseparable from the day they met.

Ryan huffed. "Fuck it we're all going to get some sun. I sure as hell ain't going to stay cooped up in this gigantic place. I suppose it was asinine to think that we would have something this large all to ourselves. The brochure made it seem smaller though. Hell I'll take it." He said before he was smashed against his driver side window. Jasmine was almost entirely in the front seat at that point. She was ecstatic and pointing

"Oh my God! Stan, they have one of those wrap around fountains. You know this place is high class when they have something like that right in front of the house! I love it!"

Maggie joined in with the feminine aesthetics of the fountain. "Look Ryan; it has cupids or cherubs or whatever peeing into the fountain. That's adorable. This actually was a steal; I really hope the inside isn't shitty."

"The chances of this place having a panic room for men seems to be dwindling Stan. Every bedroom is going to have nothing but bubble baths and rose petals decorating every square foot." Ryan sighed.

Stan offered a shrug, "It isn't that bad. It has to have something for everyone right? This place probably has a well stacked bar and some sort of game room I'd imagine. I'd hate to think the entire place was filled with teddy bears and chocolates."

"Never mind that shit; I would love for teddy bears and chocolates to be decorated all over the fucking place!" Maggie squealed.
"Ah Christ she is getting excited. The swear words are coming out like commas." Ryan said while pulling into the empty parking lot. "There's a silver lining to say the least; we are the first one's here. Maybe that means that we won't be seeing many other people after all."

"You'd think that someone would have made it here before us. We didn't leave until noon and it's almost four o'clock right now. Sundown will be in a couple hours I imagine." Maggie said as Ryan killed the engine.

Jasmine jumped from the backseat of the pick-up truck in a flash. Her feet were covered by simple sandals while her body was covered in a purple sundress that went down to her calves. "Whatever! Stan and I are calling any room that has a waterbed in it. I haven't slept in one of those for ages and this place looks old enough to have one! Did they mention any themed rooms or anything like that? You know, like a lover's suite or a beach scene?"

Ryan cracked his door open after unbuckling and stepped out in a pair of cowboy boots and blue jeans that went with his tan, plaid button up. "They didn't mention any specifics to the rooms themselves. I'm sure they are all fancy to some degree and if they aren't then I am liable to strangle someone. Seriously, this place better blow my mind if they don't want me throwing a bitch fit when the week is up."

"Can I get a few lawn chairs lined up for said bitch-fest next week?" Stan asked as he removed himself from the pick-up truck and felt a gentle breeze rolling over him. He was in a pair of black Nike's and blue jeans as well with a plain black t-shirt. When he came around the vehicle to join Jasmine and Ryan he noticed the stretch of land behind the mansion and the sudden drop off. "Damn, this is a cliff side establishment. No fences either, that isn't safe."

Maggie blew between her lips when she came around in her white blouse and cream skirt, "Oh please. Look at how far it is from the back of the house. You'd have to be drunk, blind and deaf to have an accident way out there," she pointed out and bumped her hips against Ryan's, "Or piss off your wife enough. That works too." She smiled.

"I think that is my wife's subtle way of suggesting that we carry the heavy load Stan." Ryan said and he was thankful that the front of the home was not too long of a walk, but with everything they had to carry it was still a chore to get to that front entrance. Despite the challenge ahead Ryan opened the hatchback and he and Stan managed to bring everything they had in one trip.

"Good job boys. We'll forgive you for the smaller bags we got." Maggie taunted.

When the party found themselves walking up the stairs the two massive oak doors that greeted them began opening of their own will. As they opened further someone stepped through and onto the front step.

The group paused halfway up the steps when the middle aged man came through the entrance. He was dressed in a white suit and his balding features distracted from the bright smile he had upon seeing them. His clear, green eyes had a piercing quality that sharply studied each person momentarily.

"Welcome! You must be the Freason and the McCallister family, no?" The French accent came thick along with his mannerisms. "Please come in and let me help you with your bags! My name is Jacque Collo. On Behalf of 'Fantasia Getaways' I welcome you all!" He said with his arms stretched out wide.

"Who hired the cartoon?" Ryan whispered to Maggie before stepping forward. "Well thank you for that but also you may want to inform your boss that we were told that we were going to be alone for this getaway but not even thirty minutes ago we were told that we're not going to be alone. As you can imagine that was a rather big kink in our plans." Ryan explained while he held onto the bags in his hands.

Jacque's brow rose slightly but he kept that same enthusiasm to his features while the two married couples piled into the home and placed their bags on the ground for a quick reprieve. "Ah yes! Unfortunately due to weather complications we had to re-schedule a few vacation time slots. I apologize but I assure you all that if it were just yourselves in this home that things would have been painfully quiet. There is plenty to enjoy, but being a bit social just adds onto the experience!"

"What about the people who enjoy the quiet and those who are completely anti-social? I happen to be a fan of both those things by the way." Ryan said but was shoved forward a bit by his darling wife.

Ignore him Mister Collo. I am afraid my husband can be a bit of a man-child sometimes . . . most of the time . . . all of the time actually." She puffed, blowing a strand of her bangs from her eyes.

Stan hoisted both his and his wife's bags up once more and offered a faint smile. "I said it was alright in the truck Ryan," he paused and turned to Jacque, "Though if they are available, are there any rooms that would be a bit distant from the other people vacationing?"

Jacque was quick to nod his head, "Of course! This mansion used to serve as a hotel of sorts decades ago. Its previous owner was a recluse and when he passed his younger brother turned it into a vacation home about ten years ago. It has turned quite a profit."

The four of them were relieved when the apparent butler of the establishment took a few bags himself.

Ryan's defeated sigh carried between them all. "Alright Jackie, lead the way."

Jacque led the four of them to the second floor of the cliff-side escape and stood right in the middle of the hallway. "Here at the 'Fantasia' mansion there are ten rooms in four wings of the second floor. That means forty rooms in all. I believe, off the top of my head, there are ten more people that will be staying with us. I know there will be at least three groups consisting of more than one person and then the final odd one out is just here for their own pleasure and relaxation. So you do not have to worry about anyone being too loud as I do not think everyone is going to be staying in just one wing, even though it would have been easier on me I will carry that burden without complaint!"

"Well I do not think we will have any troubles Mister Collo but," Jasmine paused, "Do you by any chance have a room that has a water bed or something that is themed?"

A broad smile graced Jacque's lips as he said nothing and pointed to the room that was behind Jasmine and to her left.

"No freaking way!" She cried out. She turned and crashed through the door and squealed. Stan smiled and followed her inside.

Stan dragged every bag they had into the room while Jasmine squealed with excitement. She was a kid in a candy store and the small bags she had were strewn across the room already as her sandals were kicked off during a short, frantic dance towards the water bed. She dove on the bed and messed the satin sheets as she rolled about on the water bed.

"I am glad the Missus approves." Jacque said as Jasmine's sounds of excitement carried into the hallway.

Maggie agreed. "She always has been the one that can find happiness in the simplest of things. She grows on people fast. Trust me."

Ryan noticed that they were still the only ones who had shown up so far. "So is everyone supposed to arrive tonight or will we be having some stragglers coming in tomorrow? I mean I imagine there is a tour of this place, or at least I would hope so considering how gigantic and fabulous this place is. It actually is. Ask Maggie. I never use the word 'fabulous' to describe something that doesn't impress me."

Maggie nodded.

"Naturally Mister McCallister. I would like to begin the tour in a few hours before the sun goes down. If the sun begins setting then I believe we will start with the back yard amenities. Do not worry, however, as if I ever had a tour that started on time I would consider myself truly blessed. I can handle a good crowd even if things start off a little late."

Maggie found Jacque charming. "I cannot even imagine trying to run a tour with people showing up late and uncoordinated. I can't figure out how a person could keep such a happy disposition as you do Mister Collo."

Jacque's laugh permeated the halls and the Frenchman shook his head. "Oh my dear, when you do this job as long as I have it becomes second nature. I am very, very good at what I do and I assure you that you all are in very capable hands. Speaking of which go ahead and take any room you wish. Consider it a gift for being the first to arrive."

Maggie knocked on Stan and Jasmine's room. "We are going to go and find our own room. We'll see you guys when the other guests start to arrive." She hollered through the door.

"Alright Maggs! Be good!" Jasmine called out as she sat up on the bed fully. She turned her attention towards Stan as her lips curled into a sinister grin. "Honey? Lock the door." She giggled and Stan had no choice but to comply after he got the bags situated.

As Stan approached the bed she scooted to the edge and let her slender legs hang over the edge where her toes nearly touched. Her legs ran for miles even in a sun dress. She looked to her husband's face and saw heavy his eyelids looked. Stan was smiling but she saw through that.

"You put up a good show there sweetie. I've known you long enough to know that you're not doing too well. Is it the depression or are you anxious Stan?"

Stan stood in front of her and let his fingers run through her straight black hair. "Am I that easy to read? I'm sorry Jazz. This place is amazing but meeting new people is still a bit hard for me. Though I am doing okay, I promise. I actually am impressed and looking forward to this."

Jasmine smiled as her own hands found their way to his hips and her fingers curled around his unused belt loops. "I love you Stan. This is going to be great for us. You're doing amazing and just remember to stay out of your own head for the trip." She broke eye contact from him and let her eyes travel downward. "And if you can't," she hummed and allowed her fingers to pluck his blue jeans open, "Then I will have to make you."

3

"Well this family vacation is off to a great start dad." Mark Sinfield sighed as he stood on the side of the road with his hand held gaming system in hand. The agonized sound of soldiers getting shot echoed out in the open. "We have a spare don't we?" His brown eyes did not leave the screen of his game.

Peter Sinfield wiped the sweat from his brow with a handkerchief. "Of course we do Mark. Could you go ahead and give me and your brother a hand while we lower it from the back? If it doesn't interrupt your game of course, would hate for you to get distracted." After wiping the sweat from his forehead the red sport's cap he had in his hand went back to covering the receding hairline that Mark had to look forward to when he reached his dad's age.

"Yeah Mark, put the stupid game down and give us a hand already!" His younger brother Daniel protested as well and pushed his black, horn-rimmed glasses up the bridge of his nose.

Stacy Sinfield piled out of the car and fanned herself off with her notebook that she had been writing in. She moved behind her husband and rubbed his shoulders. "I'll help out. I've changed a few tires in my life. Though this would be a good learning experience for you Mark, this will happen to you someday. You've only been driving with a permit for a year. God knows how terrifying that experience was in general." His mother teased.

"Well to be fair I don't want to scrape my knees up trying to get the tire on. I wasn't planning on the tire blowing halfway to this 'vacation home'. I'll turn the lug nuts or whatever but I ain't getting on my knees." Mark reasoned.

Daniel just rolled his eyes as his brother used his blue jean shorts as an excuse as to why he couldn't help with the heavy lifting. "You're buying me a new car when I'm old enough to drive right dad? I mean clearly I'll be better off taking care of it than Mark is and his beater."

"I'll beat you."

Peter sighed and shifted around the S.U.V. He adjusted his own glasses for the moment that hid his pale, blue eyes and found the crank to lower the tire. He churned the steel rod until the spare tire could be pulled free from the hidden compartment underneath the vehicle. "We'll see Daniel. Helping your father and mother change a tire isn't really worth a huge reward but we'll keep this in mind come Christmas."

"Mark, sweetie, how do you expect to become as strong as your father if all you do is play those video games? At least help your brother out with positioning the jack." Stacy sighed.

Mark gave in and placed his gaming device in the backseat of the car and slammed the door. He reached for the car jack and grabbed it from his brother and yanked it across the pavement by the handle. It wheeled along with little resistance. "I don't need to bench press a bus mom," he whined. "I'm one test away from my black belt. I would say I'm much more capable of being strong than dip wad here."

"Fuck you Mark; I'm not helping you with English or Spanish anymore."

"Daniel! Watch your mouth." Peter said. He rolled the tire over towards his younger son and gave him a pat on his shaggy, blonde hair. "Come on now. The sooner we get this tire in place the sooner we can get to this mansion. Your mother has been dreaming of this vacation for the last year so how about you two stop your bickering and work together for once? You both are talented at different things and if you two would actually use that to your advantage I am sure you could accomplish some damn good things." Peter scolded.

"We are working together dad. Daniel just doesn't know when to shut it." Mark said. He positioned the jack underneath the S.U.V to the point it would catch on the frame. He had to wiggle it around a bit and squat but he was lifting the car in a matter of moments. "See? I know how to jack up a car. I'm contributing to this family fun time!" The sarcasm oozed.

Stacy took her husband by the arm and pulled him behind to watch the two teenagers work. "Let them do this on their own. I am sure they can do it." She whispered. Her head touched her husband's shoulder as the boys began their work.

Peter wanted to get to the mansion as soon as possible but listened to his wife more often than he wished to admit. "Yes ma'am." As her head touched his shoulder he looked down to the slight amount of crow's feet that gathered near the corners of his eyes. "This is why we had kids anyway right? Get them doing the work while we relax?" He asked. He played it straight without laughing.

"I heard that dad. That's why we have child labor laws now." Daniel said. He was looking at the tire iron like it was a foreign object.

Peter's eyes narrowed. "I told you we started reading to Daniel too soon. He's too smart for his own good. Takes after his mother" he jested. Stacy jabbed him in the side with a smile.

"We've got a good couple of boys dear."

"Two sides of the same coin I would say. They balance each other out."

Mark snagged the tire iron away from Daniel and looked at his younger brother. "I'm going to smack you with this. Complain about me not doing any work and here I am doing everything." He chastised his younger brother and began loosening the first lug nut.

"Remember to go to opposite ends. Don't just go in a circle."

"I know dad. I'm not an idiot."

"Just addicted to video games right?"

"Whatever." Mark began going from lug nut to lug nut until they were all loose enough that they could be twisted free by hand. He did so and handed them to his father for safe keeping but also caught something out of the corner of his eye. Off in the distance a red corvette was speeding towards the family and their S.U.V. Mark's eyes lit up and his mouth turned into a grin while he walked out behind their family vehicle and began flagging the speeding car down.

The endless line of trees had been nothing but a blur to Clark Thompson as the wind whipped through his shoulder length blonde hair. His sandaled foot hung out of the passenger side vehicle as the music drowned out every ounce of sound either he, or the driver, could make in that moment of time. Clark's white tank top rustled against shaven chest as he let his body melt into the seat. It was a beautiful day and a beautiful occasion.

"Would you get your foot back in the car before you lose it on a stray branch or some shit? Clark? Clark!"

Clark was too busy paying attention to the music and the wind than the sound of the man's voice next to him. It was his time for relaxation and he was enjoying it to the fullest. He was until the music was shut off. "Hey! I like that song." He protested as he shifted his bare leg into the car and sat up straight. "Come on, this is our time to relax! You can go ahead and let that hard ass of yours slide now. You're in a safe place Fred. We've got a brand new car, a brand new home, and we're going to be staying at a freaking mansion all week long. We did it. This is a time for celebrating!"

Fred caved like he always did and turned the volume up by just a little. It was enough so that they could listen to the local pop station and yet still hold a conversation. "Yeah, I know we did. Against all odds and all that jazz but I guess I am still just blown away by it all." He said as he looked at the silver brand on his ring finger. "It's making me dizzy I think."

Clark laughed. "The big, burly mountain man in the relationship is getting dizzy and giddy over our most recent soiree? Are you sure I'm supposed to be the girl in this relationship? Should I grow the beard and

start chopping wood?"

"Only you could turn a week of being married into a domestic violence dispute Clark. I swear to God." Fred Thompson said while his foot was pressed hard against the pedal of his very new, and very polished red Corvette. "You can push anyone's buttons harder than any man I have ever met. I guess that is why I like you so much. I think." Fred contemplated that thought with a few strokes of his thick, full brown beard.

"I wish you would just shave that damn thing off. The ZZ top look only works well when you're, well, not being a real life embodiment of a paper towel company mascot, flannel and all." Clark plucked the short sleeved shirt Fred was wearing. "You should let me dress you. I'm serious. We could get you well groomed and maybe then you can earn a promotion at the plant." He encouraged.

"You know my boss hates *our* kind. I'm really surprised he has not come up with some bullshit reason to fire my ass. I'm even doubly surprised that he allowed me to have a week's vacation. The guy is a douchebag but I put up the 'kiss-ass' persona up well enough I suppose. That or he knows that if he fired me because of my personal life choices that he would have such a gigantic lawsuit on his ass he wouldn't be able to sit down for a decade. Now I kind of wish he had been a stupid jackass about me and you." It had been hard enough on Fred when his co-workers had found out about his orientation.

Clark rolled his eyes before his leg propped itself on the dashboard for comfort. "Let me at him for like ten minutes. I'll get you a promotion and we'll be able to take vacations like this at least twice a year then instead of once. I'm doing it. My mind is made up." Clark was stubborn when it came to those who didn't like what he and Fred represented. "Bigoted assholes; they need to get with the times and realize we're not going anywhere and that we are people too."

"Well we do have these Clark," Fred waved his ring finger around a few times, "So I would like to think that more people like us than hate us."

"Do you ever get sick of being right?" Clark asked. He took his attention to the passing trees that were whipping by. The forest around them was thick and the smell of pine and spruce permeated the air that flowed easily through Clark's open window. "I'm guessing that you don't but I really don't care. Slow down a bit, this scenery is amazing."

"That's awfully uncharacteristic of you Clark. I didn't think you enjoyed the outdoors. Anytime I actually bring up a cabin getaway you shot it down." Fred said.

Clark shrugged his shoulders and took a huge intake of the smell of the forest around them while they drove. "Maybe I was wrong or I like nature when it is actually impressive and . . . grand. This area is making me actually feel small. Not in a bad way of course but it feels untouched, you know what I mean? Shit I haven't even seen one downed tree or a branch really. It's like the nature around here respects itself; uncorrupted by men and their machines. It's so beautiful."

Fred's massive hand reached over to squeeze his husband's shoulder firmly. "When in the flying hell did you become an environmentalist?"

Clark turned his blue eyes away from the road back to look his partner dead in his pristine green gaze, "I guess I am maturing. Marriage must do that to a person. I haven't felt this high in forever Fred. I guess I am just as dizzy as you are with all of this. Sorry for giving you shit."

"You keep me on my toes. Hell I think your shit giving is why I married you." He smiled and squeezed Clark's arm.

Clark returned the squeeze by taking Fred's factory hat from his head, exposing the short, nearly buzzed hair that clashed with the bushiness of his beard. "You know you wouldn't have to wear this God awful tacky hat if you actually grew your hair out." Clark said. He placed the cap on his own head to cover those blonde locks.

Fred returned his eyes to the road and hit the pedal to the floor again to speed towards their destination. After a few more minutes of karaoke from the local pop station Fred slowed the vehicle once again and turned the music off, much to the protesting of Clark who tipped the bill of the cap up to scold Fred once again.

"What the hell is it now?"

Fred pointed up the road to where a single vehicle was pulled over to the side of the road. "Check it out. I think people are having vehicle problems." Fred said while he pointed. "We should probably stop by and help out; chances are these people are going exactly where we are if this road doesn't fork at some point."

As they drew closer they saw one of the four near the white S.U.V was waving their hands back and forth in wide draws. "Well it would be rude to just leave them. Looks like a family Fred. Try not to act too gay." Clark said as Fred pulled up behind the vehicle.

"You're such a dick, Clark."

4

Earlier that day, and nearly four hundred miles away in the same town that 'Fantasia Getaways' was located, Oswald Matthews fell out of his motel bed. He grunted as his back landed on an empty bottle of vodka and, like an angered bear, slapped the bottle away from his sore body to have it shatter against the nearby wall.

"What the fuck?" A woman still in his bed groaned.

Oswald lay on the dirty motel floor while gathering his thoughts for the day. "Never drinking that much again. At least I think I drank that much last night. You didn't fucking drug me did you? No, probably not. I'd be missing my wallet and you if you had. I also would have found you and beat the shit out of you." He didn't know the woman he had spent the night with. She was a young, attractive female that was free of charge.

The young woman shifted from the bed and put her bare feet on the ground. She drug several fingers through her pixie cut, pink, green, and blonde hair and flicked it around a bit while she wrapped the bed sheet around her petite form. "Last night was fun and all but you got a piss poor attitude buddy." She spat.

"Don't even give me that bullshit that you regret what we did last night. Didn't you say I was your daddy and I didn't even ask? You're the one with issues." Oswald fired back as he gripped the sheet she was in while she walked on by; giving it a hard tug to take what modesty she had away. "Don't be shy; I've seen you inside and out. Ain't nothing to be ashamed about there." He said with a thick southern accent.

The woman was mortified. She shrieked and covered her body up with her hands the best she could although to Oswald's amusement her small body had some large assets to it. "You pig! I bet you're just some jackass from Texas. It sounds like it!" She huffed. Oswald laughed. Her eyes were glued on him and that sheet.

"Don't be judging me darlin'. I just wanted a free show before I go. Shake your little ass out of my room. I'm late for my vacation." With the sheet still gripped in his hand he stood up and exposed himself completely to the woman with the stature and confidence of someone overtly proud of themselves. "You know it's hard to imagine I'm such a bad guy when you're biting your bottom lip like that."

The young woman didn't realize she had been gawking at him and stomped her foot on the ground. "Shut up! Sure last night was fun but I'm not making that mistake again. I guarantee that!" She said as she tried to gather up whatever underwear and clothing she could find as quickly as she could.

"I think that makes you the tenth or twentieth girl this year that has proclaimed that a guy like me won't be her next mistake the next week. That plan never seems to work does it?"

Her face was beat red from embarrassment but now it was building to an even darker red as her anger grew.

Oswald put his hands up to try and defuse the budding anger inside her. As he did the twin chains and dog tags around his neck jingled. "Okay. Okay. Calm down. I'm a jackass and you're just a sweet, innocent girl that had one too many drinks last night." He said. Oswald lowered his hands and took a few steps towards the much younger woman. "That doesn't mean we have to part ways on bad terms darlin'. I'll admit I had some biased. I have woken up with my wallet gone and that was my mistake for projecting onto you." He winked.

Biting her lower lip again was a sure sign that his sauntering was something she enjoyed. "Well . . . you were kind of charming, I think. At least I remember you were charming. I know we are both probably hung over too so okay, I forgive you."

Oswald's attention lowered from her blue eyes down to her arm. She dug her nails into her flesh, scratching deep. "Listen, you're a sweet girl and last night was fun but I want to make sure when I roll through here again that you're around that same bar I picked you up at last night. I know the I.D. you had was a fake but I've seen that scratching before in my days. Knock that shit off alright? I don't like hanging out with coke heads."

"Hey! Just because you're as old as my dad doesn't mean you get to scold me like one." She was on the defensive.

Oswald took her by the arms, slammed her against the wall, and ignored her surprised yelp. His brown eyes narrowed while hers shut tight. "I've seen shit you wouldn't even see in your most drug addled fucking nightmares darlin'. I didn't risk my life and limb so I could come back to a country where a cute little bitch goes ahead and snorts her pain away. You're lucky I don't see any track lines. I'd haul your ass into the local law myself. I loathe drug users. They turn to a needle, or a line, or a joint to get away from how terrible life is. Shit you have a bed to sleep on. I've seen little kid's necks get slashed wide open for just playing in the street."

"Get away from me you psycho!" The blonde screamed and did her best to push away from Oswald's tight grip. He wasn't letting her go.

"That's the problem with women today. They want freedom off the backs of patriotic men who sacrifice all they have to do whatever they want without consequences. It's the same story over and over again." His grip wavered on her arms for a moment before he turned his body and tossed her towards the bed. "At least give me ten minutes before you run out of here screaming that you were raped."

The naked twenty year-old landed on the bed. She trembled and looked back at Oswald after she tried to cover herself with the clothes in her hands. "You're an asshole. You don't know me; you don't know who I am or what I've went through!" She cried. She did her best to slip her clothes back on one piece at a time but she was too jittery to do so.

Oswald heard the tired stories over and over. He was sick of them. "You're right, I don't. I've heard similar stories left and right. So how about you get dressed and I'll drop you off at some detox place and you can try and get your shit together so you don't wind up in bed next weekend with another asshole just like me? Does that sound like something you would actually be thankful for or are you just going to be a pissy little bitch and cry more about how life is so very, very hard?"

Twenty minutes later Oswald Matthews slammed the door to his black Jeep and let it rumble to life. His bags were piled in the back.

"Disrespectful little whore; didn't have the time to take her ass anywhere anyway." He muttered and started on his way towards the near grand he spent for a relaxing cliff-side vacation.

5

James Newberry was inches away from slapping his best friend for the first time in his life. He drummed his fingers against the wheel of the beat up station wagon that held up, as surprising as it was, for the duration of this trip. Nothing was exploding in it. He turned his attention from the fuel gage which was near the halfway marker to the book in Jimmy Franklin's lap.

"We finally get a chance to 'party down' as you put it Jimmy and you've got your damn nose in a book. You're really helping the three of us break out of that geeky mold you know that?"

Jimmy took his middle finger and pressed it against the bridge of his glasses to adjust them a bit and made sure that the full force of that middle finger was directed towards James. "Dude, it's just a book. I'm not driving and I don't feel like sleeping." Jimmy defended himself, "Who the hell cares if we geek out in this place anyway? I mean we might find some people to play some of our role playing games. Don't be a closet geek James. You're just lying to yourself about who you are and it will look very, very sad. Besides if there are any girls here they might like your fencing." Jimmy laughed.

The commotion of arguing geeks woke Kimberly Cross from the backseat. She stretched her arms and yawned, "I didn't know you took fencing lessons James."

James adjusted the rearview mirror for a moment and captured the beauty that was Kimberly Cross. Blonde hair down to her ass, emerald eyes that still took his breath away and a figure that screamed potential model had him stammering. "I-I did. Years ago before we met you. Granted the only time I have been able to show off was during some live action role play but you haven't had a chance to get into that yet. Also screw you Jimmy, that purple satin shirt or whatever isn't going to impress any women that will be here." His eyes watched Kimberly smile while he drove down the forest lined road.

"I'm impressed by your shirt. Don't let James bully you."

"James couldn't bully me with Rick Steller's balls. I still can't believe you dated that loser Kimberly. We forgive you though." Jimmy laughed.

James let that comment slide. He did not want to get into that horrific three weeks. "You've known us for about a year and a half now Kim? You know he's like my little brother; my idiotic little brother who can't keep his mouth shut."

"I'm older than you, bro."

"See what the hell I mean?" James asked Kimberly and watched her as she tried to stifle a laugh. "You might be older but I'm bigger. Remember that the next time you want to try and kill off my barbarian who could decimate a group of rat men." James threatened as the station wagon pulled up to a large, black gate with gigantic brick walls stretching out from it on both sides. James peered forward with his jaw dropping, "Holy shit."

"Oh my God," Kimberly gasped, "This place is freaking huge!"

Jimmy closed the supernatural book he was reading and rolled his eyes past his glasses while his chin lifted. "Damn! Okay you're going to be my travel agent from now on James. This is brilliant." He mused.

James turned to his friend and nudged him with his elbow. "I told you the brochure was playing it down. Also you're not British. Stop trying to be. You're just a white boy from Philadelphia. Though I'll admit this place looks brilliant," he laughed.

"Hurry up James! We need to get in and explore this place!" Kimberly squealed.

James smiled into the rearview mirror. "Well I'm happy that you're impressed Kimberly. I know you've been stressed out at school with everything that happened so that is why me and Jimmy put this together." It was something they hadn't admitted until now.

Kimberly's lips grew tight when he mentioned that. "Wait . . . how much did this actually cost to bring me along?"

"Don't worry about it." Jimmy interjected.

"Come on guys you know I don't like being a burden on you two!" She protested as she sat back against the backseat.

James leaned forward and took a card out from his wallet that the agent from 'Fantasia' Getaways gave him and rolled his window down. "Just don't date another jackass Kimberly and we'll call it even alright? You've never been a burden on us. You've been an amazing roommate." He allowed his eyes to linger in the rearview mirror as his left hand reached out to swipe the card against the black plate attached to the cement reinforced pedestal. He caught himself staring at her pale, perfect skin and the sky blue tube top she was wearing. His eyes quickly readjusted to the opening gate.

She caught his glance like she did every time. "I know, I know. I'm working on my choice of men as best as I can. Rick was a cock to the both of you and me. Though you both know I would have been with him far longer than that if I would have been in high school. God, he was a saint compared to the guys I dated back then."

"You don't give yourself enough credit Kim. I'm glad me and Jimmy are getting through to you though. It has been a process but I think the three of us are better people for it." The station wagon sputtered several times while it crossed into the massive yard with the dozen or so maple and spruce trees. He continued on and found only one other vehicle parked in the allotted spaces after they rounded the massive fountain that poured an endless stream of water via stone cherubs.

"Well I'll be damned. Look at that! They got your likeness to a T James. The little penis, the curly hair; I never knew how adorable you were until cast in stone!" Jimmy said.

Kimberly laughed and James could only grumble while putting the car in park adjacent to the pick-up truck. "I'll contend that maybe I looked like that when I was four or five but I could still knock a wall down." He defended the manhood he had.

"If your mother visits in the fall tell her to bring baby pictures, I want to see if the resemblance is uncanny, or if Jimmy is just lying his ass off!" Kimberly giggled before hopping out of the car to get a much needed stretch in.

She wouldn't see James checking her out in the driver's side mirror. Jimmy did, however, and nudged his buddy in the arm. "You keep a good eye on her don't you?" He asked in a hushed whisper. "You aren't into her are you?"

"No. Just concerned really; I mean she hasn't been herself since Rick." James contested through his bluff.

Jimmy shook his head. "I don't know what you're talking about but alright." He said and got out as well.

James made sure he had his keys twice before locking each door separately in the station wagon. "Piece of shit auto locks," he muttered to himself before joining his two best friends at the back of the very old vehicle. "Well the important thing is this terrifying hunk of metal on wheels made it here. That's all I care about." James said and tapped the bumper with his foot, half expecting it to fall off. "Let's get our shit and get inside. I really hope the showers have a bench for relaxation. Been dreaming of using one of those all my life," he sighed.

"Need a bench for 'contemplation time'?" Jimmy's face was twisted in a grin.

James opened the back of the station wagon and heaved one of the heavier gym bags at Jimmy. "Just for that you can carry most of this shit in. Douchebag."

Kimberly flicked the two of them in the ear. "You two need to sto-" she was interrupted by a loud bang coming from around the corner of the mansion.

James turned to the sound and saw an exuberant man with his arms outstretched wide. He looked too well dressed to be a butler; too much white.

"Good afternoon! My name is Jacque Collo and welcome to 'Fantasia Getaways'!"

6

Livid was the kindest emotion that could describe what Vincent Tanner had been feeling for the last week and a half. Vincent Tanner was not a fan of a lot of things; most of which was that he hated being dicked around. His employers were doing just that but he was doing his best to be *civil* about it.

"Tanner! Get your ass back to work right the fuck now!" His boss bellowed into Tanner's ear. The cell phone he had was even a few inches away to avoid potential deafness. His other hand kept a firm grip on the steering wheel so he wouldn't end up hitting a tree head first. "I did not authorize you for shit!"

"Good thing I put in for vacation time then and not a pile of shit, boss."

"God dammit Tanner! You know the rules! It's your ass if shit goes south."

"So glad you care, boss."

"Vincent I need you to listen to me. I cannot help you with this right now. I know she's-"

Tanner cut him off. "Shut it. I don't give a fuck. We should have been moving in on this over a week ago. Period. I know the rules boss, I'm following one right now."

"Vincent!"

The cell phone snapped shut. He slipped the cell into his pocket and with his now free hand pushed his sunglasses onto his forehead as his 1967 Chevy Impala, jet black, slowed to a crawl.

An imposing black gate barred any unauthorized entrance. On either side brick walls looked to stretch on forever.

"What in the hell have you gotten yourself into?" He questioned aloud and to himself. He rubbed his eyes a little with his index finger on one and his thumb with the other while he gathered his thoughts and finally rolled down his window and dug around for his wallet.

While taking out the card labeled "Fantasia Getaways" from his wallet he skipped over the very few photos he had in his wallet. He paused and flipped back to the only one that mattered. He felt his Adam's apple bob once while he swallowed and finally reached out to scan that card against the black plastic plate. The angry, red eye turned a calming green to allow him access to the property.

As the gates parted Tanner had a sinking feeling in his gut. He always went by that feeling. As much as he hoped for the best he already came to terms with the fact that he might not find anything he was here searching for. It did not help that the mansion was that large.

"Well that is a lot of ground to cover. Fuck." He said as he continued up the pathway to find a parking spot. He saw five other vehicles, two on the right and three on the left, parked and emptied out of. As the sun began setting to the west of the mansion over the massive forest of spruce and maple Tanner stepped out and lit a cigarette.

Time to go to work.

7

Oswald Matthews had to use all the willpower he had in him to keep from sneering at two people in the large gathering of guests in the foyer. It was a force of habit but Oswald got a quick headcount of everyone that was standing around him and he counted thirteen guests, including him, that would stay for a week in the magnificent building they were in. He already made up his mind about two of the guests; the forty-five year old didn't fight in the first Iraq war so a bunch of queers could prance around with no shame or morality.

Oswald had been standing in the foyer for about five minutes. It gave him ample time to look around at the establishment. The foyer itself was bisected by an ivory staircase that was draped in brown carpeting. It was polished to a shine and looked pristine. The floor was tiled and buffered to the point Oswald almost could see his reflection in the black shine. There were a few small tables against the walls with some decorative vases that held a few exotic looking flowers. Despite the presentation Oswald was getting impatient with their host.

"Didn't this Jacque say that we were supposed to meet down here at six?" He asked the woman and man who were standing next to him. He noticed that the woman was older, but not entirely bad looking for her age. Maybe a few years younger than himself and the same could be said about the man

"Well I know this company had to cancel our plans a few weeks ago. The same for a few other people here but I don't know who." Stacy Sinfield said. She had been glued to her husband's side down in the foyer but she turned her attention to Oswald. "Oh! My name is Stacy and this is my husband Peter. My two boys over there goofing off are Daniel and Mark." She pointed to the uninterested Mark and the bored looking Daniel. Peter had reached over to offer his hand.

Oswald shook Peter's hand and felt a tight grip from him. "Pleasure to meet you both; my name is Oswald Matthews. I cannot help but feel that my late entry has held the proprietor of this place up a bit." He confessed.

Peter shook his head several times, "Think nothing of it Mister Matthews. In fact I thought my family would have been the late ones. We blew a tire on the way here and got the kids out for a good learning experience. They got halfway through, but you know how boys can be, and Mark flagged down the couple over there," he paused to point at Clark and Fred, "And they were nice enough to stop by and help out the boys."

"Oh, so they are fruitcakes." Oswald said.

"Fred and Clark? Oh, well yeah." Stacy said and smiled. "Great guys though. I guess they just got married a few weeks back and this is their honeymoon. They both knew how to change a tire but I think Fred is the manlier of the two, or however that stuff works. I'm not one to judge though, I was thankful they stopped and helped out."

"They aren't obnoxious about it, you know?" Peter asked Oswald.

Oswald knew. "I suppose that is good." He said and pulled his dog tags out from the skin tight white shirt he was wearing. It showed off his chiseled form. "I guess I am what you would call old fashioned. My father was a marine, my grandfather was a marine and now here I am. I'll live and let live but I just can't agree with what they represent." He said and noticed Stacy must have been a happily married wife. He didn't even see her eyes dash over his body.

"Like I said I am not one to judge. We all are here for the same reason, to relax and have a good time. I am sure they will be well mannered. They were very respectful when they stopped by." Stacy reasoned.

"That's all we can ask for I think . . ." Oswald paused and turned his attention to the group of threebefore turning back to the Sinfields. ". . . It was a pleasure meeting the both of you. I'll be sure to keep in touch. I may as well get caught up meeting everyone."

The sheepishness of the three is what drew Oswald to the college students. The blonde garnered his attention for the obvious attraction factor, and she was attractive. Oswald smiled to himself as he felt like the Big Bad Wolf at that point, stalking little red or little blonde in this case. If she had a red shirt or something like that in her attire he would more than likely lose it laughing. What he liked about the other two was that they looked like they wouldn't give him any backtalk if he talked to their blonde friend. One was taller and filled out more than the other but they were passive in their stance. Not a threat in the least.

"Late spring break?" Oswald broke the ice with the obvious.

James nodded his head. "Yeah in a way, there were some complications at our college and while every other college got the second to the last week of March off here we are about three weeks later. It worked perfectly, however, as it seems our previous bookings for this place in March was pushed back to now."

Oswald could respect that. "That is a mighty fine coincidence. Glad you three could make it out. Spring break was always about branching out and exploring the world in a way, so long as you have the money to do so." He said while his dog tags bounced a bit. "I'll tell you kids this much, spring break hasn't changed in the last twenty five years or so." His attention turned towards Kimberly for the slightest moment so his dog tags could clearly be seen.
"How much did you pay to come here?" Kimberly asked.

"About a thousand. Why?"

She glared at James and Oswald wanted to swim in the annoyed look that the "alpha" of the three was giving off. Clearly he answered the question wrong in some way.

"You jerk! You spent a thousand dollars on me?" She shouted a little louder than what she wanted to.

Jimmy pushed from the wall he stood at. "Whoa…to be fair we split it evenly fifty-fifty. Like James said out in the car don't worry about it. We weren't going to be going on this trip without you."

Good damage control. Oswald mused. "Hey now, that is a very nice gesture. When I was in college no one supported you. You got some good friends here little lady." He said and then snapped his fingers, extending his hands towards the group soon after. "Shoot how rude of me. My name is Oswald Matthews." Jimmy shook his right hand while Kimberly gingerly took his left to shake with her own.

"James Newberry. This is Kimberly and my best friend Jimmy."
He stood his ground and shifted a bit. He put his hand forward to shake
Oswald's hand.

The former marine gripped James' hand tight. James squeezed
back hard. Oswald squeezed harder as well in challenge. "You've got quite
a grip James." Oswald said before relenting. He knew what that meant.
James had become less passive and more aggressive as soon as he walked
over. *Lucky the other two don't know shit about body language boy,* Oswald
thought before tipping an imaginary hat. "Pleasure to meet the three of
you and if any of you have a thing for history I could probably share a few
stories about the first Iraq war."

"That would be me." Jimmy offered.

"Excellent. I'll see you kids around then." Oswald said and shook
each of their hands once more, but let his gaze linger on Kimberly for a few
seconds longer than what he had given the other two before a clearing of a
throat drew his attention from her eyes.

"Sorry for the wait everyone!" Jacque proclaimed as he came
out of one of the oak doors that led to the southeast wing of the mansion.
Oswald made a note that Jacque's room must have been in his wing that
he selected. In fact there were three other staircases that branched from the
main one to the northeast, northwest and southwest of the large vacation
home. "Is everyone accounted for?" He asked rhetorically before taking a
headcount of everyone that was there.

"Good! All fourteen of you are here." He said and clapped his
hands together.

Oswald took a glance at the two couples he had not managed to
introduce himself to. It would have to wait but he already had a passing
interest in the darker skinned woman. It was an unwelcomed passing
interest. He wanted it to be a full interest. He could tell that she wasn't
purely Middle Eastern in ancestry but he would guess close to it. *Promised
myself never to get involved with the towel heads again, damn it all; keep
it together.* The redhead with the other redhead didn't interest him as much.
She didn't seem frumpy to him, but just on the border of frumpy and he
wasn't attracted to that. *How in the hell did that mousey motherfucker bag
a woman like that? Fucking money, that's how. No other explanation.* He
rationalized in his head while Jacque walked down the steps.

"Alright is everyone ready to take the tour? The sun is going down
so I believe we should start in the back first so everyone can see what we
have to offer during the day time for recreation." Jacque offered.

Everyone agreed.

Jacque pivoted on a foot and raised one finger into the air. "Oh! Before I forget remember that on your contracts you signed a waiver. 'Fantasia Getaways' values your safety and well being above all else but if, for example, you have a few too many cocktails and slip down the stairs in a drunken stumble we are not liable! I'm sure you all are quite the agile creatures and know how to handle your alcohol, save for the younger crowd obviously, so this should not be a problem!" He explained.

Oswald turned his head when Stacy raised her hand about halfway as high as she could. "Mister Collo?"

"Call me Jacque my dear! Formalities for me mean nothing."

"Oh, okay. Jacque what about the forest outside? We saw the large brick wall that apparently keeps anyone discouraged from trying to get around and access this property but we noticed coming in that there actually is a good stretch of forest on either side of this land that is inside of the brick wall. Is it possible that one night or two that we could go out and camp?"

Oswald turned back to Jacque. He saw a twinkle in the older man's hazel gaze.

"Excellent question Missus Sinfield! Our policy remains the same even for outdoor fun. Just keep safe, keep smart, and do not go too far into the forest. While I can guarantee there will not be anything bigger than a squirrel or a rabbit that you may find even those small animals can give a nasty bite. Though if you do wish to go out into the forest for a hike or camp do let me know before you leave so I know where you guys go in case something happens. Not that it will, of course, but policy is policy!" He smiled.

"Rules are rules. I can appreciate that." Oswald agreed and rubbed his hands together. "I could be up for some camping in the middle of the week. If you guys do not mind a fifth wheel of course." He guessed they wouldn't.

Peter was delighted by the idea, "Sure Mister Matthews. That would be great. We'll let you know if we do head out there sometime."

Oswald gave an affirming nod before turning his attention back to the exuberant Jacque Collo. Even Oswald wasn't quite sure what to make of the energetic older man. He guessed Jacque looked like he was in his fifties or approaching sixty. *Glad to know I'll look forty when I reach his age. Shit.*

He tried not to smile.

"Without further adieu, shall we get to the recreation area out back?" Jacque asked the crowd.

Oswald decided to see what kind of crowd he was actually dealing with. "I have a question real quick: Where is the bar?" It garnered a couple laughs and, thankfully, a giggle from the blonde bombshell towards the back.

"This wouldn't be much of a vacation home if we didn't have a great selection for most of you to enjoy!" Jacque said while staring at Oswald. "Though we will get to the bar area in a bit Mister Matthews. Now let's, how do you say . . . boogie to the recreational area!"

Before Jacque Collo could take two steps forward the front doors exploded open.

8

The figure standing in the doorframe blinked several times.

He had a cigarette hanging from his lips and his short, black hair had been spiked up and swooped to his left side. The setting sun cloaked the front of his body in shadow before he took a step forward and shut the doors behind him. The light from the electric chandelier above the group finally displayed the newcomer's rugged five o'clock shadow and he proved to be the tallest of the bunch at six and a quarter. Sunglasses hid his eyes and his lean figure was clad in a black silk shirt which was tucked into his cream colored slacks. A black belt held those pants up and a pair of pure black wingtip shoes completed his ensemble. For now he had his black suit jacket over his left arm.

"Shit! Sorry about that folks. Those doors looked a hell of a lot heavier than what they were!" The mystery man said.

"Sir! Firstly there is absolutely no smoking in this establishment and secondly who in the blazes are you?" Jacque shouted and pushed through the crowd of surprised guests.

"Oh! Right, so sorry!" The man said and quickly turned to open the door. He drew one more drag from his cigarette before tossing it out of the window and onto the pavement in front of the mansion.

"Where are his bags?" Maggie asked.

"You could learn a thing from this new guy." Ryan whispered to Maggie and Jasmine.

"His bags are probably in his vehicle still. I don't think he walked here." Stan offered.

"Does he know that he is supposed to be on vacation?" Ryan asked as he glanced at Maggie and caught her gawking. "Or do you think that I could pull off the fancy shmancy business look woman?" He grumbled towards his wife.

"Calm down tiger. I never yell at you for checking out the racks on those hoochies we see at the store or mall; so don't even think about being a hypocrite." Maggie teased as she tore her gaze away from Tanner and back to her husband. She reached around and placed her hand in his.

The man turned around and found himself face to face with Jacque Collo; a perturbed Jacque Collo. "Who are you? I received no notice of a fifteenth guest." Jacque said. His eyes were sizing the newcomer up several times.

"Oh I'm sorry. I thought your company would give you notice. My name is Vincent Tanner and I managed to convince your company to let me get a free pass into this establishment. I had to pay double since it was all short notice but I have heard so very, very much about this place and this week was the only week I could find time away from my job. I apologize for any complications that might arise but judging from the massive amount of people here I think my extra grand might just cover any spare rooms you could find me along with food services for the week." He took off his sunglasses to reveal a set of amber eyes that almost shined like gold when the light hit it just right. "I'm glad I didn't miss the tour. I'd hate to get lost in this place.

"Has anyone got lost in this place before Jacque?" Kimberly asked. She brushed her hair a few times in a sporadic pattern.

Jacque began rubbing his temples. "Not at all my dear Kimberly. No one has ever found themselves lost in this mansion." He turned around on one foot and regained his posture. He began sauntering towards the middle of the group.

"I didn't see a hedge maze behind this place so I guess you're right." Tanner said. "My name is Vincent Tanner by the way, pleasure to meet you all and once again sorry for holding everyone up." In a sweeping glance he took in everyone that was with him in that establishment.

Jacque was too annoyed with Vincent at that point. "Well welcome to 'Fantasia Getaways' Mister Tanner. Now I am not giving anyone an option to ask any further questions. You will thank me when you see the recreation area in back of the home. Truthfully everything that needs to be seen is on the first floor. The second floor is where all the bedrooms reside and you all are pretty familiar with those, except for our late guest here." By the time Jacque turned to face Tanner his full grin had returned to his face.

Tanner didn't seemed bothered in the least by the jab.

"You can go ahead and grab a key from the box Mister Tanner. We will get you signed up in a bit." Jacque motioned to the left side of the foyer.

Tanner turned his attention to the lobby that was to his left. The desk was solid oak and barricaded a counter area where a box of keys hung above. "So this place was a hotel back in the day. Neat." Tanner said and pushed his sunglasses back down before retrieving a set of keys after a brisk walk to that desk. When he turned around the group was already heading the other way. "Hey wait up!"

"Sorry for the few boring hallways we have gone through my guests, but I assure you that after we pass through this door right here you will find the drab, blank hallways more than made up for." Jacque said, pausing by the last door with his hand on the handle. "Now to get outside you have to pass through what we call our 'Glass Heaven'. Essentially I will tell you all this just once: You must remain clothed at all times in this area. You'll see why." He turned the knob and crossed into the aforementioned room.

One by one gasps filled the massive room.

"Oh my God Ryan we are buying this place! I don't care!" Maggie cried.

The group stood in a gymnasium sized glass box. The floor was tiled in black and white checkered squares but the walls and the ceiling was nothing but stained glass. With the sun gleaming into the room it decorated everything in a mix of colors.

"It's like we're living in a damn rainbow. This must have cost a fortune to build." Ryan offered as he stood slack jawed with everyone else.

Jacque cackled in glee. He stood there momentarily before crossing nearly fifty feet of tile to one of the three doors inside of the "Glass Heaven". "Please, don't forget the pool and spa area as well," he motioned to his right to the massive pool and then to the left to the several hot tubs lined against the wall. "If you came here wanting to relax, well, the 'Glass Heaven' is where you'll probably stay most of your time. I am very proud of this room and I am very proud to share this room with you all. It is even better during the full moon and I think one will happen this very night."

"I've been in five star hotels that have cost quadruple what you are offering in this very room alone. How in the world do you keep the price so cheap?" Tanner asked from the back after he had to wiggle past Peter and Oswald just to get in.

"Considering that we only cater to private guests and parties we pretty much have little to no upkeep of this place. Our guests have a proven track record of cleaning up after themselves. We do not even encourage it but we have guessed it has to do with the presentation and how good they feel before they leave. Provide people an amazing experience at a very, very low price, give them everything they could dream and you will be rewarded as well!"

The group eventually spread out enough that Tanner could get to the front. He looked around the room with a careful eye. He noticed that other than the door that they entered, and the door across the way to the outside, there was one more door between two of the four spas and hot tubs that were offered to them. "What's over in that door?" He pointed.

"Just a storage compartment for cleaning supplies and other things like that. I have to admit that despite how clean our clients typically are it is still a, how do you say, pain in the neck to mop these floors!"

That earned Jacque a few laughs.

Jacque pulled the door leading to the outside open wide and turned his attention to the darkening sky to the east. "This room will start to dim soon." He said and then pointed to the wall that was behind the group. "There will be adequate enough light and the other rule of this room is to have those lights on if you are swimming. If you wish to enjoy some water and the natural light that comes with the night you may have the lights off in the hot tubs." He said and then beckoned them to step outside with him. "Come come, time to show you all what we have to offer out in back. I will make this quick I promise."

It was a much better view for the group when Jacque led them outside. He stood in front of him and opened his arms wide to the many activities that were offered in that backyard. "Take a look around everyone. You have about fifty yards to the cliff's edge. Never in the history of this home has anyone taken a spill off the cliffs but I must remind you all to use common sense and good judgment when it comes to this area. If I catch anyone within twenty feet of the cliff's edge, or drunk and walking towards it I do not need to tell you that there will be repercussions." Jacque then pointed to several light poles that were erected around each recreational area. "In case it grows too dark out here during your stay I will turn these lights on myself. The power is located in the basement where I have the only access."

Stacy squealed when something to the right of the exit caught her eye. "Peter! Honey! Look at the size of that grill!"

Peter turned his head towards what his wife was talking about and his jaw dropped. His eyes were glued to it.

"Oh this isn't embarrassing." Mark groaned. He watched his father pull away from the group towards the grill that looked more like a miniature iron lung. The sleek, stainless steel grill was powered by propane and Peter already opened it up.

"Dear God . . . is there a planned meal for tonight or may I go ahead and take the honor Mister Collo?" Peter asked.

Jacque turned his attention towards Peter, "I assume you enjoy grilling then, Mister Sinfield?"

Peter nodded. "I have a grill at home I use liberally during the spring and summer but this thing blows my tiny little thing away. It is magnificent! I can't wait to see first-hand how this baby handles hamburgers, steak, hot dogs; hell anything for that matter! I'll roast a tire on this thing if I had to!"

Stacy hugged her husband from behind. "I guess that means we are going to cook for everyone tonight! How's that sound for everyone? Old fashioned cookout to kick off the week?"

Stan had to stifle a laugh at the reaction of the Sinfield kids who looked positively mortified. "Sounds good to me," he offered while the rest nodded in agreement.

"Well that isn't really fair to them. I'll tell you what Missus Sinfield, since you guys are cooking tonight Maggie and I will clean up," Jasmine offered, "Ryan and Stan can help out as well on that front."

Maggie preemptively elbowed Ryan in the side before he could protest.

"Excellent," Peter began as he looked over the various knobs he would be working with, "Well I think we are all getting pretty hungry from the drive up here so once we get to the kitchen would it be alright if my family started piling things out Mister Collo?"

"I wouldn't have it any other way Mister Sinfield. I have to admit the first night is usually a tradition for the guests where I cook what I can but having a night off is surely welcomed and appreciated. I will still help and aid you both in whatever way I can, even if it is just grabbing a large table so we have something to put everything on."

Oswald stepped forward and cracked his knuckles a few times. "I'll help you get the table after all this is said and done. I'm actually hungry as hell. I haven't eaten since last night I think."

"How in the world do you forget when to eat?" Clark blurted out.

"Late night and early mornings, that's how." Oswald shot back.

Jacque, in that immaculate white suit, interrupted the two of them by stepping up to Oswald. "I would appreciate that Mister Matthews. Though for now we have three more areas to tend to real quick. The dining hall is not really that impressive, I am sure if you have seen any sort of mansion before on television that it will be just like what you have seen. It is just basically a large table, several chairs, and cabinets filled with fine china for decoration." He said and directed everyone back inside.

"I think I speak for everyone that the dining room probably is nothing special, no offense." Ryan offered. He looked around for any sour faces and found none. "Thought so! So just lead us to the kitchen so we can start getting our grub on!"

Jacque walked in front of them back into the "Glass Heaven" pool and spa area. "Well there is one other place here on the first floor I want to show you all first. It is the library we have. It is in the northern part of the mansion and some of you on the second floor might have noticed the halls end abruptly, you'll see why." He said and ushered the group into the hallways once again.

"I hate to say it Jacque but I almost think you blew the big reveal at the beginning and not the end." Maggie teased.

Jacque took it in good spirits and laughed. "That depends on your outlook on things Missus McCallister! While the previous room is quite the beauty to behold I assure you that even a room that houses nothing but dusty old books can be magnificent. You see, the previous owner of this home was a fanatic of literature. You could say that he was a recluse in some aspects when he lost himself in the very library he built. Again, however, it is better to show you and not just blabber on." He smiled and quickly led the way to a pair of massive double doors.

From his pocket Jacque produced a golden key, which, despite how shiny it was, had an intricate design that had Clark tingling. "Why is the library locked Jacque? Furthermore how old is this place if you still have to use a key like that?"

Jacque inserted the key and gave it a twist but ended it there. "Well Mister Thompson you have to understand that this library has some very, very valuable material in it. During the night this place will be locked up, no questions asked, but if you come in during the day time there will be a sign in sheet. No books leave the library and if I catch anyone here in the middle of the night they will be asked to leave, no questions asked. I am personally responsible for all the books in here so I hope you understand." He twisted the key back to the neutral position, pulled it out, and shoved the doors wide open.

The twin oak doors creaked opened to reveal a very well lit wealth of knowledge. Twin chandeliers dangled above the group as they entered and illuminated every stretch of the massive library. Potted vines dangled from the ceiling as well and above them at the top of the doorframe two large, marble sculpted male heads cast their stoic gaze upon the group.

"Holy shit!" Daniel squealed before realizing his mistake.

Peter began laughing with others but Stacy was still in mother mode. "Language mister!"

"Sorry mom." Daniel sighed.

Jacque crossed his arms and turned towards the group. "Are you a reader Daniel?" Jacque asked and then bent a little towards the blonde haired boy. "If that is the case I think I can break my rule one time and let you take a book to your room to read for privacy tonight. I am a pretty good judge of character and I think your parents have raised a good pair of honest boys." Jacque said, eyeing the young teen for a moment.

There were four large, wide windows on the west side of the library where Jacque turned his attention to next to see that there was not too much light left for the day. "Oh dear, I think I will have to turn the backyard lights on regardless I did not realize the sun was disappearing so quickly!"

Jimmy, who had been mostly silent along with James and Kimberly, pushed forward and took it upon himself to explore the vast rows of books. "I have to admit this is an amazing collection Jacque! I don't even think the university we attend has such a selection. Cripes!" Jimmy said and then paused when he came to a door located to the east of the library. The door, much like the others, was oaken and large but this one had several padlocks on it along with an intricate design embedded in the middle of it. "Creepy door though. Why's it locked Jacque?"

"That door leads down to the basement area of this place. I keep it locked because I wouldn't wish anyone to be down in that area for longer than a second. While I do my best to keep this house in tip top shape it is impossible to keep that basement clean. Apologies all around but it truly only has the breaker box to the home and a few more things for storage. Nothing special of course." He turned his attention towards Jasmine who had her arm wrapped around her husband's.

"This place feels old. I mean really old Stan. Not in a bad way of course but it just seems to emit this . . . history or something. It's a good kind of old!" She giggled.

Stan squeezed her arm gently, "You won't hear me arguing with you on that. Though there is something that just feels off about this place and I don't know why. It isn't a creepy vibe but I guess a place with as much history and age like this would give off some vibes. I am probably just being paranoid." He whispered into her ear and reached behind her to run his hand slowly down her back.

Jacque started clapping his hands together to gain everyone's attention from the various parts of the library they had explored. "I could give you all a huge speech about the history of this library but I fear that with how hungry everyone is I might get some scowls! Let us go and get this feast ready shall we?"

Aside from there being no objections Jacque did notice a few eyes observing his locked door.

9

Vincent Tanner was here on business. He was going to get in, get what he needed, and then get the hell out of dodge. He wasn't here to party, wasn't here to make friends. The only problem lay in the fact that he had no real way of finding the information he needed. While everyone was inside getting ready for the late dinner he was walking back to his car and gathering his thoughts on the whole situation. He was certain that the guests of the vacation home didn't have a clue about the place they were staying at. Tanner had several.

Back at his Impala he was busy gathering a few spare clothes and toiletries from the backseat of his car. He had much more in the trunk he might need for his trip but for now clothes and little bars of soap were the necessities. The leather seats squeaked with every movement the bag made as he dragged it from the back seat and closed the door.

"For spending a week here you sure are packing pretty light," a voice rang out from behind Tanner when the door slammed shut.

Tanner turned around and saw Stan standing with his arms crossed and his head tilted. His glasses were pushed all the way up on the bridge of his nose and his eyes were narrowed just a bit. *All this guy needs is a tapping foot and a ruler and I'll be back in grade school getting the pat down.* Tanner thought as he slung his duffel over his shoulder. "Is that a crime?"

"Not in my book Mister Tanner. In fact I was just coming out here to lend a hand with your things but I don't think you need the help do you?" Stan asked and Tanner shook his head in response.

"Stan Freason, right? I appreciate the concern but I have been rather frugal with what I bring on vacation or any business trip. I pack light and stay clean. No fuss, no muss, you know what I mean?

"Yeah, I suppose. My wife Jasmine, however, would think you are insane for only bringing one bag with you anywhere," he said with a genuine smile.

"You do have a lovely wife. I believe an honest, up front man is a trustworthy one, obviously, so I'll say it right now that you got lucky with her Stan. A word of warning though: Keep an eye on that old bastard. Not Jacque but Oswald. I noticed he didn't take an eye off of your wife or that younger blonde during the tour."

Stan offered his hand to shake Tanner's own. "Thanks for the heads up Mister Tanner, I'm a psychologist by trade so I noticed it right off the bat. Sadly I think if he tried anything on Jasmine he would have to fear Maggie's retaliation more than my own. They are sisters and Maggie would kill for Jasmine."

"I have to say they don't look anything alike," Tanner said as he shook Stan's hand and kept eye contact through it. "And looks are deceiving; I wasn't expecting such a firm handshake from you Mister Freason."

That admission tickled Stan a little and nodded his agreement. "Up until a few months ago it would have been a bit weaker, but with Jasmine and Maggie they have been sisters since they were around ten years old. Jasmine's parents were killed in a car accident. Jasmine was pretty closed off even with Maggie's family loving her and, well, it was luck like you said when I met her in college. We sort of connected in being pre-mature orphans since my parents died shortly before I graduated high school."

"You have my condolences Stan. Though what happened a few months back if you don't mind me asking?" Tanner asked and shifted his bag on his shoulder.

"Well this vacation with my family was kind of forced because of some shitty event I was involved in. They think it will clear my head or something but I think it will just take some time and several more sessions, ironically, in the chair that usually has someone else talking about their issues."

Tanner fished around in his pocket for a moment and produced a cigarette and a lighter, lighting the former after readjusting his duffel bag over his shoulder again. "I'd take their advice. There are, sadly, only a handful of moments in our life where we get to truly relax. You got yourself a beautiful setting and a beautiful woman to share it with Stan. Take advantage of it the best you can." Smoke puffed from his lips with the wind taking it the opposite direction Stan was standing.

"I suppose you are right. I wouldn't want my wife to feel neglected and run into the arms of an older gentleman, or a black suited individual who's fashionably late, right? Stan grinned.

"Precisely," Tanner said as he punctuated with a point of two fingers holding his cigarette, "Although this black suited individual won't be stealing anyone here; I already have someone. I just have no clue where they are right now." He popped the cigarette back in his mouth. "I think we should head back in and see how far along dinner is coming. I'm hungry as hell."

"Sounds good to me but if you have someone else why didn't they come with you on this trip?" Stan asked.

Tanner began walking ahead of Stan. He took a few more drags before flicking his cigarette on the ground and snuffing it out with his heel.

"Mandatory overtime screwed her hard."

"I'll tell you what sweetie, it is rewarding work but I have to say it's a good day if I don't end up with some sort of bodily fluid on me. You stick to that internet designing. Far less chance of becoming immune to being grossed out." Maggie teased Kimberly Cross as the two of them sat side by side on one of the large picnic tables Ryan, Oswald and Jacque had brought out for the evening dinner. "It was nice of Oswald to take it upon himself to get all the drinks as well. I think it was more for him than anything else though."

Kimberly smiled and sipped a bit more of her own bitter beverage before her face twisted in glorified disgust from the idea of body fluids getting on her. "Wow. I can't even handle that stuff when I'm the one who is all throw-uppy and sick. You gotta have a strong stomach to be a nurse then I guess."

Maggie cackled loudly next to the blond before nodding. "My first few weeks had me running to the bathroom whenever something like that happened but you would be surprised at how fast you can get used to something when someone depends on you to help them. Except my husband, who seemingly has forgotten that his poor wife needs something to drink?" She bellowed towards Ryan as he came out from the door that led into that fabulous "Glass Heaven" while holding a large glass full of wine while the other held a glass filled with a honey-colored liquid.

"Hey! Leave me alone! I had a hard time finding the scotch, devil woman." He growled back with a huff as he handed the glass of wine to her with a bow. "I got you your baby blood. I mean wine, yeah, wine." He teased and looked over to the only other two couples that were on vacation. "I'm really surprised a lot of people here aren't giving the Thompsons flack for their lifestyle choice. Not that I have anything against it, but Peter and Stacy strike me as a very old fashioned, 'Leave it to Beaver' type family."

Maggie sipped her wine and smiled, "The world is growing up I suppose. Or society is. Hell if I know but I think they are adorable together. Fred's the big man's man and I can tell Clark is a trouble maker. He's just got that mischievous boy-charm to him." Maggie said and glanced over her shoulders twice to make sure she and Kimberly were the only ones at the table or nearby. "Speaking of boys you came here with two of them right? Are you dating one of them?"

Kimberly's eyes widened and she shook her head. "We have known each other for like a year and a half now. Met in college and we are pretty much best friends three ways." She said and brushed a few strands of her blonde hair behind her ear. "They have always had my back and have stuck up for me when I get involved with another jerk. They've always been understanding and, as stupid as this sounds, I feel like they are my shining knights really. Though we're all nerds so whatever." She smiled.

"Oh child you don't know a thing about guys. Don't feel too bad. Before I met Ryan I used to dabble in the jerks and assholes. Granted if they smacked me I smacked back. It's ironic that I'm a nurse but I've put a few boys in the ER. I'm feisty." She laughed and took another sip.

Kimberly looked down at her feet and waved them back and forth a few times. "I don't know what is wrong with me. My last boyfriend didn't see eye to eye with what I did with James and Jimmy. Playing video games, doing some tabletop role playing games and that kind of stuff, pretending I am someone who I'm not has always been a comfort for me and he mocked them mercilessly for it until I dumped his sorry ass." She said. A random thought and name popped into her head which sent her into a giggling fit, "James always called him Timmy the Tool. He loathed Tim. Actually Tim is the first guy to actually push James so far that he got physical. He shoved Tim out of our apartment when he wouldn't leave."

"Oh wow. So up until that point Jimmy and James just would be there for you after the post-break up? Never actually got in any of the guy's faces?" Maggie inquired.

Kimberly shrugged her shoulders and looked at the woman, "Not really. I mean if any ex's showed up James always put himself in the middle while Jimmy cheered from the back for James to kick the guy's ass."

"Kid's these days are so cute. Oh God . . . You're making me feel old Kimberly." Maggie cackled again. She turned her attention towards a commotion over by the grill. "I think the first round of everything is ready.

By the time the burgers, hot dogs, French-fries, and the few steaks Peter threw on for the few not feeling the traditional cook-out food were fully cooked and ready to serve the sun was completely gone. The only illumination the group had were the large lights Jacque had turned on that lit up the eating area and basketball court and it also shined into the "Glass Heaven" pool and spa area of the home to add color into that building as well. The beautiful scenery was fitting for the first night of everyone's vacation.

The Freasons and McCallisters were sitting together at a table by themselves and watched the moon high above shine brightly.

"That is one hell of a moon tonight. I almost want to say we don't need these lights." Ryan mused to no one.

Jasmine leaned over and whispered in her husband's ear, "I think after we eat we should grab a bottle of champagne from the bar inside, a few glasses, and check out our room's bathroom sweetie."

Stan's eyebrow perked with interest as he took a huge chunk out of his steak and dabbed it into some tangy sauce. "That sounds like a lovely end to the night. Though I hope the waterbed is as great as you say it is. It looks bit hard to keep one's balance on it when they are doing various things," he echoed her whisper back before he finished off his steak.

Stan looked around and saw that Jacque was stationed at the Sinfield table, stuck between Daniel and Mark.

"Considering how amazing this food is I think I need to take over some culinary responsibilities before I have to give you a refund Mister Sinfield." Jacque laughed.

The Frenchman stood up and looked around the various groups that had begun mingling that night. He smoothed his own white suit he was wearing and clearing his throat. "Well on behalf of Fantasia Getaways I do hope the rest of your vacation is a pleasurable one for you all. You know the rules from here on out so enjoy and be kind to one another. I will be in the shadows, figuratively, but if anything is needed I am just a phone call away. For now I believe everything is in order here so I will be checking a few more things before I retire myself. Please make use of the giant trashcan I dragged out here." He walked off and turned for a moment to watch people disposing of the paper plates and utensils they used for their meal. He knew that many of them would be resting soon and that the first day of their vacation was an uneventful one. He smiled; however, as he knew that the real party would be beginning soon enough.

10

Everyone vacated the back patio area soon after Jacque made his exit and for the most part everyone was intent on getting settled in for the week. Oswald found himself taking a very sweet smelling Brandy back to his room to enjoy. Ryan and Maggie took a few flavored vodkas for themselves and Stan, along with his beautiful wife Jasmine, gathered two bottles of champagne for the night. Peter and Stacy found themselves getting an early night's rest while their two teenage sons, who were parked in their own room, discovered that the walls had to have been sound proof with how loud they were indulging in a similar interest, blowing up various aliens in a virtual environment.

Fred and Clark joined the three college kids in the "Glass Heaven" area.

"I can't believe how big these things are. They looked smaller from the outside." Clark said as he hunkered in next to Fred. They were evenly spaced out. "This is great because I appreciate the company. Fred here is great but he ends up being shy around other people, oddly enough." Clark laughed and jabbed his husband.

Fred grumbled, "It's not being shy it is just getting a read for people first hand." He corrected while Jimmy and James laughed.

"Well I don't want to say we are all cut from the same cord but I think I can appreciate how other people can treat others. It's a cruel world out there sometimes." Jimmy said as he sat closest to Clark and had James on his other side. Kimberly was the odd woman out but sat comfortably between James and Fred.

Clark looked between the three of them and looked confused. "What do you mean by that Jimmy? You guys look pretty normal to me. You and James aren't shagging are you?" Clark laughed and Kimberly burst into laughter as well.

"No! Jimmy and I are like brothers. But we are nerds. Geeks. Freaks. The kind of kids that you'll find getting their heads put in toilets in high school. Granted that has never happened but it came close once. Since we like things like Lovecraft, science fiction, and playing MMO's we aren't society's cup of tea."

Clark's lips twisted into a grin. "Well Fred here used to be a big ol' jock back in high school. I don't know how he was like back then but I am pretty sure any flack I give him will just be karmic payback then!" He said and punched Fred lightly on the arm. Fred didn't flinch.

"I'll admit I was a dickwad in high school. After I graduated though and discovered who I really was I think I was just a dickwad because I was lying to myself. Doesn't make the mocking and teasing and bullying I did any more right or am I excusing myself, but I also try to not see myself like that anymore." Fred admitted with his burly, unshaven chest wet from the bubbles of the hot tub. He was built.

Jimmy shrugged a bit. "Sounds like if you weren't into men Kimberly here would be jumping all over you if you were ten years younger or so, or fifteen."

"Jimmy you jerk!" Kimberly growled and splashed his face with that hot water. "You're a douchebag sometimes you know that!"

James did not appear to enjoy the joke either but held his outburst. "You have to forgive Jimmy. Sometimes his mouth runs faster than his mind, which is bad because he is pretty God damn intelligent. In either case college has proven to be much better than high school for sure."

"Well I am going to go ahead and be the middle man between our offbeat social standings. Anyone else want some more drinks?" Clark asked as he stood from the hot tub. Clad in only swimming trunks his body was a contrast to Fred's in the sense that he was much slimmer and much more tone than his partner.

Fred reached up and slapped Clark's backside. "Don't get into any trouble out there. I got the feeling that Oswald character might be a decent guy but I heard he was ex-military when Stacy talked to him. She apparently said he thought we were 'fruitcakes' from the get go."

"Yeah, so?"

"I'm just asking you not to be you. Don't be cocky or strut around. I may tolerate it, love it, depending on the day, but I don't want to be on some guy's shitlist for the next six days. Okay?"

Clark hopped out of the hot tub and took a towel to dry off a little bit. "Oh I promise!" He grinned and sauntered off towards the door.

Clark claimed the five drinks without fail and turned his attention back to the hallway that would lead towards that shimmering "Glass Heaven". He wasn't paying attention to what was in front of him and as he rounded the corner to the hallway that led back to the fantastic area he nearly ran head first into Oswald Matthews.

"Son of a bitch!" Oswald bellowed as the resulting near collision ended with him spilling a bit of his Brandy on his shirt. "Fucking queer!" Oswald shouted, "Watch where in the hell you are going!"

Clark shrank back a bit, "I only let people who kiss me call me queer! Relax old man, it's just Brandy." He blew it off and walked right past the fuming Oswald.

"You son of a bitch," Oswald snarled and pulled his left arm back after Clark walked right by him, "turn around and apologize to me you fucking punk!"

Fred walked into the hallway before Clark could turn around and gave Oswald a stare so cold Oswald felt his own body temperature lowering.

"What are you looking at fairy fucker? Your little princes spilled a shit load of Brandy over me and didn't say a damn thing," he said and showed off the stain for Fred to observe.

"It was an accident you old bastard. Get bent or whatever. Besides you are the one who drained half that bottle already, probably, ya drunk!" Clark spat.

Fred put himself between the two of them. "I don't give a fuck whose fault it is; I've had about enough of dealing with this shit because of what other people think about me and Clark. He looked back towards Clark for now. "Clark, apologize for bumping into Mister Matthews and you," he turned his stone gaze back at Oswald, the kind of stoic calm that always came before the storm. "You better watch your fucking mouth or I'll make sure the next 'fairy' you see you will end up fearing them instead of blindly hating them."

Clark, having no free hands, rubbed his cheek up and down Fred's shoulder while apologizing to Oswald, "Maybe after a few more drinks, Mister Matthews we can make it up to you!"

"God damn it Clark get the drinks to the hot-"

He was cut short when Oswald threw a cheap shot at Fred, he glanced the burly man's jaw with his middle finger. Fred had acted on instinct and leaned back quick enough to avoid most of the hit. Fred's hips turned and his right hand fired under and up, giving the war veteran a solid uppercut right to his sternum, knocking the wind out of the drunken vet.

"Oh shit! You just hit an old dude!" Clark said as he scampered off to the pool area.

Fred rubbed his jaw where the knuckle grazed it as Oswald coughed and panted. Oswald's efforts to compose himself came out as choked gasps.

"You . . . pansy motherfucker," he wheezed, "I'll make sure you and your bitch end up on your asses outside of this place in the morning!."

"Sleep it off you homophobic prick. Though go ahead, go and tell everyone that a 'fairy fucker' beat your ass if you want. I'm sure that will do wonders for your pride." Fred said before turning his back to Oswald. "If you'll excuse me I have a lovely evening to attend with my husband. I'm not going to let you ruin that for me and him after all we've done to finally be fucking happy."

Fred opened the door for Clark who still had his hands full and entered back into the pool house. The painted glass ceiling and walls were brightly shining in the moonlight and illuminated the entire area in almost a disco ball color palate without the constant moving lights.

"Hey what was that all about? We heard a commotion in the hallway." Jimmy said as the three college students continued to relax.
Fred's eyes narrowed on Clark and the smaller of the two men shrank back and handed the drinks out to everyone. "Just a misunderstanding, that's all. Problem solved." Fred offered as an

explanation.

"Actually kids I think me and Fred are going to call it a night. I'm getting all pruney as it is from sitting in that hot tub for so long." Clark said and could feel Fred's eyes scrutinizing him.

Kimberly frowned and sank herself down a bit after taking the drink. "Well damn. I was hoping we could make fun of James' and Jimmy's 'brotherhood' a bit longer. Well we have all week! You guys have a good night!"

Clark pulled Fred into the hallway and licked his lips for a moment. "I want to do some exploring of this place starting with that library. I mean what kind of person makes a huge library like that and then close off a door just because it leads to a 'basement'?"

Fred leaned his head back and groaned loudly. "Clark, why can't we just relax for a change? I mean just really have an enjoyable vacation?"

"Oh come on you know it will be fun. Besides I have not seen one security camera around this place. No one is going to know if we did a little snooping. After tonight you and I can do everything you want. How's that sound? I'll be compromising this time around!"

Fred lowered his head back down and in defeat, followed Clark back to their room to get properly dressed.

Clark and Fred stood in front of the massive library doors. They both were dressed in blue jeans and while Fred had a solid black t-shirt on Clark had a white tank top to complete their nightwear. Clark had a few metallic pins in his fingers and he rolled them around in his grasp.

"Nervous? Seriously Clark why are we doing this? We could get kicked out of this place and boom, there goes two thousand bucks." Fred scolded as he held a small flashlight towards the doorknob and keyhole.

Clark rolled his eyes and took a knee. He inserted one of those metallic pins into the door and checked to see where the pins were that he had to push down. "This won't take any longer than ten minutes, twenty at the max."

It was just the two of them in that darkened hallway. The only light they had been from Fred's flashlight. "Yeah but why are you so interested in this library? You're not a thief; at least I don't think you are. Damn it Clark you should have just told me you were one so I at least had time to process it before marrying your ass."

"Oh calm down. I just do not think it makes much sense to keep a library locked up regardless of how many books are in there. That and he skipped the door that apparently led down to the basement. That door looked way too fancy to just lead to some dingy basement." Carl argued while his fingers were working at the lock with his tools.

A few moments later Clark inserted another metallic pin and the clicks picked up as his fingers arched and twisted with every newfound pin to push. With one final twist of both fingers a larger click echoed through the hallway and the doors opened slightly after being freed. "See? If it was that important to keep this place locked up tight then they wouldn't have made it so easy to get in, simple as that."

"So what do you want to do now? Are you that curious to see if there is actually a damn basement beyond that other door?"

"Of course . . ." Clark paused while popping his tools out of the keyhole ". . . we already got past one door and that was my goal after all. You just need to relax honey, we weren't the only ones drinking you know," he said, taking his own flashlight, flicking it on, and pushing the library door open further.

11

Stan closed his eyes and breathed deeply while Jasmine rolled off the top of his body in a heap of sweat and blankets. The waterbed jiggled as their bodies wiggled around to get situated after their coupling.

"That was," he began but needed to stop to get some hard earned breaths in, "An experience to write down. My God, how did we not fall off this damn bed?" He smiled as his chest rose and fell in rapid succession.

Jasmine pulled her hair back behind her ear before lying on her back next to him, staring at the ceiling as their night was slowly coming to an end. "I have no clue honey but I think I'm going to find us a waterbed and buy it. I don't care if we have to put it in the guest room. We'll lie to any one that asks. We'll say we don't use or we hate it, I really don't care."

Stan rolled to his side so he could look at his wife and pulled his free arm around her waist. He pressed his lips against her neck and tasted her sweat-kissed skin. After the kiss he sat up and pulled the blanket to the side. "Do you need a drink?" He asked as he bent over to put his pants back on.

"I think I could use a glass of water if it's not too big of a trip honey," she said as she sat up as well with the blanket covering her modestly. "You should go and get me some water without a shirt on. That would be sexy." She smiled.

Stan stood still for a moment before fumbling with the white shirt he had on before their fun. "I don't think I'm feeling sexy enough to try that; especially with people walking around this place." He said and slipped the shirt on.

"Well maybe tomorrow night then. I can imagine Ryan and Maggie will want to get pretty wild tomorrow or sometime during the week but if you want we can make sure we don't remember our nights here. It has been forever since we've been able to act like stupid college kids." She smiled.

Stan buttoned his pants and nodded his head. "I think if the days here lead into such a night then sure, we can get stupid drunk as often as we can," he said and turned back towards his wife. "You're perfect, you know that? Why are you sticking with an idiot like me Jazz?"

She gave him a simple shrug of her shoulders while she sat and rocked back and forth lightly in the waterbed they shared. "I don't know really. I guess the money? I'm a gold digger you know. A big ol' gold digger." She teased and winked her playfulness at him.

Stan rolled his eyes and smiled before he walked into the hallway.

Blackness filled the halls that had no natural light to them. It was a safety hazard. "Need some damn light in this place," Stan muttered to himself and made a mental note to bring it up to Jacque the next time he saw the Frenchman. "At least they had the foresight to not put any clutter." Despite the darkness that enveloped some of the hallways Stan managed to locate where he was when he entered the hallways that had windows that provided some precious moonlight.

He managed to get to the grand staircase that led downstairs. He noticed that there was a large glass window above the doors that led out into the front yard from the foyer. He descended the staircase only after his eyes got used to the moonlight that came pouring in from that large window. At the bottom of the staircase Stan stood bathing in the moonlight, clearing his mind. Flashes of Jason were still in there. The scars of his nightmarish ordeal were still there, still healing.

He heard whispers.

The voices trailed from the hallway near the kitchen. He silenced any urge to shout his surprise and swallowed everything down. It felt like heartburn. He adjusted his glasses before turning his full attention to the noise.

He kept the balls of his feet the focal point of his steps as he snuck up to the hallway that led to the kitchen and library. When the voices grew louder and closer Stan paused and poked his head around the corner for a scant moment. In the darkness he saw Clark and Fred hunched over the library door. He whipped back into the shadows.

After taking a moment to compose himself Stan stole another peek and watched the two disappear into the library and close the door behind them. Stan breathed a sigh of relief and turned the other way to head into the kitchen. He scratched his head and looked concerned while all alone in that kitchen. Shuffling around in the refrigerator, he could not understand why Clark and Fred would be breaking the rules already. *Maybe they are thieves,* he thought while taking two bottles of water out for himself and his wife.

He arrived back at his room minutes later with his gift for his wife. He shut the door and put his back against it, "At least the trip back was uneventful." He muttered.

"What?" Jasmine asked as she stood up from that waterbed bereft of clothing. She crossed the room to meet her husband and took one of the bottles from him.

Stan's gaze never left his wife's eyes even in that darkened room, "Well when I went down to the kitchen I saw Fred and Clark by the library doors. They broke in Jazz."

Jasmine gasped, "No way. I can't believe it! Those two? Wow." She said as she took a few steps back to sit on the edge of the bed. They seemed so nice." Jasmine twisted the cap off the bottle and took a few sips of water.

"Well I don't think they were breaking in to steal anything. That Clark seems like the trouble making kind but Fred is down to earth. The two of them don't scream 'criminal' either. I should know." He said and sat down next to his wife on the hard bed edge. He took a sip of his own drink before his shirt came off again for the night. "In either case I am going to mind my own business unless they get caught. If anything I'll just say I went downstairs without my glasses and didn't see exactly what happened." He rationalized before his hand ran slowly up Jasmine's right side from her hip to her breast.

"Honey?" She asked feeling what he was actually touching.

Stan paused and turned his attention to her eyes again. "Oh, sorry. I didn't mean to."

She shook her head and turned her body toward his own and kept his hand placed against the foot-and-a-half-long scar that went from her underarm to her thigh. "Don't be sorry. This is nothing to me anymore. It may have taken a while for me to grow comfortable with having it but we both know how well I can kill it in a bikini." She smiled and then took her hand and put it on her husband's chest. "You'll learn to live with yours as well. They are not an ugly part of us, but a reminder of how strong we are as people."

Stan nodded his head and leaned in to kiss her on the lips. He pulled away after the short peck and smiled, "It's weird you know? I've said the same thing to dozens of people pretty much but I can never learn to follow my own advice, but here you are putting me in my place and telling me how it is. Maybe we should change careers or something, like switch."

"Oh yeah Stan, I can totally see you designing clothing and cutting fabric. Sweetie you are an amazingly talented and smart man but you are just all thumbs when it comes to anything involving your hands and fingers."

"Well if that isn't the most sexist comment I have ever heard in my life I don't know what is!"

Jasmine smiled and took their water and set it on the nearby end table, "I didn't mean to offend honey! If you want you can punish me for being such a callous, insensitive . . ." she paused and was stumped ". . . what is the opposite of misogynist?"

"You know I have absolutely no idea, but you are the best thing that has ever happened in my life Jazz. Not a single day goes by that I am not thankful Maggie and the girls dragged you out of the house that night."

Jasmine tucked a few strands of her dark-as-night hair behind her ear, "Don't say that. I didn't want to leave you alone at all after that happened. It turned me into an over protective mother more than a wife. You should not have had to go through that alone." She said. She pulled her legs up and tucked them in before she rolled into the waterbed and patted the spot next to her side.

"Are you kidding me Jasmine? I don't even really have nightmares about the event, well, I do but they involve you in that chair and not me. I think that night changed me somehow and I'm thankful you've put up with my ass for the last few months. In fact I know I haven't been myself." He said as he joined her on that wavy mattress.

Jasmine draped her naked body over his chest and gave him a soft kiss to his jaw. "You haven't changed, just shifted. Anyone in your situation would have. You can't blame yourself if you have an off time with your patients still. It's alright to be afraid, I just think you tried to be too 'manly' about it and bury everything deep inside. I know you want to continue helping people; I know you still have a heart. It's still inside of you and you just have to find it again honey."

"See?" Stan asked and draped his arm around her shoulders, pulling her in close to his body, "I honestly think that in the broad spectrum of things you and I were meant to be together forever. Stay with me always, okay? Stay with me even if I have a little trouble getting back on my feet after this vacation."

Jasmine kissed him deeply on his lips, a fierce kiss to compliment her body sliding on top of his own.

12

Inside the library there were several switches right inside of the doors and to the right but they were unresponsive no matter how many times Clark fiddled with them. Up and down, up and down, and nothing. Not even a flicker. The flashlights they had bounced off the numerous bookshelves and walls though the shadows it cast made everything look twisted in comparison to what they had seen with the lights on. The floor creaked with every step the two of them took.

"Dammit Clark," Fred began, "This isn't like me but I am kind of freaked out by this place.

"Oh hush. We are almost at the door anyway. It isn't as if the bookshelves are going to come alive and get us. There is no such thing as the boogeyman."

The two of them approached the single door with that padlock securing it to the wall. Fred and Clark drew close and let their flashlights roam over the odd design that was on the door now that they were close enough to observe it for what it was.

"Okay this is just weird," Fred exclaimed as he looked at the middle of the door.

There were symbols on the door carved within a large circle on the door. Crosses, chalices, and other Christian signs decorated the door. There weren't any signs of Jesus hung on the cross, however, but some were completely upside down in how they hung.

Clark placed his hand on the door and began tracing a few of the symbols with the tip of his finger.

"Hey, Clark, look at that. There isn't any keyhole or handle. This door is just held by that latch apparently."

Clark pulled his flashlight up to the padlock and gasped. "It's unlocked! The padlock isn't even there!" He reached up and gripped the latch and pulled the door open.

Clark and Fred stood there slack-jawed. In front of them were two more doors. This time the door was showing the exact same designs that the first door had but they were between both doors and evenly spaced out. There was a split down the middle, however, and hinges on both outer sides of the doors.

"Is this even a door? What the hell?" Clark asked.

Fred took his finger and slowly ran it down the split in the middle and shrugged. "Yeah, I'm pretty sure it is. It'd be silly to have hinges just on a wall or some shit. Maybe it's a French thing or something," he said as he began tracing some of the other symbols as well.

Clark and Fred found their fingers tracing around two circular indents in the door. On Clark's side it was an imprint of a sun. The rays were curving away from the indent while Fred traced a symbol of a half-moon with the other half acting as a shadow. It startled the two of them when the two circles began rotating when their fingers trailed around each shape.

"Whoa," Clark began as the doors creaked open towards them. The two circles continued spinning, one clockwise and the other counter clockwise until a click echoed from the crack in the doors. Their automatic movement stopped along with the click.

Clark was pulling at his side of the door and Fred slapped his hand. "Are you crazy? This is fucked up Clark. I mean who the hell puts this kind of shit in a place like this?"

"You're no fun, you know that? This is probably part of the deal! A hidden adventure package or something Fred! Come on, what company is going to risk a lawsuit on something dangerous?" Clark reached to the door again and yanked it as hard as he could.

Both doors were on the same latch mechanism as the other door swung open with the same force when Clark pulled so rough on the other side.

Darkness spilled into the mysterious area before them. Each flashlight was centered on the darkness before them which revealed nothing but a set of staircases made out of solid stone. Fred knelt down and ran a few fingers across the surface and discovered it was cold as ice.

"There doesn't seem to be any heating down there," he said.

Clark pouted, "Some secret room. It's like it's been cleaned recently. That's no fun, but hey, if people sweep the steps between vacations let's see what's going on down there."

Clark inched his way into the darkness. Fred followed in suit and used the side of the submerging corridor as a way to keep his balance from step-to-step. With each step taken the air seemed to chill a degree.

"Christ, did they build a freezer area for meat in the wrong damn area of the house? I bet that's why Jacque brushed this place off; they screwed it up in the planning."

Fred and Clark stopped when their flashlights hit something shiny. It reflected the light right back into their eyes, blinding them for a moment.

"Is that a mirror? Is the floor made out of fucking mirrors?" Fred exclaimed. He had to clear his throat soon after.

Clark shook his head as he pointed the flashlight up and away from the direct line they had with the floor below. "No, I don't think it's a mirror but something extremely glossy. Look, the floor is pitch black. It might be tiled, see?" Clark pointed at the small strips of white that he could see between the large squares of the shiny black that reflected their light back at them. "I think these tiles are made out of some shiny rock. I always enjoyed geology in school. Anyways I think this type of material is called onyx. That might be it I'm not sure. It is like marble but it's slick and black. If this floor is made out of this onyx shit then this floor is expensive as shit Fred. We are talking huge payday for a carpenter."

Clark finally stepped onto the black floor. His flashlight pointed forward fully and revealed a long stretch of hallway before them which had several other branching hallways attached at an angle from the main one they stood in.

Fred joined Clark and proceeded to shine his own light down the branching corridors that went too far for his flashlight to reach. "Freaky," he said; his voice only a whisper.

"Your life would be boring as hell without me and you know it," Clark said and leaned over to steal a kiss from Fred's cheek.

"Whatever."

"Well I don't think we should go down any of these corridors. The idea of getting lost down here doesn't sound like a fun time at all so how about we just venture to the end of this hallway, look left and right, and be done with it?" Clark suggested as he stepped lightly towards the end of the hallway that the flashlight could reach. It was all made of the same onyx material.

They each made their way down the cold, yet breezeless hallway until they came to the T-intersection at the end the hallway which housed the staircase to the now less-than-creepy library. Fred and Clark looked in opposite directions when they got to the end and found two doors that were only a few feet into each hallway; just normal, wooden doors and nothing more.

"Okay they are fucking with us; all this glitz and glamour for two fucking doors that look like they were bought from a fucking hardware store?' Fred asked as he looked to the door on the left and Clark inspected the one on the right.

"Maybe they ran out of funding? Or maybe the whole 'adventure' thing will be implemented at a later date?" Fred asked and stepped up to his door. Jiggling the handle a bit he found, to his surprise, that it turned without a fight and the door opened without any other lock or latch catching it. No squeaking sound emitted from the hinges either. Clark's door opened in a similar fashion.

The two of them were each bathed in light as soon as the doors swung open. They had to shield their eyes for a moment to adjust to the sudden brightness that filled the hallway they were in.

"Do you think it is some sort of motion sensor Fred?" Clark asked as he blinked a few times.

"I don't know but I'm still trying to see what the hell is in here," he replied before pushing into the room. His eyes took their sweet time adjusting to the bright light but the doorway did lead into another room. His vision was still blurry but he spotted a single pedestal in the middle of the room. In all the brightness it was hard to miss since it was a solid black object. "There is something in here Clark!"

"Same here Fred! It's like a storeroom of sorts. Just a bunch of boxes," Clark announced his findings when the light became bearable to look at. The room was full of boxes and most of it was marked with grocery items for the week. "Lame, it's just a store room for the food."

Fred, meanwhile, was able to make out the pedestal that sat in the middle of the bright, white room when his vision cleared. On the pedestal was something he wasn't expecting to see. It was a book; a simple, leather-bound book. Before Fred could say anything about it he felt his body drifting towards the out of place object. His arms felt numb as he reached for that very book.

As he touched the leathery tome he felt a stinging sensation shoot from his fingertips to his heart. A silent scream escaped his lips as his body felt on fire for a brief moment before it all just went away. The room went black.

13

"Fred? Fred! Talk to me babe!"

Fred's head ached as he stirred awake. The light was bright again but there was warmth to it. His eyes fluttered several times but remained closed. He felt someone tugging on his arm to help him into a sitting position. He had not realized he was lying down.

He realized something was amiss when he felt grass underneath his hands instead of tile.

Fred's eyes shot wide open and he was outside. He was in the sun and the voice that was constantly echoing in his head was Clark's. It took him a moment to figure out what was going on.

"Fred! Come on, snap out of it! You took one hell of a tumble!" Clark's voice rang in Fred's ears.

Confusion fell over Fred's face as he whipped his head around. "What? Where are we Clark? Why is it sunny out?" He asked with a groan as he tried to stand up but fell right back down on his ass. "We were just in a basement; a weird one-," he said before Clark cut him off.

"Damn you really did hit your head. You've been out for a few minutes," Clark said as a few other people surrounded the downed, burly man.

Another voice boomed behind Fred, "Hey, sorry about that man. I wasn't even looking where I was going. Are you alright?"

Fred's head whipped around and he saw that the voice belonged to Vincent Tanner. Fred sprang to his feet and wobbled around as he eyed a one story house, a white picket fence, and other cookie cutter homes around him. They were in a suburban area and from the decorations which hung on the house behind him and the trees, along with the various tables and the grill that had been fired up it was a house warming party. Fred was beside himself as his eyes jumped from Clark, to Tanner, and even Oswald Matthews.

"Whoa slow down there tiger! I don't need you falling over and knocking your head against the ground again. We have to break this home in tonight," Clark said as he pressed his hand against Fred's back and chest to help stabilize the grizzled man. "Tanner here wasn't paying attention to his surroundings when he was tossing the Frisbee around."

Fred turned to the Frisbee in Tanner's hand and then shot his gaze to the rest of the people standing around. The three college kids were there, the family Sinfield, the Freasons and the McCallisters were there as well. Fred shook his head back and forth.

"No! This ain't right! Where the hell am I? Clark we were just in a fucking mansion!" He shouted as his pulse escalated and his body spun around several times in his panicked state. The sun was beating down on his flesh something terrible and perspiration rolled down his forehead and over his nose and lips. He could feel it, taste it.

Before Clark could grab him, or anyone for that matter, Fred sprinted for the home they were all parked in front of. The sound of the grass crunching underneath his feet was almost as maddening as the frantic shouts for him to stop. The sun grew warmer against his skin while he vaulted up the steps of the wooden deck that was built on the back of the house. As his hand glanced against the wood he felt a splinter slide right into the palm of his hand. The pain was excruciating but he ignored it.

Fred's hand gripped the chrome handle of the door and shoved it open after turning the knob. He exploded into the home and felt something snap. It wasn't s body part; it wasn't the wood from the doorframe from his violent entry either. He was happy. He was ecstatic that he was finally moving into his very first home with his newlywed husband. The pain from his hand hurt but he was calm, at ease. He realized that this was his dream life, that this was his goal. This was all he ever wanted in life and he wanted to eat it all up.

Blood dripped from his hand but as Fred's mind took in the magnificent home along with the calming feeling he felt as soon as he opened that door the blood trickled less and less. As he smiled and felt the need to greet his family and friends, ones he and Clark had known for years, the sliver was soon non-existent; it disappeared from his flesh as the door slammed shut.

14

Clark huffed when a fog of dust kicked up at him after he dropped one of the supply boxes. He coughed hard to clear his lungs of the foreign invaders, "Fred!" he grumbled, getting agitated that the man that hadn't responded to him for the last minute or two. He hadn't heard anything from Fred since they entered each room.

Clark was fed up with calling out to his husband. He turned towards the door he entered with the storage room light still shining from above and discovered that the light which spilled so brightly on the other side of the hallway had been completely snuffed out.

"Fred?" Clark called out as he poked his head out of the storage room. He stepped towards the other side of the hallway with careful steps and called out again, "Fred? Come on, this isn't cool! Are you okay in there?" He asked as he stood in front of the darkened room and leaned forward to see if he could get a glimpse inside.

A hand shot out of the dark attached to a hairy arm. It was Fred's but it still caused Clark to jump out of his skin. The hand beckoned to Clark, fingers dragging back in a silent petition to coax Clark into the room.

"Christ! Don't do that to me Fred! Say something you jerk!"

Fred's arm melted back into the blackness of the room. As it retreated into the dark it looked more like the blackness was swallowing his arm more than anything else. Clark could not, for the life of him, see into that darkened room. It didn't look or feel like a natural absence of light at all.

Creepy images and thoughts entered Clark's brain. He shook his head several times to shake his head clear of his own imagination. He didn't need his creative side perking up at that point, but he did not imagine the fact the area was getting much colder. "Fred! It's starting to get cold as hell down here!" He said as he inched his way to the dark room and stopped just inches from the pitch black area in front of him. "F-Fred?" he stammered, "Let's go back upstairs. This is freaking me out!"

While he peered into the darkness a force slammed against the front of his face, square into his nose. The cartilage shattered immediately upon impact and the burning sensation of his nose breaking caused Clark to cry out in pain. He stumbled backwards from the hit and tripped onto his backside.

Blood flowed from his nose down to his upper lip and tears welled in his eyes from the sudden assault. Fred's arm vanished into the dark.

"Fred! What was that? You broke my nose!" Clark screamed as he tried his best to get back to his feet.

One leg stretched from the darkness and then the other. Fred stepped out from the black and Clark, trying his best to clear his eyes of the tears, wanted a better look at what was happening. His mind was playing tricks on him, he had to be dreaming; he was hysterical and that was all. It was an accident and nothing more.

When the haze from his tear stained vision cleared Fred was off. Different. What stood in front of Clark was something he could not comprehend. It looked like Fred, it certainly felt like Fred but a fog was surrounding him, a black fog that swirled around his body. It flowed like smoke. His body could be seen through it but his face was wrong. The defining features of his face, his nose, eyes and mouth were all obscured somehow. Clark could make out the stubble on Fred's face but his face was blurred. Clark closed and opened his eyes numerous times to see if his head had just been knocked too hard. It was useless. Fred's face looked permanently censored.

"Fred? Fred what happened to you?" Clark's voice trembled. He choked back his tears the best he could. "My nose hurts! You busted my nose Fred!" Clark cried out and reached for Fred's hand for help.

The grip Fred gave Clark's own hand forced a scream from Clark. Not only was it crushing his hand but it was also freezing it to the point of pain.

Fred yanked him to his feet with that steel grip. When Clark was fully on his feet he began beating on Fred's chest as hard as he could while his other continued to chill in that freezing grip.

"Let me go Fred! God damn it, what are you doing?" Clark cried as he did his best to wiggle away while hitting Fred square in the chest.

The struggle ended when Fred cocked his arm back and launched a right hook across Clark's Jaw.

Blood shot across the adjacent wall as Clark's jaw cracked and his skin was cut. It left the man dazed while on his feet.

Fred let go of Clark's hand but before he could feel any relief from the agonizing burn on his hand his body was slammed against that onyx wall. He felt his breath leave his lungs from the force of the push against the wall and Fred's hands wrapped around Clark's shirt to keep him standing.

Clark could finally see Fred's eyes through the blurred features of his face. The no longer held a gentle brown tone to them but were iced over, glossy. He had no irises and the eyes showed no emotion, just neutrality. No expression to once vibrant eyes. That lasted for only a moment before Fred's face began shifting wildly. The once censored features were now slid across the surface of Fred's face until it was a whirling mass of flesh.

Another solid hit glanced across Clark's jaw, splitting his face even more while blood coated the front of his body. One hit after another pulverized Clark's face. His resistance was weakening.

The pounding echoed through the black hallway several more times before an ugly sound of shattering bones and skin tearing took its place.

15

The sound of a car roaring to life in the middle of the night alerted Tanner from his slumber. He jumped out of his bed and stumbled along his blankets in his scramble to the window to get a glimpse of who was leaving. He tore the curtains back to catch a vehicle driving along the paved pathway. He couldn't make out who was in the vehicle but the silhouettes inside showed at least two dark figures inside.

Tanner tossed his shirt and pants on and slipped his shoes on without socks before he dashed out of his room. He rushed down the hallway and bounded down the lavished staircase two or three steps at a time. He slipped on the rug below but caught himself just in time so he could slam his body against the large double doors that led outside.

He fiddled with the knob before he yanked the door open to see the car already halfway down the lot. Tanner launched himself into the moonlight night and landed with a loud thud that made his knees quiver.

His feet padded on the pavement for five solid lunges before a voice brought him to a skid. He stopped dead in his tracks.

"Tanner? Tanner!"

That voice. It came from behind him but from a distance. The car didn't matter to tanner at all now. He spun around, nearly tripping himself in the process.

The voice belonged to a shadow that was just peeking around the corner of the building where all the vehicles, including his, were parked. He stood there for a moment to look at the shadowy figure that called out to him again in the same familiar tone.

"Helena?"

He gathered his courage and took a step forward. The shadow disappeared around the building.

"Helena!" He cried out and dashed after the vanishing shadow. He rounded the corner and found nothing.

Resisting the urge to curse for now, and seeing absolutely no activity between the cars, he knew the only other way the shadow could have gone was over the cliff side and that was still a good distance to sprint. He would have caught the person by then. He had imagined it. He felt like a fool as he looked back to see the car make its exit.

"Fucking hell!" He cursed as he reached into his pants pocket and pulled out his cigarettes and lighter. He lit one up and turned the corner to head back inside.

The figure standing around the corner didn't make Tanner flinch in the least.

Jacque was wearing a ridiculous outfit for a grown man. It was a one piece pajama with a night cap that was reminiscent of a character from a Charles Dickens' novel. He looked annoyed.

"Hello," Tanner muttered, "You're a sneaky little bastard, you know that?"

Jacque's annoyed features curled into a sickening grin. "I will take that as a compliment Mister Tanner. Though did I not strongly recommend no one goes out alone?"

"When you gotta' smoke you gotta' smoke. It's an addiction I'm not proud of it but at least I'm not contaminating the inside of this lovely establishment you have here . . ." he paused and gave the building a good pat with his free hand, ". . . question is: what the hell are you doing up and about?"

"We all have our vices Mister Tanner. I won't judge you for that. I am awake at this hour because those two gentlemen who were together had to leave the establishment without a refund.

"That was Fred and Clark?" Tanner asked as he took another drag from his smoke. "Well damn. I hope everything is going okay with them."

"Unfortunately they violated one of the rules that were outlined in the contract you signed. Just a simple defiance is all. It isn't that uncommon, really, I have had to evict a few from this establishment in the past. It never stops being awkward."

He watched Tanner's cigarette continue to disintegrate every time he took a drag of it.

"I understand. You have to do what you have to do but will you be kicking me out now that you have caught me outside after dark?" Tanner asked as he finally finished the smoke down to the filter. He reached into his pocket and procured a silver case that flipped opened and acted as a portable ashtray. The symbol on the front of it looked like a pentagram but had two golden swords bisecting it diagonally. He closed the lid with the disposed cigarette nestled inside and slid it into his back pocket.

Jacque spun on a heel and walked back to the entrance of the mansion. "Not at all; going outside was never one of the rules, I just strongly suggested that you do not. We are on the edge of a very large forest Mister tanner. Naturally, I would hate for one of my guests to encounter a stray forest denizen that could cause them harm."

Stan woke up when the sound of a car engine lit up and pulled out of the drive. He observed the car from his window but he also he watched Tanner shoot out after it only moments later. It was a curious thing to see. Tanner had exhibited behavior of a loner and to see him running after a vehicle that wasn't his in the middle of the night confused Stan.

Just as he began drawing the curtain back he saw Tanner, who appeared flustered, turn and begin heading back for the establishment before breaking off to the left. He almost thought he heard Tanner shout something even from the second floor.

"Stan?"

Jasmine had woken from her slumber. The curtains closed together while Stan turned around to join his wife in the bed once more.

"I thought I heard a noise but it was nothing," he began and then smiled, "Hey, you know what? I didn't have a nightmare tonight." He said and knocked on the wooden headboard gently three times in a row.

16

Jacque had called for a meeting for everyone to attend to in the indoor recreational area when the morning sun poked over the ocean to the East. Tanner was the only one aware as to why Fred and Clark were not there with them but Stan also had an idea as to why they weren't with them.

While the group waited for Jacque to make his own appearance after making the announcement over a pager system James, Jimmy, and Kimberly were off in the corner of the room and dusting off a few pool cues to pass the time while they waited.

Oswald walked towards the group and chalked a cue. He watched as James set the rack. "Let me do it son." He commanded and James obliged.

"Here's how you do it kids," he began as he started popping the balls around the proper way, ensuring that every single orb was tightly held together before carefully pulling the rack up and away from them. "The key to a good break is always in the racking. The tighter the rack the better the crack."

James and Jim looked at each other with uneasy eyes before Jim cleared his throat, "Alright, well I have no problem with teams. Though who's on whose team?"

Oswald perked and beamed, "Well I am not a world champion at pool, and my hustling days are far behind me but I think I can still play a decent game."

"Well then I am the worst here by far. I haven't even shot that white ball or anything!" Kimberly perked a bit, "Though you boys are lucky there isn't a dart board in here. That was the game I was raised on."

Oswald looked towards the boys. "Well that is settled then," he said and came around to chalk his cue once more. "Go ahead and break."

James stepped up to the pool table and shot. The break was clean and the balls scattered in a chaotic beauty. James sank a striped ball into the corner pocket which gave them something to start with. He missed the second shot something terrible and nearly sent the ball over the rim of the table. He put too much power into the shot.

"Too much power is a common mistake in pool. Don't worry about it." Oswald watched the cue ball settle near a solid which was lined up at an angle with the side pocket.

"You go ahead Mister Matthews. I don't want to take this shot; I know I'd screw it up," Kimberly said.

Oswald looked at the solid colored ball and the cue ball that was at such an angle that the shot would be a pain in the ass to make, "Nonsense Kimberly. Pool is a game of finesse really. Put the right spin and angle on a shot along with the perfect amount of power behind the thrust and you can sink any shot. Here let me show you." He said and set his pool cue on the table. He lined the cue up with the white ball and showed Kimberly the angle he was situated at. "You have to envision the angle you want the cute ball to hit the colored ball to get it where you want it to go." He took the cue away from the ball and stepped back. "Go ahead and line yourself up and I'll adjust you to make sure you get it right."

Kimberly did as he instructed and bent over the pool table. The inviting curve of her ass had a draw to it that challenged him more than any other woman had before. He kept his eye on the prize, however, which was the tip of her cue.

"Alright your form is looking good but make sure you are twisting just enough to make sure the cue ball hits more to the right of the red ball there," he said and finally set his own cue down to help her adjust. He made sure to make his touches feel innocent in nature.

When he let go over her hips and her arm she swallowed hard and nodded her head. "Is this good then?"

"Looks good to me Kimberly and now all you have to do is ease it right in there."

Kimberly was still nervous about missing the shot and while her arms shook a little she pulled back slightly and jabbed the cue forward; her eyes closing along with a single bite to her lower lip.

The three males watched on as the white cue ball slapped the number three. The sphere rolled at an angle right at the side hole and stopped right on the lip.

"Damn it!" She blew a strand of her blonde hair that had been hanging in her eyes after the shot.

Oswald laughed, "Hey now, if you would have made the first shot you ever made I would have to call you a liar about never having played before. I would have to call bullshit quick."

"Not bad Kimberly, though I am afraid I won't let you guys get another shot in," Jimmy said and swaggered up to the pool table. He lined up the cue and sank the striped four ball in the corner pocket.

Jacque made his way into the recreational room about halfway through the pool game and when he arrived he cleared his throat as a means to capture everyone's attention. When he got that attention he looked solemn.

"As you may have noticed the Thompsons are not joining us this morning or for the rest of the vacation. They, unfortunately, broke the rules and had to be removed from the premises for doing so."

"What rule did they break? It seems a bit harsh to throw them out after one day," Stan said from the back of the crowd as he stood hand in hand with Jasmine.

"Who cares what rule they broke? Rules are rules. If you break them you deal with the consequences," Oswald interrupted before Jacque could even speak.

"I have to run this establishment by myself Mister Freason. If I allowed everyone to get away with one rule break then this place would be unruly. Though the fact is they broke into the library for whatever reason.

I have an alarm system in my bedroom that is tied to the library and other locked doors of this establishment and I caught them sneaking around in there. It is unfortunate but they understood that they had done wrong. I do not think badly of them and I am sorry that that I had to end the contract they signed due to their own curiosity."

"That's a shame. They were a pretty nice couple I thought," Maggie whispered as she stood between Ryan and Jasmine.

Jacque continued on, "As I mentioned I have an alarm system in place during the night for the library. I hate to repeat myself but if you wish to go into the library all you have to do is notify me and then sign a sheet showing that you were indeed in the library. I mean it is a simple rule that is not that hard to follow. I am sorry that we are now two guests down but I assure you that as long as the rules are followed you all will have an amazing time in this vacation home."

As Jacque left the recreational room Stan slipped from Jasmine to stand next to Tanner while everyone else dispersed as well. The four at the pool table continued their game.

"So," Stan paused as Tanner turned, "did you rat them out or what was the deal last night when they left?"

Tanner shrugged, "Actually I find it odd that they were kicked out because of that. Clark and Fred do not strike me as the breaking and entering type."

"So I think we are both thinking that Jacque is full of hot air?" he asked Tanner through his thick rimmed glasses.

"You got that feeling too? For the life of me I didn't see any cameras around that area or any other for that matter. Let's take a walk Mister Freason."

17

The early morning sunrise had a sobering effect on Tanner. That, combined with the fresh breeze that rolled in from the ocean past the cliff side aroused Tanner's mind better than a cup of coffee. The two men went all the way around the side of the mansion and back towards the outside recreational area where the basketball court and other amenities had not been used aside from the grill. It was going to be a hot day, judging from the humidity Tanner felt in the air.

"So if Fred and Clark weren't kicked out for breaking the rules what other reason do you think they could have been evicted for?" Stan asked as they came to a stop near the cliff's edge. "You know chances are if they were kicked out for that we could be yelled at for being so close to this cliff," he said as he looked over the massive body of water. He could not see what resided under the cliff's edge. "Figure there is a bunch of sharp rocks? Think anyone has actually fallen off?"

Tanner laughed, "I doubt it. Maybe back before this place was a house some pilgrims may have been chased off by the tribes around here, or vice versa, but in any case if you slip I'll try and catch you." Tanner said as he too looked over the ledge, "In any case, Mister Freason, normally I wouldn't care if people got kicked out of an establishment for breaking the rules. The fact that they were kicked out in the middle of the night without causing a fuss is what has me twisted."

"I have to admit it wasn't that much fun waking up in the middle of the night because of car starting up and driving off."

Tanner took his cigarettes out of his pocket and lit another up. After he put the pack away he drew his silver case from his pocket and traced his thumb over the design on the side of it away from Stan's vision. He slid it back into his pocket.

"So you saw me running after the car and talking to Jacque afterwards?" Tanner asked as he watched the sun continually rise. The ocean was pristine and the view offered them nothing but a clear blue sky without a cloud as far as they could see. It was natural, fresh. The gentle wind offered a breeze that rustled each of their shirts.

"Yes. I didn't hear what you two were talking about thought. How was Jacque acting when you spoke to him?"

"For someone that was apparently angry enough to evict two people from a very expensive vacation he looked amused more than anything. Giddy kind of. He also was suspicious as to why I was out there so late at night."

"Psychologically I cannot put a finger on the man. He gives off sort of a megalomaniac persona. A strict person for rules and punishment but he also seems to be carefree and exuberant about everything in general," Stan said.

"You're not a shrink are you?" Tanner asked.

"Psychiatrist; and yes, I am," Stan said as he looked back to the mansion for a moment, observing the backside of the building and the well-trimmed grass surrounding the foundation.

"Whatever gets you a paycheck dock," Tanner said.

"I know we get ribbed for not seeming like actual doctors. You don't have to tell me how much it seems like we don't' do any work at all. It's why my wife and I are here actually."

"You don't see that every day: a psychiatrist who doesn't defend his profession to the death. Something happen?" Tanner asked.

Stan let out a ragged breath as he looked over the cliff again. "You ever get that feeling that you are doing a good job; that you are doing your best for those that depend on you but then one slip up, one bad case and it just throws your entire world into a downward spiral?"

"Every single God damn day my friend."

"Well a patient of mine was having a turn around. A real breakthrough, you know? He went against my advice and some awful things happened. Not just to himself but to me and his ex-wife."

The wind blew a violent gust and the men each took a step back from the ledge.

"Remind me to never bring Jasmine out here if it is too windy out."

"Hell Stan after that gust I don't think I'm going to be coming this close to the ledge again."

Stan took his leave from the cliff and came back inside. He was halfway up the stairs to his room when Ryan, Maggie, and his wife rounded the banister.

The three of them were ready to enjoy the pool. Ryan had a pair of swimming trunks on with Cupids and hearts decorating the fabric and it clearly was a gift from his wife. Maggie was wearing a one-piece suit that hid her body modestly. Ryan had no issue with that. Her dark blue outfit looked like an athlete's suit.

Jasmine, on the other hand, knew she had a body and was not shy on showing it off. Stan looked to her side and, as always, saw that she had used some waterproof make-up to cover up her scar.

"Stan! Baby I gotta show you something in our room. That and afterwards I'm making you swim with me," Jasmine said as she took his hand and pulled him past Maggie and Ryan.

"Are you legitimately going to show him something Jazz?" Maggie asked the corner of her mouth turned upwards.

"Shut up Maggie! And yes, something legitimate," Jasmine huffed. She drug Stan through the door that led into the dank, dark hallway before it spilled into the more illuminated path that led to their rooms.

"I really wish they would get some lamps for that first damn hallway," Stan muttered. "So what is this all about? I didn't think there was anything worth showing in our own room. We sort of already have seen everything it has to offer."

Jasmine huffed and pushed the door open before letting his hand go. She moved to the side of the water bed and knelt down. She opened a drawer that was under the bed and pulled out a plastic card. "Check it out sweetie; I think someone left their I.D. here or something!"

Stan took the card from her and looked at the picture offered. The picture showed a stunning redhead with piercing blue eyes. Her face was thin with high cheekbones and little make-up from first glance.

"I was making the bed from last night and when I pulled the sheet up to rearrange it a bit this fell out from underneath it. That is what was so freaky. It was like that woman, or someone, put it there on purpose. I mean it looks like a driver's license but doesn't offer any information on it. Just a barcode on the back of the card," she pointed out and had Stan look on the back. Sure enough there was a barcode with an eight digit number above it. "I mean an I.D. card just doesn't fall out of someone's wallet or purse and floats around until it finds a nice sheet it can tuck itself into."

Stan thought it over, "Keep it inside the drawer. If anything we can ask Jacque or someone else later on."

He kissed her on the cheek and slid the I.D. back into the drawer. He then kicked his shoes off and began taking one sock off after another.

"So who do you think she is?" His wife asked him as she watched him hop around on one foot trying to get his other sock off.

Stan shrugged and flopped onto the bed after he lost his balance. "Honestly I don't know, but I find it very strange that someone would just put their I.D. card there and never came back to get it. For that matter how Jacque or the cleaning crew missed it as well."

"Well then let's ask Mister Jacque about it then! He might know considering he runs this place by himself all the time."

Stan shook his head and looked to the open door. He slid over and pulled her down onto the bed so his lips could be near to her ear. "I don't think so. Not yet at least. I mean that man kicked Fred and Clark out of in the middle of the night. I do not want to bring up any problems that we don't have to."

"How about we try and figure out whose I.D. it is? Make a little game of it and pretend we are detectives or something?" Jasmine suggested with a little bounce of enthusiasm.

"Sounds like a plan to me. Can you do me a favor and don't

bounce around too much when we get down to the pool? Especially if those college kids or that older man are hanging around down there? You might make the boys into men and give that old guy a heart attack."

Jasmine reached over and pulled Stan to his feet with a coy grin. She pushed him back down onto the bed and sashayed her way towards the door. "I wouldn't worry about that honey, you're the only boy here I plan on making a man later on."

Tanner's pants began vibrating. He closed and locked his door before digging around to pull his cell phone out. He didn't have to look at the screen to see who was trying to get a hold of him.

He debated on letting the phone go to voice mail. After a few more rings he finally flipped it open and held it a few inches from his ear.

"Tanner? God damn it are you there?"

"Can you tone it down a little boss? I mean my hearing is going bad already without you blasting my eardrums with that amazing baritone voice you have."

"Tanner," his boss sighed, "Vincent. I need you to come back."

"I can't do that boss. I honestly wish I could but there is something very wrong going on here. You ever get that feeling that everything is too perfect? That's how this place feels. The guy running this place is creepy as all hell and I heard her voice last night boss. Helena is here somewhere."

"Jesus Christ Vincent. You're hearing her voice? You're upset. You're becoming more than a bit delusional. I understand you are worried about her but without solid evidence that she did not just up and go AWOL on us I cannot do a thing Tanner. You know that."

"Yeah, I do Ralph. I am telling you there is some legitimate work to be done here. I know it. I mean for fuck's sake boss this Jacque guy kicked two other people out that were staying here for apparently going into the library after dark. He kicked them out and they didn't make a fuss! There was no argument, no screaming, and no shouting."

Ralph sighed, "So what? If they broke the rules they broke the rules. Some people are not as lenient as I am on some matters."

"Why in the hell are you so worried about me and what I am doing if you think Helena just went AWOL on us? On me? Shouldn't you not give a damn if everything is sunshine and lollipops?"

"I'm not worried about your safety Tanner. I'm worried about what you might do if you find out the answer isn't the one you have made up in your head. Our job is dangerous Tanner, you know and I know that but that also is why we can't just send people out on a hunch."

"This is Helena, Ralph, I trained her. I taught her everything about this job and this life and you cannot ask me to abandon her Ralph. You can't. It's the same reason you're not giving up on me. Why you haven't sent anyone to drag me back kicking and screaming."

A breathy, deep sigh escaped from the other end of the phone. "Just promise me if anything comes up you don't get stupid, that you don't lose your head."

A smile graced Tanner's lips, "Trust me Ralph, if anything has happened to Helena you better bet your ass I want the hammer dropped on this place with every God damn resource you can provide. If something did happen I will get you the evidence you need."

"I'll be here Tanner. Regardless of what happens your balls will be in a vice when you get back."

"Love you too boss," Tanner said and snapped his phone shut.

18

Stan flinched as the water sprayed in his general direction from Jasmine leaping in and splashing into the gigantic pool. Stan huffed and ensured she got a face-full of water before he set the other buoy up so that they could get a game of water volleyball going with Peter and Stacy.

"I'm trying to work here woman!" Stan shouted as Jasmine came up from hiding under the water behind him.

Ryan and Maggie were at the other end of the pool hall enjoying the warmth of the hexagon shaped hot tub that they had bubbling on high with some champagne in their glass that they had smuggled with them.

Jasmine wrapped her arms around her husband and kissed him on the neck while ignoring the chlorine taste on his skin. "I'm sorry honey. I know how fragile you are to splashing."

Stan grumbled at the notion and reached under the water to grab the back of her knees that were near his own thighs. With a huff he was diving back, sinking both him and his wife under the water.

He dunked her under the water for a second before he let go of her legs and resurfaced. He swam to the right a little bit to get some distance from her and realized she hadn't come up yet.

"Jazz?" He called out, unable to see under the water. He looked at Peter and Stacy who shrugged their shoulders after his little stunt.

From behind he felt something grab his legs and pulled him down. He almost choked.

The couple both popped up at the same time and Stan was sputtering and spitting water as Jasmine laughed. "Fine, you got me. You win. Happy now darling?" He asked his wife as he rubbed his eyes from all the water that had managed to collect there. He was almost as blind as a bat without his glasses on but he still would see a giant, multi-colored, beach ball coming at his face when he needed to.

Jasmine rolled her eyes and turned her attention to Peter and Stacy for now. "Don't go too hard on the macho man over here," she teased.

"I'll spike the ball on your head woman." He protested as Peter served the first shot up while he laughed.

Jacque sat in his room, his office, watching the monitors. He grabbed at a small joystick and aimed the hidden camera in the "Glass Heaven" room towards a specific target. Jasmine's features, her beautiful face and wet hair, filled the screen. He hit a button on his keyboard and the image sat frozen on the screen. He sat back and smiled before leaning forward and switching the monitors off. He ensured the password protection was active before he disrobed completely on his way to the other side of the room.

The Frenchman approached the opposite wall of his room and stood in front of two small statues mounted about three feet across from one another. Each little statue was designed in the shape of a snake wrapped around a woman's hand. The snake on his right was curled around an empty hand while the one on the left was wrapped around a hand that held a stone apple. Jacque pressed down on the left serpent's head. In front of him the walls bisected and opened to reveal an elevator shaft. The elevator itself pulled open via steel gates and the shaft was exposed on all four sides due to the fact the only thing keeping a person inside the elevator was a single horizontal steel bar that ran across the back, right and left sections of the elevator. Jacque stepped inside and slid the iron gating across. It locked in with a click and he was on his way down.

The elevator ride was always slow.

The iron gate opened once again when the elevator came to a full stop. In front of Jacque was a dimly lit hallway where the black surface on the floor and walls shined against the light and offered a glossy version of Jacque as his shoes clicked through the corridor. The narrow hallway soon spilled into a much wider room.

The space was split off into ten separate rooms on each side where walls would divide each one side by side but the front had nothing more than a simple gate. Each room was longer than it was wide but the spaces were still quite small. It was more of a stable than another set of rooms and currently nine of the twenty rooms were occupied.

"Good morning my very special guests, how are you today?" Jacque asked as he began going from stable to stable area.

The entire area sang out in a chorus of cries and moans. To Jacque's right was a man who was blindfolded and chained by his arms and his legs. He was shaved from head to toe and bereft of clothing. His ribs poked from his malnourished body but he pulled at his chains that bound him hard. The blindfold would not conceal the rest of his face which twisted and swirled around like water down a drain.

The first two stables on Jacque's left were a young man and a young woman, "I'm sorry my dears, but I think I have a new favorite couple." When he mentioned that at the end of the room a loud, bellowing roar shook the walls of the stables. "Not you! I'll be there in a second!" Jacque fired back as his hands gently slapped the blurry faces of the two teenagers that were chained to the walls of their rooms. The male, much like the older man behind Jacque, was bare of all hair. The female next to him was allowed to keep her shoulder length black hair and eyebrows intact. They were painfully thin but like the man in the other stable they were having no problem in shaking the thick, solid iron chains and shackles around while they cried and moaned.

Skipping a stable on his right he peered in on a much larger woman. He sneered for a moment while the chains did not rustle or move at all as the woman was sitting in a puddle of her own filth. "I can see that you are going to be the first one I replace. Such a lazy and filthy creature; it was a mistake to keep you and I can see that now. I am disgusted at how you never grow any smaller. Shame!" he taunted and berated the woman. Several stables down there was another bellowing roar and something slammed against the wall so hard that it shook the other rooms.

"God damn, you are one angry beast, aren't you?" Jacque asked as he skipped past two more rooms to come to the final row. He looked upon his newest collection, a burly man who was salivating all over his lips and chin as his neck, waist and arms were chained to the wall. He was violent, full of rage, and had to be restrained. Jacque reached over the fence and dug his fingers into the freshly shaved head of Fred Thompson and yanked his head and blurred face in Jacque's general direction.

Jacque shook his head and looked past the large man to the back wall. "I cannot see why you are so angry. I was gracious enough to give you a gift!" He said as he twisted Fred's head around entirely, snapping the man's neck to show him the body that was chained to the wall around the waist. The figure groaned, jawless, and was constantly reaching out towards Fred. He was fully clothed still; a trait the body on the wall did not share with the others. Jacque twisted Fred's head all the way back around with the massive man's bones cracking each time.

"You are going to be more than impressive. You are going to be my shining star." Jacque said and slapped Fred across the face as hard as he could. There was a loud slam against the stable wall that came from the stable that Jacque skipped over so he could calm his new pet down. After the bang a feral, yet feminine scream echoed throughout the corridor and stables. The wailing of the female next to them was filled with anger and sorrow. She wasn't pleading as much as she was demanding with her guttural grunts and moans as she swung her body into the wall again and again.

"For heaven's sake," Jacque exclaimed, "You are becoming the most troublesome whore!"

He slid to the right and in front of the stable next to Fred. The immaculate cleanliness of the stable housed a rather filthy young woman. Her fiery locks of hair hung over her eyes like a curtain as her entire body was suspended in the air by four chains wrapped around each limb.

The chains wrapped around her flesh so tight that it pressed in and indented her skin. The chains seared into her flesh like the fires of hell yet preserved her nerve endings for a constant stream of pain and suffering. Her wrists up to her forearms, and her ankles up to her knees were red and welted from the chains that burned her.

"You were a nosey young woman. Beautiful, but nosey; very beautiful indeed actually," Jacque said as his fingers pressed against the woman's cheek. He could feel the warm tears of her painful capture running down and staining her flesh in a different way than he already had observed several times in the last week.

19

"Holy shit James," Jimmy exclaimed as he grabbed a dusty book from a shelf in the way back, "Fuckin' H.P. Lovecraft! This looks like a God damn original!" He was careful as he pulled the book from the shelf.

It was almost lunch time but James and Jimmy had received Jacque's permission to enter in the library. They followed the rules and signed into the book that was chock full of names from others that had come before them. James had made his way to the science fiction section of the massive library while James drifted to the supernatural and horror section.

"What are you talking about? We both know it would be damn near impossible for that to be true. Even if it was you should probably put it back since Jacque is so damn touchy about his shit." James said. He was flipping across some of the classics and found nothing, "Well, then again, there isn't much in the sci-fi area to write home about. Maybe the fantasy section has a better selection." He did notice the shelves were high enough that one would need a rolling ladder to see anything that was offered at the top.

Jimmy sat the book down on the table and traced his fingers over the front of the book. It was bound in leather and while it was no book of the dead, that was for certain, the symbols and etchings on the front cover were strange and foreign even for Lovecraft.

James rounded the corner of the rows which offered the science fiction section and scratched the back of his head, "So how is this Lovecraft?" he asked as he inspected the side of the book.

"Well," Jimmy paused as he turned the book around and inspected it, "I found it between some of his other works and I just figured it was his. This Jacque seems like the kind of guy who would be rather meticulous about the order of the books in his library if he was going to kick people out for entering this place after dark. I mean that guy puts a new meaning on the term 'anal'. I actually don't like him that much but I guess owning this place and being secluded can turn someone into a creepy person."

James fell silent, lost in thought.

"James? James!"

"What?"

"Dude you spacing out or something?"

"Yeah, I'm sorry. I was just thinking about other shit."

"What? Kimberly?"

"We've known her for a while Jim. The three of us have been pretty damn inseparable over the last year and a half or so. That Matthews guy gives me the creeps though. I mean you saw the look in his eye. We've seen that look in other people's eyes plenty of times and shit, I'm willing to bank you've had that look in your eye about her and so have I."

"Don't start that shit James. Come on. I mean I agree with you on Oswald but Kimberly is smarter than what you think she is. She is just being polite and conversing with him. Sure she's had her boyfriends over the last year but she hasn't been close with anyone but you and me."

James sat back and rolled his eyes, "That is beside the point. Most of who she deals with is just college kids like us. We've studied disorders like hers and an older man is someone she'd find appealing I guess, or whatever. I just don't trust the guy."

"Dude, are you jealous or what the hell is going on?"

"Maybe I am Jim. I know we both like her and that is why neither of us has ever attempted to show an interest past friendship. I guess I'm afraid she might just make a mistake here on our vacation because of it."

Jimmy sat back and crossed his arms. He bit down on the left side of his lower lip and shook his head, "Well fuck. We've known each other from high school. I mean I like Kimberly as a friend but I'd rather work on college than work on my social life for now. If you have feelings for her then just go for it. Don't sit here talking to me about it."

"It might be too late."

"She knows that this is a vacation dumbass! Mister Matthews isn't going to be here next week. You are. We are. Well fuck you know what I mean. If you think she might feel like you are trying to take advantage of her you need to get that thought out of your head. You have done a lot for her you know, I don't think she's the kind of bitch to forget you nearly took a shot in the jaw from her ex."

"You're right. Maybe it is about time I grew a pair."

"That's the spirit. I don't know if I'd go out trying to find her right now, it might be a little awkward if you did," he said while thumbing through the pages of the odd, leather bound book. "I also don't suggest bringing her here to show her this afterwards, as awesome as this book is."

Jimmy looked through the book and saw that it was a collection of previous works from some unknown author. While it felt and read like a Lovecraft horror it wasn't completely about any demons or supernatural Gods that would bring ruin to the Earth and universe. Instead it spoke about demons that walked amongst humans by blending in with societies and culture throughout the ages. "This book is trippy. It's reading more like a non-fiction book."

James scooted next to Jimmy. The two eagerly looked at the illustrations that accompanied some of the text through the book. None of the images were really new to the two of them.

"These look just like the standard cliché that we've seen before Jimmy. I mean look, pictures of torture, demonic effigies, tools of destruction, all of the horror tropes are here." James said while Jimmy flipped through the pages. James gripped Jimmy's wrist when he was halfway thumbing through the pages, "Wait a second. Look at this."

The illustration on the left side of the page had a drawing of a book paved in black. The drawing did its best to portray how shiny the book was, but it was the illustration in the background that made James stop Jimmy's flipping.

"Holy shit, that is creepy as fuck," Jimmy said.

James studied the image in the book intently, "I have never seen anything like this. How many do you think they are trying to portray here?" He looked at the numerous beings that were behind the book, "This is hard to look at. It's like their faces have been slightly erased, or something like that," he added.

"Hey, look at that guy holding the book. Doesn't he look familiar?" Jimmy asked as he pointed to a person that was actually holding the book in the drawing. It was a male figure in a business suit with gleaming white teeth. His features were defined whereas everyone else appeared behind the man like twisted shadows.

James agreed, "Yeah, it does."

"Hello boys."

Each of the two college students nearly leaped from their seats. They hadn't even heard footsteps approaching them. In the startle Jimmy's hand accidently flipped the book shut while they spun around. They were face-to-face with Jacque who gave them a charming, warm smile and reached in to take the book from them.

"Now where in the world did you two get this?"He asked. "This is from my private collection. Oh those tricky devils! The Thompsons must have stashed it here before I caught them!"

"Sorry Mister Collo. I mean Jimmy found the book right there wedged between some H.P. Lovecraft books. We figured it must have been by him but clearly it isn't." He said and pointed into the row of books that Jimmy got it from.

Jacque nodded his head and held the leather bound tome to his chest. He took a quick glance back to see that, indeed, the area that James pointed out had enough space for the book to fit in.

"That's understandable. I'm not upset in the least. I have to admit though you boys have a fascination for the supernatural don't you? I was a big fan as well and still am in some ways, although I haven't really browsed this section in some time. I have no clue who authored this book either, but I picked it up when I was down in Tennessee a few summers ago."

"Again we are sorry if we disturbed anything Mister Collo, we didn't mean to." James said.

"No harm no foul boys. You did not break any rules. I know that what I did with the Thompsons may have put a few of you on edge but I assure you that I am quite the reasonable man."

Jimmy spoke up, "Thank you Mister Collo. Do you mind if we stay in the library for a bit longer? I mean your selection is amazing. I am doing my best to not geek out."

"Of course I don't mind. Just remember to sign out when you leave and make sure that you lock the doors."

"I'm fine with locking up. It is a nervous habit of mine anyway," James said.

"Alright boys, have fun." Jacque said. He spun on his heel and made his way out of the library without another word.

20

Jacque stopped a few feet before his office door by the husband and wife Sinfield. They were parked right in front of his office door and looked like they were going to venture into the forest. Jacque saw that Peter had a baseball cap on and a tight white t-shirt on and knee length mesh shorts along with a pair of brown boots on. Stacey had black tennis shoes on and had a pair of matching pink short shorts and a tank top on. Her sunglasses were sitting on top of the visor she was wearing.

"Good afternoon Mister and Missus Sinfield. Is there anything that I can do for you?

"Hello Jacque and well yes, actually," Peter said as his eyes met Jacques, "Stacy and I, along with the boys, were hoping to do some hiking and exploring in the forest out there. We saw that brick enclosure at the front and it looked like it stretched pretty far into the forest so we were wondering if there was a barrier all the way around this place. If it is alright could we get a number we can call you if we need you for any reason? We would be back before dark of course."

Jacque allowed his peripheral vision to look at Stacy while Peter addressed him. He knew she was the oldest woman of the bunch but her curvy body was accentuated by her outdoor wear. Jacque mentally approved, "Of course Mister Sinfield. In fact I have three radios that are all set to the same channel so if there is any trouble you can contact me and you can let your boys take a radio as well. 'What if's' tend to be cautionary visions. It is best to be fully prepared right?"

"I agree completely Jacque," Peter agreed and stepped to the side so Jacque could access his office.

"That's a creepy looking book Mister Collo," Stacy commented.

"Yes. This is a book that Jimmy and James found down in the library. It is part of my personal collection and as much as I hate to point fingers I believe the Thompsons were trying to make off with this at some point. It is a very old and very expensive collectable." Jacque said. He disappeared into his room and shut the door before Peter and Stacy could look inside.

A minute later Jacque opened the door and handed the two of them two fully charged radios, "Here you are. Since I handed these to you two personally do not worry about signing them out or anything to that extent." He paused and licked his lips, "If you need anything at all just let me know. Also you have about five or six hours before sundown."

Tanner was surprised to see the library open in the mid afternoon. He wasn't surprised, however, when he saw Jimmy and James huddled around a couple of books and despite the clacking of his shoes the two boys were not drawn away from the books for a moment.

"What do you two have there?" Tanner interrupted as he showed up wearing a suit and tie along with some black khaki's.

"Oh! Hey Mister Tanner, James and I-"
"Please, call me Vincent or just Tanner."

"Oh, alright, um, well me and James were just looking up some stuff. I tell you what Vincent, Jacque seems to be a huge fan of the supernatural. He has some books in here that read out like non-fiction more than anything Stephen King or Anne Rice could make up."

James cleared his throat and nudged his best friend, his head canting back towards the empty space between the Lovecraft texts.

"Oh! That's right! Mister Collo was in here about five or ten minutes back and found us reading this funky leather-bound book. I mean this thing look old and authentic. I mean there was dust caked to this thing.

He explained to us that the Thompsons more than likely are the ones that put it there since he said the book was part of his personal collection."

"Did Jacque tell you guys where the hell his personal collection is? I mean I find it peculiar that he would keep something of sentimental value in the open and not under lock and key. What was in the book anyway? If it was old and leather-bound there must have been something interesting in it." Tanner said.

"Yeah, I'll say. I mean the book was not inked in blood or anything like that but whoever illustrated and wrote the book either inspired a lot of authors or he had a rather vivid imagination and twisted some horror clichés into something terrifying. There were tools of torture, monsters, standard horror stuff, but everything had a certain sort of humanity to it."

"There was something in there that was brand new that I had never seen before," Jimmy interjected, "I mean like there were pictures of obvious monsters like zombies and creepy ass dolls and whatever but there was one section we saw right before Jacque came in."

"Go on," Tanner said while taking a seat across from both of them.

"Jimmy sucks at explaining shit. Basically there was a picture on the left side of a man holding a book; the book was portrayed as metallic or something because the drawing made it seem like it was shining."

"A metallic book is an odd thing to see but not as weird as sparkling vampires," Tanner insisted.

James suppressed a laugh and shook his head, "Yeah but there were people in the background of the picture. They were human in shape but their faces were distorted. It was almost like their faces were like those, damn it, what do you call them? The kind of pictures that you look at closely and then slowly pull away to see a shape in the pattern?"

"I know what you are talking about. Are you saying that their faces were blurry or something? Like you couldn't quite see what they looked like?" Tanner asked.

James nodded his head.

"They were called 'The Bleak' or something like that. I saw the title before Jacque snagged the book from us," Jimmy blurted out and lowered his voice soon. "I think he is a writer in the off time Vincent. I mean he has all these books by King and Lovecraft and others but he has an ego to him."

"The man that was holding the metallic book in the picture looked like a younger version of Mister Collo." James said.

Tanner said nothing for a moment. He looked down towards the table and put his chin in his hand and narrowed his eyebrows. "Maybe that is why he considered it to be special. Perhaps he is an artist and a writer and he didn't want his work taken from him. It is stereotypical to think that way about artists but they can be eccentric and over the top. That is the perfect way to describe our host I believe."

"It takes a special kind of confidence to make yourself into the leader of some creepy ass looking people though." James pointed out.

Tanner slid back from his chair and stood up to look down at the two college boys, "I wouldn't read into it too much. If I was cooped up in a mansion this size just waiting for random people to arrive who will complain, want service, and otherwise treat you like a ghost I am sure I would develop an imagination pretty quick." Tanner turned and made his way out of the library. He waved back to both of them and pulled out his cigarettes.

Jimmy turned to James and nudged him, "Well that was weird. I didn't think that guy would be interested in anything like that. He's in a business suit."

James shrugged, "Everyone has their interests Jimmy."

21

"So why in the world is that Tanner fellow still wearing a suit?" Jasmine asked as she dried her hair with a towel after she and her husband got out of the pool. They had stayed and played in the chilly water for a good thirty minutes after their volleyball game with Peter and Stacy.

Stan shrugged his shoulders and toweled off the rest of his wet body. He watched as Jasmine wrapped her body with the large beach towel she brought with after scrubbing most of the water from her frame. The make-up she used to cover her scar had washed off after the prolonged exposure to the water and despite Ryan being family she was still self-conscious to let anyone see that scar.

"Honestly I can't say for sure. I mean there are some people who wear suits down in Bermuda. People tend to grow comfortable in what they wear on a daily basis."

Jasmine smiled and wrapped one arm around his shoulders and neck and kissed him on the cheek, "I guess that makes a lot of sense. That's why I come to you about people; you know how they behave better than anyone I know. I mean sure you have your Master's in psychology but even when we met I felt like your talents were a gift."

"Well I have to admit that it's a super power. One that I just cannot seem to use on you since I learn something new about you every day; you are my beautiful puzzle and I'm not going to solve you for a long, long time I don't think."

Jasmine giggled, "Probably not. Then again I think I am somewhat crazy so that could make things hard," she said and glanced down and then back up to his eyes, "right baby?"

Stan sighed, "You are going to put me into a coma."

"Well I don't think you'll be complaining on how I do so! Though have you figured out what you want to do about that I.D. that I found? She asked while another, larger towel wrapped around her body.

"How about we do nothing about it until the final day we are here?" he asked and smiled. He wrapped his arms around her shoulders and pulled her into a gentle hug before pulling away.

"Shouldn't we really report it honey? I mean if some poor woman is frantically searching for her I.D. then we owe it to her to at least give it to the man who runs this place.

Stan put his hands on top of his head and expunged a large breath of air, "Sweetie I know that you want to help out. I know you care a lot about people but sometimes you care way too much about nothing. Besides," he paused, "I don't like him Jazz. There is something about him that I just cannot . . ." he stopped for a moment and looked around to see if Jacque was in the vicinity, ". . . see."

Jasmine cocked her hip to the side and crossed her arms underneath her breasts, causing them to almost pop out of her top. She never meant to do it but somehow she always managed to flirt with her body language even if she was annoyed or angry. "Stan you have to learn to trust people again. Honey, he is just a manager and a care taker. That's it. It is his job to monitor things like this and make sure that people don't come back here upset and disgusted with the way this place is run."

"It isn't that baby. It really isn't. I mean for example I trust Mister Tanner. I've interacted with him and I can tell he's lying about something. He isn't here on vacation but he has the telltale signs of having a reason to be here. I just don't know why he is."

"So why do you trust him, when you know he is lying about something, instead of Mister Collo who just seems like a lovable weirdo?"

"Because even though Tanner lied about why he is here he isn't a dishonest man. Also how long has it been since the last guests were here? If I lost my license then I sure as hell would have known to look in the last place I had it. We both agreed that it did not just fall under the sheets either."

Jasmine narrowed her eyes, "Well, you are right about that. I mean I had to pull the sheet off the bed and it was pretty much right there in the middle of it. Do you think Mister Collo is hiding anything? I mean should we get Ryan and Maggie and get out of here?" She asked.

"Of course not Jasmine, we still have a few days of vacation left and you are right, I did need this. I am feeling much better already," he said, bringing her back in to hug her tight this time. He kissed her hard on her lips and ignored the taste of the chlorinated water that washed over them previously.

Jasmine's lips reciprocated every ounce of love he gave her in that kiss. Her arms wrapped loose around his neck while they shared a substantial amount of public affection. She broke away from the kiss and smiled. Her arms hung around his shoulders as her hands rubbed the back of his neck, "So day two of our festive vacation and we have the whole day left; what do you want to do?"

"Well how about we go ahead and spend the rest of the day outside? Not in the forest or anything like that but just lie outside and enjoy the cliff view?" Stan asked as he held his hands on her hips and felt the damp fabric of the towel that covered her.

"If you two are going to head outside today would be the day to do it," Ryan's voice called out from the hot tub he and Maggie were in.

"Well it's a nice day out but I don't think it's the perfect day," Stan said.

"Wrong bucko, storm is coming in tonight and apparently it is going to be lasting a few days. Sudden change in pressure or something to that extent," Ryan informed him.

Maggie nodded and splashed Ryan a little, "Yep. We saw it on the news while hanging out in the game room when everyone left."

"Well crap," Jasmine said and stomped her bare foot on the tiled floor, "I was hoping to explore the forest tomorrow," she whined.

"I didn't think Stan was one for pitching tents and being the outdoorsy type," Ryan smirked and then groaned when Maggie elbowed him in the sternum.

Stan shook his head and turned with one arm wrapped around Jasmine's shoulder. 'Well maybe it won't be too bad. I mean this house is still an amazing place and we could swim under the rain and the lightning if it starts storming too much. I mean you don't hear of glass getting hit by lighting too often do you?"

"That is beside the point honey! I wanted to enjoy the outdoors a few days this week. This sucks," Jasmine muttered under her breath while she stood with her husband.

"You know how wrong weather forecasters suck at their jobs though Jazz. I swear to God I wish I had a job where I could be wrong ninety percent of the time and make over a hundred grand a year. So much bullshit," Ryan grumbled.

"Dip-wad here has a point there Jasmine; it might not actually do anything. Keep your chin up sweetie." Maggie smiled. The older of the two sisters sat back in the hot tub and relaxed with a sigh.

Jasmine offered a small smile to the two of them and nodded her head. She tugged on Stan's shorts, "Well let's get a shower in and head out to enjoy the rest of the day in case we don't get another."

"You're reading my mind. I figured the same thing. This chlorine is making my hair too damn gunky." He said and hooked his arm in hers, "Lead the way m'dear."

Stan and Jasmine made their exit so they could enjoy what the rest of the day offered, leaving Maggie and Ryan in the "Glass Heaven" room all alone.

"Hey, Maggs, what is the punishment for skinny dipping?" he asked as he kissed his wife and popped out of the hot tub to stand next to the pool.

"Oh shut the hell up Ryan," she grinned as she followed him from the hot tub to the pool's edge. She pressed her hands against his bare chest and kissed his cheek, "You know I love it when you get all wet in anything," she said before shoving him in.

22

"See kids? Isn't this a bit better than being cooped up inside of that mansion for the entire week?" Peter asked as he extended his arms and did a small circle in the forest area they had trekked into. Thick maple and oak trees populated the area they immersed themselves in. The sunlight barely escaped from the thick leaves and branches that the trees offered and the forest floor had its spots of high grass but it was easy to traverse through the natural ground.

A passing blade of grass that was too tall, a bush that stuck out just far enough, or a branch that allowed leaves to brush up against Mark Sinfield had the teen constantly scratching and itching at his skin, "This sucks. I think I've brushed up against seventeen dozen different types of poison ivy Dad."

"Suck it up woman." Daniel smirked as he brushed a few low hanging branches away from his face and ducking over a larger one that could not be moved. He was trailing behind the other three.

"You wouldn't have brushed against so many leaves if you were paying attention to where you were going dear," Stacy chimed in, "I cannot believe your father caved and let you bring those hand held games with you." She turned back to make sure Daniel was doing alright, "Be careful now, I can't even see the mansion anymore so don't trip and fall."

"Whatever. As long as we have lotion back at the mansion I'll be fine." Mark said.

Daniel landed the killing blow on Mark's beast and laughed, 'oh he is almost out of lotion since he's been spanking it constantly since we've been here."

"Daniel!" Stacy roared.

Peter laughed and continued through the forest out in front. He led his boys and wife through the thick branches and bushes that littered the area north of the mansion. "You know I noticed we haven't seen very many critters. I haven't even heard a squirrel or rabbit scampering about."

"Well we are intruding in a forest that probably does not see a lot of people. They probably smelled us coming a while away dear," Stacy said.

"You have a point hon. This forest is getting thicker and thicker I think," Peter said as his fingers spread through thicker leaves and branches that provided a natural obstacle to get through.

Daniel shut his game system off and tripped on a branch. He stumbled a few feet forward but caught himself, "Cripes. Well we have been walking for a while now Dad, don't' you think we would have come to that brick wall fence or something by now?"

"Suck it up, woman," Mark mocked his brother back, hopping over a log to keep up with his father and mother.

"Let's take a little bit of a break Peter. We've been out here for about an hour now and I don't think we've walked more than a mile or two," Stacy said.

Peter stopped and turned to his family. He looked at the log that Mark had vaulted over and pointed towards it, "Right there. Let's sit for a while. The log looks sturdy enough for all of us."

The family of four sat down on the log and Peter dumped his backpack on the ground. He pulled out a water bottle for everyone and relaxed by leaning up against the tree the log was against. He looked up towards the little bit of sun that shined through the leaves and sighed, "This feels amazing. I mean really just take it all in. It might be a bit warm, we might be sweaty, but just take in the natural smell of everything. No factories, no fumes, no nothing," he said as he breathed the smell of the forest around him. The crisp bark combined with any sap that might have been leaking from the maples around them, "Breathe it in kids; this is what the actual world smells like. Your mother and I used to go camping a lot when we were younger. Then technology butted in."

"Wasn't it a bit dangerous with the Tyrannosaurus Rex and other dinosaurs running around?" Mark quipped, which got his arm smacked by his mother.

"I am not that old mister."

James fiddled with his pockets. He stood outside of Kimberly's room and rocked back and forth on his feet. A dollop of sweat formed on his forehead and he wiped it away with his finger before finally digging in, "You can do this," he whispered to himself. He knocked on her door.

Kimberly heard the knock at the door while she listened to music. She took her ear buds out and got out of her bed. She looked through the peep hole in the door and smiled. "Hey you," she said when she opened the door to let James in.

James smiled when she answered the door. Her pink tank top and her short jeans shorts took his breath away this time around. It did not help his condition that her tank top accentuated her upper body. "Care if I come in?" he asked while he stood right outside of her door. Her looked into her room and didn't see anyone else.

"Sure, come on in," Kimberly smiled and stood to the side to let him in.

James looked around the room and saw that she hadn't decorated it in any way. Her suitcase was in the corner next to the drawers and no clothes were thrown anywhere that he could see. She had a small laptop sitting on the desk next to the bed that had a playlist up and running. He could see her ear buds were connected to the computer. He sat down on the edge of her bed and felt the hair on the back of his neck start to stand on end and the pinpricks of nervousness stabbed his flesh. Even though the bed was only a queen size he felt an ocean separating them.

"So what's up?" Kimberly asked.

"Nothing really; did everything go alright with Mister Matthews? He asked.

She shrugged her shoulders a bit, "He and I didn't have too much to talk about after leaving the lounge. I mean I guess he was politely hitting on me but I don't think he was too happy when I made it clear I wasn't too interested in learning how to play pool like a pro."

"You know I had the feeling he was going to pull that 'older man' shit on you. I would have stepped up but, honestly, I think you're a big girl now Kim," he said, looking over his shoulder to smile at her.

Kimberly scooted from the head of the bed to the foot of it and returned the smile James gave her. "I am glad you were there though. I mean you and Jimmy. I know if I got into any trouble with him you guys would have had my back."

"Maybe. Maybe we feel that you really don't need us shielding you from people anymore. I mean things are a lot better than what they were a year or two back."

"Don't even talk like you two are going to ditch me or something like that. I'm not going to allow it." She smiled, pushing him a little with her hand.

James smiled but looked to the ground as that smile faded.

"James? Is there something wrong?"

He shook his head quickly and put the smile back on, "No, nothing is wrong but can we talk about something a bit more adult-like? I guess?"

"Well yeah, what's on your mind? I mean Mister Matthews really didn't try anything sleazy with me. He'd be out on his ass if he did. Like you said, I'm a tough girl!" She said and showed him by punching his arm a few times.

He feigned pain and blocked a few of the shots before he shook his head. "That's not it really. I mean it has to do with you, me and Jimmy. I know how close we have been and the truth is I have been kind of keeping something inside for a while now." He said and tried to meet her gaze.

Kimberly found his eyes for a moment and then looked away a little.

James bit down on his lower lip and then inhaled a large breath to calm his nerves. He stood up and turned away to pace the ground in front of her and the bed now.

"James if it is something between you and Jimmy you should know I don't care. I mean I guess I had my suspicions."

James stopped dead in his tracks. He looked over his shoulder and his right eyebrow cocked high.

Kimberly smiled and stood up. She came over and gave him a tight hug, "It's not that bad being gay guy in this day and age!"

"What? No!" James protested, hugging her back but pushing away right after.

Kimberly giggled and sat back on the bed when he separated from her, "I get it! I know seeing how happy the Thompsons were before they were kicked out inspired you and Jimmy to finally discuss your feelings! Its fine, I'm happy for you two!"

James pressed his fingers to his temples and rubbed them hard, "It ain't Jimmy! It's you Kimberly! I like you. I like you a lot actually; maybe more than just like," he said, sighing as he slumped onto the edge of the bed. "I guess getting called a homosexual took some of the fear out of telling you that."

"Oh. I see."

"Jimmy and I, at least I thought, had an unspoken bond that we would keep this group together as long as we could. I mean come on Kimmy, you're beautiful. Jimmy and I are two dorks that specialize more in fantasy than reality. Science Fiction more than science itself you know? It isn't really that big of a secret that having you around was about the only female interaction either of us has ever had."

Kimberly stayed silent. She sat there on the bed with her hands behind her to support her weight as she allowed James to get everything off his chest.

"I guess seeing you with that Oswald broke my typical poker face. Jimmy saw it and encouraged me to do this. I guess he likes you as just a friend and nothing more."

Kimberly tapped his side with her foot, "You were jealous of Mister Matthews? I mean did you think I would just cut loose and get with some guy twice my age? I don't think I have any daddy issues James."

He shook his head, "No that isn't it. I guess with the location, the situation and everything else I suppose I couldn't hold it in any longer. I guess Jimmy's pushing finally brought me to this point. I have been jealous of them all Kimberly. All your boyfriends, all the guys that have flirted with you; I just kept to that silent vow or whatever and never attempted to sabotage any attempts for you to have a decent boyfriend."

"Well, have you been sabotaging yourself?"

"I think I'm doing a pretty bang up job doing right now I think."

Kimberly leaned forward and wrapped an arm around his shoulder and neck, bringing him towards her for another hug. "You idiot; you and Jimmy have been more to me than I could ever hope for. You two have been there for me through a lot of hard times and you guys liked me for who I am. Not just my looks or anything like that. You guys are my friends and will always be my friends. I'm not the easiest person to take care of and be around even and I just thought you two were, well, not being true to each other if you know what I mean." She smiled.

"Well we aren't gay or anything. I guess this is the part where I ask if you think we could be anything more than friends."

Kimberly pulled back from the hug but kept her arms around his shoulders, "Well it was certainly unexpected James, but not an unwelcomed one. If Jimmy pushed you into this and since I know you're not batting for the other team, which is the right term, right? I suppose it couldn't hurt to see where things go after this vacation here." She leaned in and pressed her lips to his. It was a short kiss and her forehead pressed against his, "Or maybe we can just say 'fuck it' and make this a damn memorable one. How does that sound?"

She ignored his nervous nature and pushed him onto his back. She smiled, stood up, and locked the door.

23

"We've sat here long enough guys," Peter said while he stood from the toppled log. He put the empty bottles of water everyone drank back in his pack and patted the log several times while the dense foliage around them swayed with a gentle breeze. "Feel that? The wind is picking up so we should get some relief from the heat. It isn't all that hot out anyway, honestly."

Mark exhaled a disappointed sigh, "Dad can we seriously just head back to the mansion? This is all fine and dandy, really, but there is nothing but trees and more trees around here. I wasn't expecting to see a deer or a bear but hell there aren't even birds in the damn trees! This forest has been silent save for our stomping feet."

"You know Mark you're right. I haven't heard one bird chirp or anything but just the trees and leaves around us. I thought you boys would have been complaining about the mosquitoes right now but even they aren't here." His father said.

Stacy stood up and stretched her legs and arms out wide, "Um, which way is it towards the mansion?"

Peter came up behind his wife to rub her back and shoulders, "Its fine. Jacque told me that we could contact him by radio if anything happened." He continued rubbing her shoulder with one hand and used the other to take the radio off his belt buckle.

Daniel pulled out the radio he had and waved it in front of his father and mother, "We're alright. We were heading in that direction," he said and pointed north, "so we should just go ahead and start heading back through the clearing we made. I mean since there are no animals or anything around here there should be no other broken branches and crushed bushes right?"

"See how your brother is learning how to survive in the wilderness Mark? This isn't just to bore you guys or anything," Peter laughed and brought the radio to his lips. "Mister Collo? We're about fifteen or twenty minutes into the forest. I didn't think it would get so thick."

Peter waited a few moments for a response. There was only silence.

"Over?"

Still silence.

Peter double checked the radio he had and the battery icon showed full bars and the signal strength was equally full.

"Mister Collo? Are you there? This is Peter Sinfield." He growled.

Mark turned on his heel and headed back the way he thought they came from, "Screw this; we'll just walk back. I mean it can't be that freaking big of a forest." When he looked directly to the south he saw that there was no path or trail that had been made. He looked to the left and right and did not see any bushes, grass, or branches disturbed by their walk to the log. "Where the fuck did we come from?"

As Mark took a step in the direction he thought was the right way back to the mansion a huge figure stepped out from behind the nearby tree Mark was about to pass, forcing the teen to stumble backwards. His foot snagged a renegade root sticking up from the ground and tripped right onto his ass.

"What the hell!" He shouted as he looked up at the massive shape in front of him.

Peter and Stacy had been picking up their equipment to head on back when they heard Mark shout.

The light that broke through the tops of the trees showed a man well over six feet tall. He had a black t-shirt on that looked darker all over the front of the shirt, and crusted. The blue jeans the figure had on were stained as well in various areas. Large, hairless arms flowed from the cutoff point of the t-shirt and the knuckles and fingers were coated in a dried red, clenching and releasing and forcing numerous veins to pop out from the man's forearm and the back of his hand.

Mark tried to scramble to his feet but his eyes were locked on that face, or what should have been a face. It was too real to be a mask and the way the facial features swirled where the man's face should have been simulated water going down a drain. There was a split second where the blurring stopped.

Fred Thompson's mouth was locked in a silent scream.

"Mark run!" Peter hollered as Mark tried to get to his feet.

Mark's leg jerked back when Fred took a step forward and grabbed his ankle. He shook his leg as hard as he could and Mark could hear his brother behind him doing his best to contact Jacque.

"Mister Collo! Oh shit! Mister Collo!" Daniel cried, with shaking hands, into the radio.

Peter dropped his backpack to the ground and before Fred could yank Mark away by the ankle Peter tackled the much larger man to the ground.

When Peter had tackled Fred Thompson to the ground it allowed Mark to get to his feet in an instant. He was about to help his father with Fred when he heard his mother scream.

A decrepit hand gripped her shoulder from behind. She turned around, and with her momentum, swung her own backpack into her assailant's head, knocking the figure off balance and into the nearby tree.

"Jesus fuck! What the fuck is that?" Mark screamed when he saw the broken face of Clark Thompson. The man's lower jaw had been removed from his head and his tongue flopped around with no control. After he hit the tree his arms came back out once again, grasping at Stacy but getting nowhere close to where she was standing. His eye sockets had small spirals of black smoke billowing out. Mark noticed that only one of his hands was empty, the other held his missing jaw, and that his face was not blurred like Fred's was.

He swung for the fences with that makeshift weapon, the sharp edges of bone slashed upwards towards Stacy. She took a hop back to avoid the boney weapon but it still caught some of her shirt, tugging her body forward before it sliced through the top. When she jerked back she stumbled, much like her son had, and fell to the ground.

Clark was on top of the woman in an instant. His knees straddled her waist and he raised his severed jaw high into the air.

Adrenaline pumped through Mark's veins and it overloaded his brain. He closed the gap between his mother and her attacker and brought his leg back and high into the air. His shoes clipped the ground, kicking up dirt and leaves that covered his mother's flailing body but none-the-less the pendulum force of his leg swung in front of Clark's body up towards his missing jaw. Before the ghastly man could swing his arm down to pierce Stacy's throat Mark's foot had driven straight up and into Clark's head. The boy cried out in pain as his foot connected through the rest of Clark's skull and brain, breaking his own foot as it spilt Clark's skull in half and sent brain matter and blood splattering everywhere.

The force of the kick had sent Clark's body backwards off of Stacy Sinfield. She clawed the ground several times to get her legs out from under Clark's own before she vaulted to her feet and wrapped an arm around Mark, who had been hopping up and down on one foot, favoring his other.

As Clark's form flopped around on the ground and spasmed Mark tried to limp over to finish the job. He growled as pain shot through his foot with every step he took. "Daniel! Fucking break his shit," Mark growled.

Daniel couldn't move. His hands were pale around the radio and he had the transmit button held down but said nothing. He couldn't stop shaking as the scene unfolded around him. He could see Mark yelling at him, but as much as he wanted to move his body he couldn't lift his leg or move his arms.

"God damn it Daniel!" Mark cried out before he reached over for Daniel's backpack. His hand gripped the strap and brought it up and over his head to smash down on Clark's already disfigured head. He repeated the motion several times until Clark's head was unrecognizable.

Mark's breaths were ragged. Sweat poured down his face as he tried to collect himself. His mother's screams were nothing but echoes in his head and time slowed. He turned his attention to his father who had been slamming his fist into Fred's face. His father's knuckles were bloody but it was from cuts and scrapes in his own hand and not from Fred's face. Mark flinched when he watched his father's hand break from the last strong hit to Fred's face.

"Run! Get back to the mansion!" Peter screamed. It wasn't a scream of pain from his broken hand either.

Fred's massive hand wrapped around Peter's throat and his other hand shoved upwards into Peter's chest and disappeared. The sound of bone, muscle, and sinew snapping was the loudest sound Mark had ever heard in his entire life.

"No!" Stacy cried out. The three of them stood in terrified shock as Peter's body was thrown off of Fred's. The vicious attacker had something in his hand, a trophy from killing his opponent. Blood from Peter's heart flowed down Fred's forearm before it turned black as night. The black blood receded from Fred's arm and back into Peter's heart. The red muscle grew black as well and Fred growled as he shifted on the ground and slammed his hand back into Peter's chest, placing the heart back where it came from.

"Oh my God! Oh my God Peter, no!" Stacy sobbing continued. Tears were blurring any vision she had and Mark was grabbing at her arm to pull at her, limping away and favoring his right foot.

"Come on mom! We need to get the hell out of here," Mark said, gritting his teeth. He shifted to his right and turned his attention to Daniel, who was already running past Fred and his dead father towards the south. "Daniel! God damn it we have to stick together!"

Fred was preoccupied with Peter's lifeless body. The creature that used to be the stoic, man-of-few-words slammed Peter's body against the ground as that black heart settled back into place with each shake and slam.

Black blood began flowing throughout Peter's body and the hole in his chest was sealing up, marking the large black spot where Fred had punctured his body. Peter's head was twisting back and forth and his eyes and mouth opened in a silent scream which began blurring and twisting.

Stacy and Mark started chasing Daniel in the direction that he fled but Peter's transformation was complete and the man that used to be Mark's father sprang to his feet. Dirt went flying into the air with Peter's kicking feet and the sudden burst of speed sent him sailing in front of his retreating family. Grasping hands were aimed right for Stacy's arm.

Mark, pivoting on his bad foot, swung his mother's body around, sending them spinning counter clockwise. Mark's last good foot shot out and sent his heel right into Peter's sternum, knocking his father backwards and onto the ground. "Go after Daniel! I'll be fine; my foot is starting to feel better." Mark yelled at his mother, pushing her towards the direction his brother ran off.

Stacy's trembling figure took a few steps away from her son, tears streaking her face as her boy stood his ground against his father. With quivering lips and vision blurring with fresh tears her steps became strides and taking off after Daniel she wished this was all just a nightmare.

Mark, scanning the ground around him, found salvation in the form of a tree branch that was thicker than his arm. His body continued pumping adrenaline through his form and healing his foot until the pain was no longer there. Out of the corner of his eye he saw Fred turning his attention towards his fleeing mother, "Hey! Come and get me you son of a bitch!" Mark screamed, picking the branch up.

Ignoring Mark's taunts Fred continued his pursuit of the frightened woman.

Running past his father to stop Fred a shooting, ice-cold pain ran through Mark's ankle, up his leg, and through his spine. He turned his attention back to his father that had a tight grip around his foot. The crushing pressure forced Mark's hand and he took that branch to Peter's head in several hard, sledge-hammering like whacks to his father's skull. Peter relinquished his grip on his son's ankle and took chase after his fleeing son.

Daniel had run so far and so fast that he did not recognize the area around him when he came to a stop. He placed his hand against the nearest oak and his breathing was labored. Gasping violently, with his fingers scratching down the tree, he sobbed. He took only a few moments to catch his breath before he was off and running again through the many branches and bushes that littered the forest in front of him.

His legs, bleeding from the many thorn bushes he was crashing through, left breadcrumbs behind him. Through the leaves that were busily blocking out the sun Daniel cried in joy when through those thick trees he saw the dark brown siding of the mansion in the distance. It forced his legs to pump faster and faster, his hands reaching forward to try and grasp that safe haven.

It was less than a football field's distance away, only one hundred yards to go before Daniel would be among friends. He felt weightless a moment later and a sudden pain in his right sight had him coming back to reality. Crashing onto the ground, Daniel's body rolled until it slammed against the nearest tree, banging the back of his head against the hard wood. The resulting smack to the back of his head had his vision fuzzy, confusion setting in and least of which the force that hit him knocked the wind and energy right out of him.

"W . . . What?" He croaked as his eyes tried to adjust from the violent crack he took from the oak behind him. Reaching to the back of his head he felt wetness across his fingers.

Several hands wrapped around his legs and yanked him from the tree he sat at and dragged him to the ground. Trying his best to scream, Daniel found his voice locking up. He couldn't call for help and his eyes were setting in on what had assaulted him.

It wasn't just one thing. Four people stood around Daniel, each looking down at him with a crooked neck. One of them was a large woman; her obese form hanging over Daniel's much smaller body. Her face twitched and swirled, but a thick, prehensile tongue dangled from the blackness where her mouth would be. Her flabby body was slower than the others as fat fingers pawed at Daniel's clothes.

To his right was another woman but she was much more lithe and toned. She had black hair that fell to her shoulders and her hands reached for his leg. She gripped it roughly and sent a cold chill straight up his leg. Wiggling it back and forth Daniel could not find the strength to get his leg free from her grip.

His left arm felt the same chilling grasp. He shifted his attention to the naked man gripping his forearm. The same blurry, out of focus facial features danced across the man's hairless head just as Fred's had, just as the rest of their faces had. He couldn't stop the two of them from lifting him from opposite ends.

The obese woman grabbed his right arm and his left leg was gripped by a younger, hairless male. All four of Daniel's limbs felt frostbitten and he could not will them to move.

Each of them started swinging Daniel by his limbs back and forth. After a few initial swings they were slamming him against the same tree he had smacked his head against. It knocked the wind out of him with that first connection with the tree and in three more rough slams his ribs were cracking and breaking, stabbing into his lungs, and causing him to spit up blood moments later.

The only sound from Daniel's lips was the gurgling of blood

exiting from his mouth. The four stopped slamming his body against the tree and each figure at his limbs pulled in a different direction. Jimmy's head was swimming as he barely heard his flesh and skin tearing before each of his assailants gave one hard, final tug.

24

Jimmy sat down outside the mansion a good fifty yards away. He situated himself under the shade of the several oaks and maples that represented the frontline of the sprawling forest. Behind the tree line there was a security fence comprised of hip high bushes that sprawled from the brick wall behind Jimmy all the way out towards where the forest met the cliff.

It was a warm day out and Jimmy wanted a change. He was going to get some sun but he also needed to see the screen of his laptop. The shade the trees offered was a best of both worlds. His legs could get some color while he cruised the internet. He fired up his favorite search engine and got to work.

"The Bleak," he whispered to himself as he entered it into the search engine. He browsed through the hits he got and nothing matched what he had seen. There were plenty of books and movies that had it in the title but nothing supernatural or even close to the spooky.

He almost gave up on the search for the same image of a single man in a white suit with a legion of faceless beings behind him until he thought about the book that was illustrated with the man in the suit. He remembered it being shiny and metallic, but he thought about other shiny surfaces and began searching marble and porcelain covered books.

It was a fruitless search.

The only other material he could think of was a shiny, black glass. He entered in "obsidian" into the search engine and hit enter.

The search engine showed more results than he thought he could get through in a day. There was one link that caught his eye about three pages in; it was a supernatural website.

When he clicked on the link he was brought to a single page reference on possession. Jimmy scanned the page and the information was all about a being that walked the earth carrying an obsidian clad book. The book had the power to grant anyone the perfect existence. It would give anyone what they wanted at the price of their soul becoming one with the book itself. It described the event as an unwilling deal; that the person was raped of their soul because just one touch from the book was enough to set the deal in motion. It was a single touch and a person was lost in the pages.

The paragraph broke and the illustration that was in the leather-bound book Jimmy and James had read was recreated by the person who designed the very cheap website. Without any interruptions Jimmy could take his time and study the man holding the book and the faces behind him. "Creepy . . ." Jimmy groaned.

The faces behind the man in the white suit had faces that looked blurry. Marks around the faces and heads had the same connotation as something vibrating or shaking very fast. The heads were not moving at all.

Underneath the picture more text was offered:

'The simple ideology of The Bleak is a simple one. It seeks to gain souls for sustenance and will power itself through those very souls the book consumes.

Once a human loses his or her soul the book creates a puppet out of the body that is controlled entirely by the master for whatever purposes. To signify this puppetry the victim will have a forever shifting visage of torture to it ever shaking and creating a fuzzy resemblance to the person it once was.

The Bleak may separate itself from its beloved tool just as any human would separate themselves from a dinner plate. It should be noted, however, that the larger the will of the victim that touches the book the longer it takes *for that person to be fully consumed by The Bleak. Full gestation can take anywhere from a matter of seconds to a month depending on how powerful the soul of the victim is.'*

Jimmy was enthralled with the entire mythology the website offered. Enthralled as he was with the website he turned his head to the side when he heard heavy breathing and footsteps coming from the forest, which drew his attention away from his laptop.

Mark had no idea where he was going. In the struggle with his chasing father he was mixed up in his direction. He wasn't sure if he was going north, south, east or west at that point. He shoved his hand through leaves and bushes, running as quick as he could towards the mansion.

His father was hot on his heels. The branch that Mark assaulted Peter with had broken off during their scuffling and now had been impaled through Peter's stomach. It didn't slow the being down at all as he slammed his hands against the trees and used it to propel himself closer and closer to Mark as the teenager ran and hopped through the downed logs and bushes that impeded his path.

"Shit!" Mark growled and snagged a tree root. Stumbling against the root, he corrected his direction and turned his body, shifting it just enough so that he could grab the branch end that was about to crash into his kidney. Mark felt his father slamming his body and sent the two toppling to the ground. Mark's hands were gripping roughly on that branch that had his father impaled and, while on his back, got his feet underneath his father's stomach and shoved as hard as he could on that body and the stick.

His strength sent Peter flying backwards. The branch pulled free from the man's stomach and from that gaping hole black blood oozed. Mark used the branch to pull himself up fast and held it horizontally against his body when Peter's hands tried wrapping around Mark's shirt. Despite the branch blocking the grasping hands Peter still shoved Mark against the tree behind the teen and held him against the oak with inhuman strength.

The branch slid towards Mark's throat, threatening to cut his air off if it reached his neck. Mark put his foot against the tree behind him, and bracing himself for whatever would come of it, drove all of his strength forward.

Peter shoved him back against the tree easier than Mark expected,

"Son of a bitch!" he shouted and made the decision to use his father's immense strength against him. Against the tree, bringing both of his legs up, started kicking both feet into Peter's chest at the same time to try and beat his father back. Mark's shoes continuously crashed into his father's chest and sternum several times before knocking Peter back.

Mark almost fell on the ground but caught himself with both feet. Steadying himself for another attack Mark brandished that tree branch like it was the only thing keeping him alive. Mark placed the branch end firmly against the tree, huffing ragged breaths as he watched his father lunge again.

Peter's body went flying into Mark again but this time his eldest son stepped to the side at the last possible moment. Mark had made sure to keep that branch tight against the tree he had been pressed against firmly when Peter charged. The branch went clean through Peter's body, but the inhuman being acted like a makeshift hammer, pounding that branch into the tree and his own form. His father was stuck.

Mark, sliding around the tree as soon as he was sure his father was stuck, took off running through the forest once again. He knew he bought himself some time, but hearing the branch cracking in half meant he did not have that much time to gain distance.

Mark pumped his legs harder and faster, running on empty and yet never feeling the burn. Exploding out of a thicket of bushes and trees Mark's feet skidded to a stop, "Holy shit!" he cried out as he looked over the edge of the cliff he nearly toppled over. The edge was a straight hundred foot drop into nothing but jagged rocks. The edge of the cliff was rocky but also had thick patches of green scattered about it.

The trees and bushes behind Mark were not rustling with the gentle breeze. Turning to face the noise behind him Mark's eyes widened as his father came exploding from the foliage just a few feet behind him.

Peter took both himself and his son over the cliff.

Stacy stumbled over the scattered debris the forest floor offered. Her strength was sapped from the traumatizing experiences she just suffered through and the only thing keeping her on her feet was the hopes that her boys had made it back to the mansion in one piece.

The thought of stopping, of just lying down and giving up crossed her mind but only for a moment. She could see the mansion from where she was at. It was close. With fresh tears streaming down her face she found the strength to start running once again.

She had made it. She was yards away from the forest's edge when a body rose in front of her. She couldn't scream. Her throat had closed up and she found it hard to just breathe at that point. When she realized it was Jimmy, the polite college boy, she could do nothing but sob.

"Missus Sinfield, are you okay?" he asked, looking at the staining dirt on her clothing while she limped towards him. He could see the tears running down her face and her hair was chaotic. "Holy shit what happened? Where is your family?" Jimmy asked, taking a few steps towards her to help her past the forest edge.

He froze.

From the foliage above, perched on a branch, was the hulking body of Fred Thompson. Jimmy's eyes widened as the massive man dropped from the branches to the ground without a sound. His clothing was ripped and torn and that black t-shirt was covered in grass, dirt, blood and flesh. The smell of decay made Jimmy gag. The vein in Fred's arms were pulsating with hate, the black blood pumping rapidly and discoloring patches of Fred's skin in a sick purple hue.

Stacy saw Jimmy just stop. She sobbed without looking behind her. Limping towards Jimmy, ignoring the threat behind her, she reached out to the college student with her hand and pleading eyes.

Fred closed the distance between him and Stacy with one step. His gigantic hand gripped Stacy's hair and wrenched his arm back. Stacy cried out as she tried twisting away from the iron grip locked in her auburn strands of hair. Several clumps tore from her scalp but she escaped that grasping hand. Her stumbling towards Jimmy continued when she was free, but was halted again when Fred yanked the woman back by her shirt.

The fabric tore from its seams from the violent yank. The shirt didn't break away from her body despite the tearing and caused Stacy's body to collide with Fred's.

Jimmy couldn't move. His feet were locked to the ground like invisible forces were holding him down. His eyes were focused on Fred's face, or what it had become. He saw the blurriness; he saw the silent scream and twisted agony when the face froze for the slightest of moments. His knees quivered, his arms felt heavy, and his mind fought with itself while the scene unfolded right in front of his eyes.

Stacy whimpered and her eyes widened. She kept her arm stretching towards him, pleading silently for help with her tear streaked eyes.

Instinct and survival went out the window.

Jimmy lunged forward and grabbed Stacy's hand in just a few long bounds with his lanky legs. He held tight onto her hand and arm as he did his best to pull her from Fred's grasp.

"This can't be happening!" Jimmy screamed, tugging on Stacy's arm to help free her from the monstrosity behind her.

Fred brought his other arm around Stacy's neck and closed it around her throat. He squeezed roughly with his new grasp on the woman and his other hand relinquished the hold on her shirt and reached over her body, backhanding Jimmy with an upward swing that sent the young man sailing through the air.

Jimmy slammed against one of the oaks near the edge of the forest. The branches and leaves rustled from the impact and the transfer of force had him bouncing back to the forest floor right on his face. Dirt and grass filled his mouth when he landed, causing him to sputter and cough while his chest ached from the hit, and his back, protesting any movement, throbbed as he picked himself up from the ground.

He watched as Fred spun Stacy around. He had a firm hand around her throat and her cries became whimpers as he squeezed, crushing her windpipe. Stacy went limp. Fred tossed her body to the ground and knelt over her with that faceless face staring right into her own.

"H . . . Help! Somebody help me!" Jimmy screamed at the top of his lungs, his cry reverberating through the forest and the open spaces that surrounded the mansion.

Fred, using that insane strength he had, gripped Stacy's jaw and pulled it down, sickly breaking it from her skull. Now that her mouth was widened by force Fred's hand slid between her teeth and over her wiggling tongue, descending into her throat. Widening that broken windpipe the outline of Fred's arm was seen through Stacy's throat and mouth. Over half of his forearm buried into Stacy's gullet before stopping. The crunching sound of her ribs internally parted turned Jimmy's stomach until he vomited on the ground before him.

Composing himself from his nerves he turned around to run and stopped dead in his tracks.

"No . . . No! You get the hell away from me!" Jimmy screamed.

Jacque Collo laughed as he held Jimmy's laptop in his hand, tinkering with it and sighing as he did so. "Jimmy, my boy, you are far too inquisitive for your own good," he said while Jimmy backpedalled into something solid.

Two large, hairy hands gripped Jimmy by his arms. Jimmy screamed again as Jacque pulled a book from his business suit. The glassy blackness reflected the sun right into Jimmy's eyes.

As the book was pressed against Jimmy's chest the screaming stopped.

Stan and Jasmine enjoyed the sun on a cloudless afternoon day. They each had a reclining, plastic chair that they laid in while soaking in the sun. Stan had a pair of khaki shorts that extended past his knees along with a thin, buttoned up white shirt. Jasmine decided it was warm enough to lay out in a very short jean skirt and a yellow tube top that showed off her cleavage and midsection.

"This actually isn't too bad. I mean it's kind of warm but with that breeze coming in from the ocean it feels like a good spring day, it's actually pleasurable," Stan said as he lay there with his eyes closed. His hand was stretched over, holding his wife's as they let the breeze that traveled from the vast ocean in front of them.

"Well it is rather odd that we are laying right here on the basketball court but it doesn't really get in the way now that we are out here." Jasmine smiled and looked over at Stan, flipping her sunglasses over her head and squeezed his hand, "Next time don't argue with me when I tell you that you need a vacation."

Her hand squeezed hard when they heard the screams.

Stan shot up so fast that he knocked over his chair. He looked towards the forest.

"My God, is that Jimmy?" she asked as she onto his arm. Stan said nothing.

The screaming abruptly stopped. Stan, feeling his wife tugging on his arm and yelling at him to follow him towards the screams, felt sick to his stomach and dizzy when that night came flooding back into his mind.

His attention came back to him when his wife gave him a swift slap across his face.

"Stan, come on honey get it together. Something is wrong," she said as she ran towards the thick forest edge.

Vincent Tanner, making his way towards Jacque's room, stopped for a moment next to a window near Jacque's room when a figure outside caught his attention. He turned and drew back the curtains that hid some of the window so he could get a clearer view of the dense forest that surrounded the mansion home. He had to squint to see Jimmy Franklin sitting underneath the shade of the various trees that littered the entrance into that thick, green wonderland.

"Whatever trips your trigger kid," Tanner muttered under his breath. He shifted his attention to Jacque's room and took a lock-pick out of his suit jacket. He didn't bend over the knob, but he slid the device inside it and prodded inside of it gently. Again his attention shifted when the faint sound of someone screaming reached his ears.

Pulling the lock-pick from the knob, Tanner rushed to the same window he had observed Jimmy from just moments ago. Jimmy was gone but his laptop remained on the ground.

"Shit," Tanner cursed and pulled the curtains closed. His feet stomped through the hallway on the second floor and not even the carpet lining the floor could muffle the urgency in his bounding steps. He slammed his body against the entryway door that led to the staircases and threw it open, taking three and four steps at a time. The motions he made the previous night were reenacted leap for leap before he slammed into the massive oak doors that led into the vacation home.

Throwing the door open and not bothering to close it, Tanner kicked up grass and dirt when he hit the lawn, scrambling towards the area where Jimmy's laptop had been. Out of the corner of his eye he saw the Freasons sprinting towards the same spot.

"Stan! Wait!" Tanner shouted as a familiar burning in his legs started registering in his mind. Tanner reached into the left side of his suit and pulled his hand free. In his hand was a double action revolver with a four inch barrel on it. The same design on his cigarette case was etched into the handle of his silver revolver, two golden swords slicing through a pentagram.

Jasmine shrieked and Stan, oddly enough, put himself in front of her when he saw Tanner pull the gun, "Tanner? What the hell?" Stan cried out as he and his wife stepped back from the forest line.

"This isn't for you dumbass!" Tanner scolded and leaped over the bush and into the forest.

"Should we follow him?" Jasmine asked as she tried to follow where he was going.

Stan thought about it for a second before taking a deep breath in, "I hate myself for thinking this, but I really want to know what the hell is going on."

25

There was nothing on the other side of the forest wall where Jimmy's screams echoed loud enough for them to hear. There were no footprints, no broken branches, and no trail to follow in the dense forest Tanner stared into. He scanned the forest floor and didn't see a bush disturbed in the least and if there were any signs of struggle he wasn't seeing them. It was just a quiet, unassuming mass of flora and fauna. There wasn't even a bird chirping in the trees.

"God damn it!" Tanner screamed, slapping the rough wood of one of the trees next to him.

Stan and Jasmine followed moments after Tanner told them to stay put, "Tanner? I hate to sound like a broken record but why in the fuck do you have a gun?" Stan asked, sounding a little less panicked.

Tanner ignored Stan for now as he cupped his hands around his mouth, "Jimmy! Jimmy!"

Stan stepped up behind Tanner and placed his hand on the man's shoulder, gripping it tight "Tanner for the love of God what the hell is going on?" he asked.

"Damn it Stan I'll explain later. Just trust me on this; I'm not here on vacation if it isn't obvious already." He holstered his gun in his suit jacket and continued looking around.

"Are you a cop or something?" asked Jasmine.

A crack of thunder almost deafened the small group. Stan's almost jumped out of his skin.

"Okay what the hell was that? Wasn't it sunny out like two seconds ago?" Stan asked.

Another crack of thunder sent shivers down Stan's spine. Even though they were in the woods, the sound of an engine had them each turning their attention back towards the mansion. Each of them saw a white S.U.V tearing out of the parking lot and down the drive. Its tires squealed as it made a beeline for the exit.

"Shit," Tanner cursed and began taking off towards the vehicle before Stan gripped him hard by the forearm. "This is the last fucking time I'm going to ask you what the fuck is going on."

Tanner wasn't going to catch up to the car on foot with the way it was speeding towards the gate. The white S.U.V stopped and the gates opened for it. Tanner tried to see who was in the vehicle but could not see anything from that distance. He turned his attention back to Stan and Jasmine and shook his head.

"Alright, alright," he began as the sky above them started to darken. Black clouds rolled in from the ocean and lightning streaked the sky, turning the previous dark sky into light for a split second. Thunder followed that shook the ground and Tanner shook his head, "I'm not here on vacation or business. I'm looking for someone that came here a couple of weeks back."

Droplets of rain splattered the group as they stood on the forest's edge.

"Let's finish this inside honey. I think it's about to get very wet out and you know I'm prone to colds." Jasmine said as she tugged on Stan's shirt.

"Jimmy might still be out here Jasmine."

Tanner shook his head, "Fuck it. You two head back inside and start asking if anyone has seen Jimmy. Maybe he was playing a prank or something and is a sneaky little bastard. If that is the case I am going to wring his neck."

"Are you going to stay out here and look for him then?" Stan asked as the temperature felt like it dropped ten degrees in just a matter of seconds.

Tanner felt the temperature drop and grit his teeth, "I don't like this one bit Stan. I'll try and find Jimmy but you and Jasmine keep an eye on each other. Like I said I'm looking for someone and the last time anyone heard from her she was out here investigating something."

Jasmine's eyes beamed as she rose on the balls of her feet and dropped back down, her chest bouncing with enthusiasm as well, "Oh! Oh! Is she a redhead? Real pretty green eyes too?" she asked while tugging on Stan's arm several times in her excited state.

Tanner swallowed hard and looked at Jasmine with disbelief in his eyes. "Yes! Her name is Helena Kyarsgaard. She checked into this place about two weeks ago and the company she and I work for hasn't heard from her since. We suspected this place would hold some clues but I haven't found jack shit. How in the hell do you know about her?" he asked as another streak of lightning and a horrible crack of thunder illuminated the ominous black sky. It was turning to night at three o'clock in the afternoon on a summer's day.

"Well we found some sort of I.D. thingy tucked underneath the sheets of our waterbed. I mean it was pretty much smack dab in the middle of the bed. We were going to tell Jacque about it but Stan advised against it," she said, blinking several times when she realized how dark out now was.

"God damn it Stan you are amazing! Thank you," Tanner said as he whipped his cell phone out and began dialing.

The phone did nothing. He had no signal.

"Son of a bitch . . . Ain't this fucking typical?" Tanner slipped the phone back into his pocket, "I'm going to look for Jimmy and I hope he is alright. You two head back in and talk to everyone but Jacque. I don't trust him in the slightest but just play it dumb if you encounter him. Maybe ask about Jimmy but don't give anything away about Helena's I.D. or who I am."

Jasmine tilted her head to the side, "Well, why should we trust you Mister Tanner?"

Tanner licked his lips before taking a deep breath in. He took his revolver out once more, "You shouldn't really. I'm not the nicest man in the world, or the greatest, but if shit starts happening that your mind can't fully comprehend I'm going to end up being your best friend," he said with a smile before heading into the forest.

"Well what in the hell was that supposed to mean?" Stan asked Jasmine as she, in turn, shrugged her shoulders.

"I hope we don't find out baby. Come on; let's get back inside before it starts pouring."

Jacque was standing on the steps of the mansion home with his arms crossed. He was looking up at the blackening sky and watched as the first few drops of rain splattered against the pavement before him. He watched Stan and Jasmine running from the edge of the forest back towards the entrance. He did not look pleased. The doors behind him were open but he was blocking the entrance as the rain fell a little harder.

"I assume you two heard the screaming," he said as his eyes lingered on Jasmine a little longer than she was comfortable with.

Stan cleared his throat several times, "Yes we did, in fact, can you explain who the hell it was that was screaming? It sounded like he was getting murdered."

Jacque's face took a solemn turn. "I am afraid Mister Franklin accidently hurt his leg. I do not know if he broke it but thankfully the Sinfield family found him and volunteered to drive him to the hospital in their car. Jimmy didn't want his friends to be affected by what happened to him." Jacque was relaxed in his body but he licked his lips several times already. His arms were crossed over his chest and while he should have been under stress about the potential backlash of an injury he looked almost too relaxed for what had happened.

"Well how did he get hurt? Aren't you afraid he is going to sue you or something?" Stan asked as his eyes were glued to Jacque's.

Jasmine took a step to her left and put Stan between her and Jacque.

"Oh no, of course not," Jacque began, "While it is sad to see that he injured himself our contract that each of you signed before coming here has an injury clause that states that any injuries sustained, unless it happens inside of the home, like a large tree falls on your head is not our responsibility. The woods cannot be controlled, obviously."

"I guess that is understandable Mister Collo. Though did the entire family have to take Jimmy to the hospital?"

"It isn't up to me who comes and goes Mister Freason. Though I would like to suggest that we go back inside because I believe the weatherman was very, very wrong."

Stan and Jasmine walked up the stairs with Jacque Collo, narrowly avoiding the torrential downpour of rain that followed a few seconds later.

Tanner had circled around the back of the mansion and snuck along side of the building next to the parking lot. He just caught the end of the conversation between the three and had to bite his tongue with how nonchalant and convenient Jacque made it sound.

Tanner grumbled when the three went inside and the rain began dropping on his head and body like a hurricane. He dashed to his car and hopped inside of it quickly as the rain battered his suit.

Another crack of thunder disguised the sound of him starting his car and in a matter of seconds Tanner was tearing out of the parking lot and down the driveway. He paused at the pedestal and scanned his card so the gates would open for him. As the gates opened his tires squealed as he chased after the white S.U.V.

26

Tanner caught up to the SUV relatively quickly. Then again, he had been careening down the paved road going about ninety miles an hour as soon as he got past that gate. He kept the car in sight and it even with Tanner's headlights shining on the car in front of him the driver showed no signs of slowing down.

He wasn't expecting the S.U.V to turn off the road about eight miles out of the mansion. With the rain pelting his windshield, even with his wipers on high, he almost missed the white vehicle cut a hard right into the forest. Tanner did not miss a beat and turned to follow, realizing that there was a path that he missed on the drive in.

Tanner slowed his Impala to a crawl as he drew closer to the vehicle in front of him while tires crunched leaves and twigs in that dirty forest road.

He hit the brakes when the bright, red tail lights of the S.U.V flared to life. The dense forest around him soaked up the rain that had pelted his vehicle beforehand, allowing him to see much better in the forest than he could on the road. He had to squint but past what the Sinfield's were driving there was a large, gaping strip of nothing between the edge of the forest they were on, and the start of the forest on the other side.

Three doors of the S.U.V. opened and three figures emerged. Tanner could barely make them out but two were male and the other was a woman. The shadows played in the favor of the three that got out of the vehicle and their backs were turned to Tanner and his car's lights.

Tanner steadied himself by taking several deep breaths. He reached over, opened his glove compartment, and pulled a lengthy, and bulky, flashlight. When he was ready he opened the door to his Impala and flicked his headlights onto hi-beams. The light didn't get their attention.

Tanner stepped out of the car and left the car door open, "Where is Jimmy?" he shouted as a crack of thunder almost drowned out his voice.

The three stood their ground; backs turned away from Tanner and ignoring him.

Tanner grumbled before shining his light at the one who had come out of the backseat. Tanner's eyes narrowed when he saw the young man wearing Daniel's clothing but the clothes were too small on the figure; the shirt was tightly wrapped around the person's body and Tanner could see that the shorts were unbuttoned as the button hung off to the side.

The clothes were also stained with blood.

The figure turned its attention towards Tanner. Its face came into the light and the swirling, chaotic mess screamed its silent song at Tanner. The shifting flesh and whirl of painful expressions gave Tanner all the answers that he needed in the short moment the flashlight was drawn to the male's face. He knew it wasn't Daniel and he knew Jimmy wasn't in that van. Tanner swallowed the knowledge that Helena was onto something new, something unique and he had to push past the sinking feeling in his heart as the teenager in the tight clothing dashed at Tanner. The screams never made a sound, but the figure reached out as it sped towards the human with a flashlight.

The sound of gunfire echoed through the forest as Tanner quickly drew and fired, placing a sizable circle right in the middle of the teenager's forehead with the accuracy of someone who had fired countless amounts of ammunition in their life. Tanner watched as the assailant's body hit the dirt after the shot. The defiant act agitated the other two creatures on either side of the bulky vehicle. Before Tanner could fire his weapon at them they separated from the vehicle they stood by and dove into the forest to shed the light of Tanner's vehicle.

Tanner, retreating to the back of his Impala, reached down to the bottom of his revolver and popped latch that was on the handle. A hidden key fell into his hand from inside the weapon and he slammed the key into the trunk of his car, unlocked it, and popped it open. The trunk revealed a treasure trove of weapons. Inside he had shotguns, rifles, and even and assortment of melee weapons ranging from daggers to a battle axe attached to the roof of his trunk.

Out of all the items available in his trunk Tanner reached for a flare gun, some rounds for it, and several handheld flares as well. He slid the flare gun into his belt buckle and popped the rounds in his suit jacket. He had one flare out now and he unscrewed the bottom of it, slapping it so that it extended to its full length.

When he turned to his left, to look into the forest for any sign of the other two, the teenager was face-to-face with him, the bullet hole in his head oozing black blood. Tanner reacted by jumping back the best he could but the teen brought a hand up and latched it around Tanner's throat.

The steely grip around his throat forced Tanner to look into the horrific, shifting gaze his attacker stared at him with. The unknown male had his fingers and thumb squeezing Tanners' trachea to crush that essential airway Tanner needed to breathe. Choking and grunting, Tanner slammed the active end of the flare into the black haired teen's chest, pressing it hard against the boy's heart and used his other hand to slap the base, igniting the intense flame.
The flame burned through the shirt it was wearing like a hot knife sliced through butter and with the added pressure of Tanner pushing in on the boy's chest ensured that flare melted the flesh and with a sickening squish bored through the teen's chest and right into that black, tortured heart.

The thing released Tanner's throat and the boy finally screamed. The shriek was shrill, high pitched, and as that fire burned and pierced its heart it began spitting up blood as dark as night. It dripped down its chin as it hit the ground, convulsing and gurgling while Tanner took in labored breaths, coughing violently as his sore throat ached.

The erupting flames from the teenager's chest died down and the blurring image that was his face stilled. The boy was no longer moving and tanner let that twinge of guilt flow through him for only a second before concentrating on the task at hand. There were still two of them out there and he was alone. The teen's strength, as unbelievable as it was, wasn't something Tanner hadn't seen before. He sure as hell did not want to fight the other two head on after just the teenager attacked him.

On either side of him the rustling of branches and bushes grabbed his attention and he struck three more flares, throwing them out into the forest and one on the ground a few feet away.

The flares in the forest did not reveal the other two, but Tanner knew he needed stopping power. Inside his trunk he wrapped his hands around a double barrel, sawed-off Mossberg twelve gauge shotgun. The illegal design of the weapon made it much easier to use in situations where one needed to be quick and did not need a long, bulky barrel getting in the way. He loaded each barrel with a round as quick as he could.

He kicked the barrels of the shotgun up and locked them into place, but as the gun clicked he felt a hand on his shoulder gripping him tight. Tanner was flung from the ground and into a nearby tree; his back cracking against it as he fell to the ground. He never lost his grip on his weapon as the hit had him dazed.

As the flares illuminated the area around his vehicle and the surrounding forest, Tanner watched as the remaining two people, a man and woman Tanner had actually never seen began systematically wrecking his Impala. They smashed the hood of his car with their bare hands and ripped rubber straight from the tires, causing those bloated rings to blowout louder than the cracks of thunder in the sky.

Tanner pulled himself to one knee and shook with an adrenaline fueled rage. He afforded himself a few deep breaths of air to steady himself. Holding the shotgun in his left hand, his right reached into his suit pocket and pulled his revolver out once more. He lined the shot up while the two continued to destroy his vehicle. Several shots rang out, disguised by the near-constant stream of thunder that rattled the earth with each dance of lightning above, and hit the back of the male figure. His back exploded into several chunks of flesh as the rounds pierced lungs, bone, and that heart, forcing black blood to ooze from each side of the man where the ammunition struck clean through. The powerful shots had knocked the man forward, toppling him over the hood of the vehicle.

The shots didn't do much harm, however, as the man stood erect and turned towards Tanner who groaned in disgust, "Seems like I gotta take your fucking hearts out completely." He muttered and slipped his revolver back into his pocket.

The man charged Tanner head-on. Whatever had happened to those poor souls gave them the same strength and speed the teenager had exerted on Tanner minutes before, and that consistency made Tanner smile. The being rushing right at Tanner made the man even happier as it allowed him to simply raise the shotgun up at the last moment.

The freaky individual leaped at Tanner and the shotgun jerked in Tanner's hands. He pulled both triggers of the double barrels right as the body was about to dive on him. The force of the shotgun ripped through the man's body and blew out the other end, severing his chest from the rest of his body in a show of gore and blood. It splattered Tanner's expensive suit and pants in a messy red paste and the upper body, which consisted only of the male's head, shoulders and arms, smacked against Tanner's shoulder, knocking him off balance but the body fell lifeless to the ground. The lower half of the possessed man flopped around a few times before that black blood turned red.

Tanner stepped out of the man's intestines with disgust on his face, "Never fails." Tanner's shoulder ached from the blow he took from the man's bisected upper half and he shook the pain away, he did not have time to worry about it.

The female, stopping her incessant beating on Tanner's Impala, realized what had happened and growled at Tanner. It was a mixture of a painful scream and some rabid animal which sent shivers down Tanner's spine. In a flash she was running at him; ducking, weaving, and generally becoming a much harder target with her speed.

Tanner reloaded and kicked the shotgun up once more. A deafening blast of gunfire echoed through the dense, rain soaked forest when he fired another round at the woman's chest, much like he had done with the man previously. She evaded the buckshot.

She almost was on top of him at that point. Her hand slashed at him with nails that were much longer, and much sharper than any woman's should have been. The nails raked through his suit and his t-shirt under it, slashing several thin gashes into his midsection. Tanner doubled over and twisted his wrist that held the shotgun around and up.

Tanner let out his own growl when he shoved the barrel of the gun under the attacking woman's chin and pulled the trigger. Tanner's wrist jerked down and he risked the break to end the encounter. The last buckshot that was loaded in the gun fired from the pull of the second trigger and the female teenager's head was gone. It was a nasty display of power that had his Impala draped in blood and body parts that should have been kept inside. The last of the twisted faces were done with and Tanner stumbled back a few feet after dispatching her head and fell on his ass.

The shotgun fell to the ground and Tanner checked his wrist. He could still move it around, so it wasn't broken, but it hurt like hell firing the weapon like that in a pinch. He shook it off and used the shotgun as a makeshift cane to pull himself to his feet. Checking to see how deep the gashes in his stomach were, Tanner pulled his suit jacket off and raised his shirt, showing off toned abs that were not that worse for the wear;

only a little blood was trickling from his wounds. To be safe he tied his jacket around his stomach tight, grunting at the sharp pain from the sudden pressure.

The rain was relentless and the lifetime on his flares had ended. Draped in darkness, along with a car that might not even bother working, Tanner favored his stomach while walking back to his car. He situated himself in and placed his head against the steering wheel. He turned the ignition several times and heard a disappointing chugging sound each time.

In front of him, from the S.U.V, came the sounds of violent banging. The back of the vehicle screeched and thudded. Metal crunched and twisted as the car bent inwards from the violent dents put into the back and the tops of the vehicle from whatever was still in it. The metal tore from the violent bashing at the back of the S.U.V before half of the back swung out and swung back with a crash. Another dent was put into the metal and it tore off from the car with a sickening whine of shredded metal.

Tanner's head shot up when the commotion began, turning the ignition on and off to try and get his beat up vehicle started. Blown out tires and rims aside it would still be faster than walking or running. The metal back of the S.U.V had landed on the hood of his car and through the flickering lights of his Impala Tanner could not mistake the massive body of Fred Thompson appearing from the back of the wrecked sports utility vehicle.

Still wearing the black shirt and blue jeans that had fresh blood over the front of them, Fred's face was twisting and shifting faster than ever. The flickering lights caused every movement Fred made to appear more surreal than it should have been, and made those blurry, shaken facial features even more terrifying. Fred bent forward, and Tanner expected nothing but silence from the creature, instead Tanner and his car shook from the ear splitting wail that emitted from that dark abyss. When the scream ended Fred charged.

Tanner turned the ignition several more times and the third time was the charm. The engine roared to life but it had been too late. When Tanner slammed the gears into reverse Fred Thompson slammed into the front end and curled his fingers underneath the bumper. With straining veins the possessed man hurled the front end of the car into the air.

Tanner had no time to escape as the roof of the vehicle crashed onto the forest ground.

27

Jacque sat in his office watching everyone who was left inside of his lovely establishment. One monitor showed Kimberly and James still in each other's arms and under the blankets. They had been that way when Jacque had to take care of their little friend Jimmy and he was glad he did not miss the scene starring Kimberly, who was eager to show James what it was like to be with a closet whore. Jacque knew a whore when he saw one, and he could spot one a mile away. They were all the same; a shy demeanor hiding a wildcat that wished to be free. He had been surprised when she refused Oswald's advances.

It aroused Jacque to watch; even if it did not involve sexual situations. He slid from his chair and double checked the numerous locks on his door. It was secured by two deadbolts, a chain, and the knob itself. Erect and needing, he tugged on the snake's head once again, disturbing it from its otherwise still slumber. The grinding gears from the elevator shaft squealed with protest from the old design until the walls shifted out of the way and the gate to the elevator opened for Jacque. He stepped in and rode the long ride down, a smile gracing his lips as he felt so full of his new collection.

Jacque wandered through the obsidian halls, tracing his fingertips against the cool, shiny black stone. His nails dug against a few lines in the wall, sending a high-pitched screech through the hallway and into the subsequent room where his new pets were.

The stable looked a little empty but that did not put a damper on Jacque's spirits. "How are my new pets doing? Jimmy? Miss Sinfield?" he asked the two newest people to his collection.

Stacy was bound with her bloody clothes still on her body. She wasn't the concern at the moment so he did not strip her down. She was already broken, her mind and soul already lost to the book's insatiable hunger. Her once attractive, middle-age features were now just blurred lines shifting across a tortured canvas. Her arms and ankles were shackled to the walls and she hung there without a fight. No rage, no anger, just an agonizing sadness with the way her body hung.

"Still have those pesky memories in your head Miss Sinfield? You should be happy with your family in here." Jacque spat, gripping her hair by the handful in his hand and slamming it against the wall to liven her up. It was a futile attempt; a small, insignificant part of her still fighting the illusion that took her soul.

The stall behind Jacque sang to him as a body slammed against the wall, "L-Leave her!" a choked gasp yelled at Jacque. Jimmy Franklin was another surprise. Jacque turned around and noticed that the boy's face had over a fourth of purity left in it and it was untouched by the swirling mass that covered the other three-fourths of his face. His body was wrapped in the same burning chains the rest were wrapped in but Jacque went into overload on the meddlesome teen. Those chains were wrapped across his naked body and also covered his crotch several times in a painful, sadistic act for discovering things he shouldn't have. Jimmy could barely move, let along speak, but he continued fighting.

"You are one sneaky child. I should thank you though, I will be looking for the author of that 'web site' you kids call information today. I am shocked so many true things are on such a thing where anonymity runs rampant. Such a shame my power does not run through ones and zeros," he said and slapped Jimmy across the face.

Out of the twenty stables only eight of them were occupied now. Jacque had sent his previous pets he spent some time with out with the Sinfield vehicle but instead of sending the overweight, nasty sack of flesh with them he sent Fred instead. Jacque stopped in front of the overweight woman's stable and sneered. "You are truly disgusting," he said and thought about the new acquisitions he could make. He made up his mind, "Your services are no longer required," he cackled and reached right into that stall and punctured the woman's chest. She didn't scream, didn't cry out at all, and was silent as Jacque crushed her black heart. He pulled his hand back and stuck his tongue out, revolted that he had to even touch the woman. He reached a finger over to a blue button on the side of the stall and pressed it. The floor below the woman opened and her body dropped into blackness along with the chains that bound her. "Good riddance."

Between the stables where Jimmy and Stacy were held and the last stables which housed a rather disgruntled redhead laid Jacque's all-stars. They were the first of many corrupted, a family of four, much like the Sinfield quartet, only it consisted of a father, a mother, and two daughters who, over time, proved to be more loyal and more lethal than any others Jacque had taken a hold of during the last few years. The corruption had coursed through them all for so long that their bodies were still bound to the stables but their flesh had been flayed from their skin, their features, once recognizable, were now all the same images of muscle and dried blood. Their heads still had flesh on the top of their head and back, but that black swirling of facial features was nothing but a whirlpool of blackness. Fingers were now boney claws, same with their toes; they were perfect killing machines that only the best torture could design.

At the end of the stables the redhead struggled in her bounds. Jacque came to the conclusion that she had been the one who had broke free before and, despite fighting her innermost fantasies and gluttonous desires for over three weeks now, managed to gain clarity long enough to steal his own leather bound record of what he was and place it in such an open and obvious spot.

He was starting to fall in love with her.

Helena screamed as half of her face remained. The beautiful redhead continued her struggles against those burning chains. One bright, blue, eye centered on Jacque and her brow narrowed. Wrinkles decorated the right side of her nose and the corner of her eye as she screamed and bounded against the walls with renewed vigor. Her red tresses had matted together in clumps in several areas.

"You are so unclean," Jacque said and looked at the buttons on the side of the stable. He had stripped Helena down to nothing like the others and had no problems in pressing the lighter blue button under the blue one he had dispatched the overweight woman with before. When he pushed the button a small square hole opened above the stable Helena was in. A small nozzle extended from the hole and sprayed a fine mist of ice, cold water over her head and her body. He cleaned his pets often, but the last few days had been quite busy ones.

She squealed when the water hit her body, freezing her flesh and soaking her hair in the mist which covered her head to toe back and forth for several minutes. A drain underneath her body disposed of the water that dripped down her form. Jacque, feeling that she had an adequate cleaning, stepped inside of her stable and drew several of his gangly fingers through her tangled hair to straighten it out.

"You are quite the little trouble maker Helena."

Helena spat at him the best that she could. She growled and snapped at him, biting at him despite the bit that was in her mouth along with her chains.

"Fuhhk-ou!" a metallic, graveled voice echoed from her stuffed mouth.

"Well aren't you the most surprising little thing I have ever captured. So verbal too! You have to be, by far, the longest person to ever fight never ending happiness. Color me impressed my dear." Jacque said as he stroked her hair. After he yanked a few matted clumps of hair free he reached down to slap her across the face hard. She thrashed and that fueled the anger she had, the rage, the ferocity.

As her body dangled from the restraints, Jacque crept behind her. He disrobed his lanky, decrepit body entirely. Even though Helena was not entirely corrupted, just like Jimmy, the corrupted parts of them were etched in Jacque's flesh, joining the dozens, hundreds of individuals that were devoured by Jacque and his demonic book.

Jacque took his liberties with Helena's body as the tortured faces of everyone whose souls he had stolen rolled across his limbs and his body. They swirled around, blinked, cried out in silence on Jacque's flesh. They were in hell, forever bound to disgusting flesh from ankle to wrist.

28

Stan, dragging Jasmine past the threshold of their room, shut the door behind them and locked it quickly. He placed his back against the door and tried to calm down by taking labored, deep breaths. He slid down the doorframe and to the bottom of it, keeping his back placed against it as hard as he could against the hard wood.

"He was lying to us Jasmine. He only showed a few signs but he was lying through his teeth baby. Worst of all is that he's good at it, I almost believed what he said." He warned his wife while she went to the nearby window to observe the storm that was coming in from the east.

"Stan? What kind of storm comes in from the ocean? I mean hurricanes do but we are pretty far up for a hurricane to develop this quickly right? I mean the weather said nothing of a storm coming from the east."

He joined her at the window, sighing, "I am about to take back what I said earlier."

"Don't think like that honey. So things are getting a bit odd; isn't it exciting through?"

"You and I have a drastically different definition of exciting. I would call mine more freaking out."

Jasmine pulled back and closed the drapes to keep the sight of the worsening weather from their eyes. She turned to him and gripped his hand, smiling bright. She was his optimism when he had none.

"Stan, come here." Her hand tugged his towards the bed. She sat down before him and crossed her silky legs, patting the bed beside her in the process. "You have to live a little Stan. Now I know what happened. I have been worried to death about you ever since that night. I'm not growing tired of it, but things are never perfect. The only thing close to it is our marriage. You are, and forever will be, the perfect man for me but that doesn't mean I want you acting defeated all the time when things look down and out."

"Jasmine I-"

She put a finger on his mouth, "Hush. I wasn't finished." She smiled and brushed her finger to his chin. "You are strong. You are a survivor Stan. Just like me. That is all that matters do you hear me?"

"This isn't fair. You are just using what I told you when we first met," Stan said and looked down to his hand that was held in hers.
Jasmine's lips curled into a deviant grin and she nodded her confession, "I had the most amazing man to set me straight. One that needs to listen to his own advice and realize that he is so much stronger than he thinks he is."

"Who is he? I can't believe you've been cheating on me Jazz. After all we've been through," he said with an exaggerated quivering of his lip.

A moment later a pillow smacked him along side of his head, forcing him to laugh.

Jasmine huffed and pouted, crossing her arms while tossing the pillow back behind her. "Fine, go ahead and don't take me seriously. I will never help you again and I am cutting off all sex." She said, stomping her foot on the ground to make her point.

Stan leaned in and kissed her neck as his hand pressed against her chest, pushing her down onto her back with a little push. "Don't say that Jasmine. Thank you. I love you."

She giggled and allowed him to push her onto her back so she could look up at him, "You're damn right you do butt-head."

The door knob jiggled several times. Stan shot off Jasmine and lurched towards the door with a few long, silent steps and looked through the peep hole.

"Well fuck."

"Open the door Stan! You two have had enough time to fiddle fuck around."

Stan sighed and unlocked the door. Ryan and Maggie were standing out in the hallway when he opened the door; Ryan was wearing a beach towel around his waist and was dripping water onto the ground where he stood. Maggie had a similar towel wrapped around her entire upper body and waist and had a beige bath towel wrapping her hair. Maggie, at least, had sandals on.

"We weren't really interrupting anything were we?" Maggie asked as she entered the room and sat down next to her adopted sister, "How is everything going for you guys so far?"

Stan licked his own lips, "Everything is going fine so far. We kind of had a scare before this storm hit out of nowhere though. Jimmy hurt himself in the forest and it sounded like he was quite distressed but the Sinfields took it upon themselves to take him into town, or that is what Jacque told us."

"We thought we heard screaming but we just thought it was something else entirely. That sucks."

"See that Stan? If Ryan can grow a heart with just two days of vacation you should be right as rain by the end of all of this."

"I've got a heart of gold woman. It isn't my fault you can't see how much it shines."

"Yeah, a dull shine if anything."

Ryan bent over, gripping his wife around the waist and tossed her over his shoulders. Her fists beat against his back lightly in protest, "I'm going to have to teach this woman a lesson. Sorry if we intruded on anything." Ryan smacked Maggie on the back of her bubbly bottom while turning to carry her out of the room.

When the door slammed shut Stan and Jasmine looked at one another and sighed in unison.

James fell onto his back and panted several times. His body was covered in a thin sheen of sweat and his chest rose and fell with slow, laboring breaths.

"Did that just happen?" he asked the blonde woman next to him who was busy crawling up his body, laying her head across his arm and letting her hair tickle his sides and chest.

Kimberly huffed, wrapping an arm around his midsection while nodding her head, causing her hair to brush against his body even more. "Yeah, it did. For a nerd you were damn good." She closed her eyes while nestling her head more into his lanky body.

"I can't even tell you how amazing that was. My God, that thing you did on top. I can't even process how you did that."

"Well, Mister, I was very surprised and happy when you went ahead and took the reins and did your own thing. That was sexy as hell James.

He leaned in and kissed her on top of her own sweaty brow and squeezed her tight with his arm, "Are you kidding me? I was so nervous I thought I was going to ruin everything. Instinct is one hell of a drug though."

"Well then you have great instincts James. I guess it just needed a little encouragement." She giggled as her hand danced down his chest and to his stomach and finally to his spent manhood.

James groaned as she tended to his flesh again and looked down at the confusing situation they had on their hands. "Does this mean we are going steady?"

Kimberly nodded her head and squeezed him down below, "Steady? Sure, got any other terms Mister Seventies?"

"Groovy, tubular, radical; well one of those are from the seventies. I think I'm getting my eras mixed up but my head is spinning right now," he said, smiling as he kissed her again.

She placed her hand on his stomach to stop him, "I know what you want to feel and I just want to take things a little slow right now. We both like each other a lot, and I love you as a friend, but do you think we can just let these things between us grow slowly? I've been where you are and, well, I guess I just want to ensure things go right and in a mature way. I know we went from crawling to the high jump, but I think we both needed this."

"You know I actually agree. I want to say the obvious thing to you right now but I know if I did it wouldn't be a mature thought, I suppose. I want this to grow and God damn it, I am going to be happy every single moment while we grow together Kimberly."

"This also means no telling Jimmy what happened right here. I won't be all bitchy if you let it slip but if you tell him anything I did to you technique wise I'll have to cut you off for a month. I don't want to do that to you James, I'm a nice girl," she said with a coy grin appearing on her lips.

"The best girl ever, no doubt about that; your secret is safe with me, don't worry."

"You can tell him one technique. The one where I spun around on you like that? Thank gymnastics for that."

James swooned for her again and dove on top of her body, kissing her hard on her giggling lips.

The lights in the kitchen were on when Jacque Collo stepped in front of the kitchen door that swung both ways without any sort of handle or knob. It was the same set up anyone would find in a diner or expensive restaurant where busy busboys and an overworked wait staff would do their best to not smash into one another as the door had its constant sound of swooshing back and forth. The door was still in this massive home with its small population. The door had been lifted from a diner, after all, and Jacque peered through the plastic square. He stole a glance to see who was rummaging around in there and a small grin graced his lips.

The pots and pans hung above the large stove that had more than the standard four ranges and Jacque saw James Newberry pouring himself something to drink, a soda of some kind, off to the right of the stove. No ranges on the stove top were active that Jacque noticed and the swinging barrier eased open without a squeak or creak. He slithered into the kitchen like a snake, creeping towards James who finished pouring that orange, fizzing drink into his glass.

"Mister Newberry?"

James shot into the air. He almost knocked over the glass of soda he poured just moments before as he turned to address the sneaky man "Jesus Christ! Mister Collo you have to be a ninja or something to sneak up on people like that. I nearly just spilled everything across the counter here."

"I apologize. I do have a way of walking silently without even thinking about it," Jacque smiled on the inside, "I am also sorry to inform you that your friend Mister Franklin hurt his leg in the woods. The Sinfield family graciously offered to take him to the hospital in town."

James looked at Jacque like a deer caught in the headlights, "Well shit, is he alright? What happened?"

Jacque's hands were in front of his body, crossed at the waist where one hand held a fist. It was a common way an authority figure addressed someone, "Simply put he tripped and twisted his ankle. He may have even broken it. I am not sure of the seriousness of the injury but he told me that you and Miss Cross didn't need to be interrupted and I was honoring what he wished for. He said he would be fine."

James looked to the ground and nodded his acceptance. He put his hands on the counter behind him and leaned back, careful to not spill that drink he had, "Damn. Well that would have been awkward if you did come and get us but thank you for seeing that he was taken care of. I suppose that Kimberly and I should go ahead and get packed up to go see him."

Jacque shook his head and took one step towards James, "Mister Franklin said he'd probably, how did he say it? 'slap you silly' if you came for him and ruined a 'special' vacation you could have with Miss Cross."

"Will he be back by tomorrow at least?"

"Mister Franklin is a surprisingly strong lad. I think he will be back before you know it. I mean when I looked at his injury I did not see a bone sticking out of it so that is a good sign."

James shuddered.

"I will leave it up to you to tell your other friend about Mister Franklin. I think she will take it well, considering it could have been much worse if he was out in the woods alone."

James drew his gaze from the polished, black and white checkered tiles that decorated the kitchen floor to look back up at Jacque, "Why was he out in the woods anyway?"

"Your guess is as good as mine but he was enjoying the day from what I could tell. I found him with his laptop and some water. Maybe he wanted some alone time?"

"Alright, well thank you again Mister Collo. I'm going to go and tell Kimberly about it. Oh and before I forget do you care if we have one of the frozen pizzas in here?" he motioned to the freezer underneath the gigantic refrigerator.

Jacque shook his head, "Not at all Mister Newberry; as I mentioned before all of the food and utilities and everything is covered in your initial payment."

"Cool, thanks," James said as he took his leave with his drink in hand. When James left the room Jacque's smile only grew wider.

29

Vincent Tanner woke to the sound of metal grinding on the ground underneath him. He reached behind and felt a large welt on the back of his head but the peculiar thing was the feeling of wetness trickling up his face. He also felt his hair brushing against the top of his car. His vision was blurry but he felt an uncomfortable pressure against his shoulder and waist all the while that annoying grinding echoed in his ears.

He realized he was upside down.

The last thing flashed through his mind like a bright flare. Before he blacked out he remembered the gargantuan body of Fred Thompson, his face nothing but a literal blur, slamming into the front end of his Impala and tossing it into the air. Tanner realized Fred Thompson only flipped it onto its hood.

Judging from how his blood was flowing Tanner knew he had to have hit his head on the steering wheel and had been knocked out for a moment because of it. The seatbelt against his shoulder and around his waist ambiguously played both the devil and an angel with how it held him in place.

Looking out from the broken passenger side window of his busted ride, Tanner watched as the tires of the S.U.V pass by. He was getting pushed along the ground and the scraping metal sound was the roof of his car grinding along rocks and dirt.

Tanner grunted while he started thumbing the seatbelt release. He slammed the button down and moaned when his head and back smacked against the roof of the sliding vehicle. He had remembered the black crevice that those things had been taking the S.U.V to and he knew that it was not going to be a simple, shallow drop down a hill.

Tanner did his best to adjust his body around from inside of his car and grabbed his revolver from the holster inside of his suit jacket which had been tied around his midsection. Twisting just a bit more so he was on his stomach, Tanner looked in front of his car and saw Fred Thompson's legs digging into the dirt, kicking it up with every step and shove he gave. Tanner ground his teeth together and pointed the gun right at Fred's shins. His hand shook and it took one solid, deep breath to calm his nerves before the gun fired once, shifted, and then fired again. The shots hit their mark and the large, corrupted male stopped the labored task of shoving that car around.

The bullets to Fred's shin did not impede any motor functions in the male's legs. Tanner watched Fred's steps take the large man from the front of the car to Tanner's right where the driver's side door and in response Tanner shimmied his own body to the passenger's side on the left, breaking the remaining glass out of what was left of the window before sliding from mangled steel to grainy dirt.

Tanner allowed himself two quick breaths before he shot to his feet and stumbled backwards with the rush of blood to his head. He was dizzy with adrenaline and the blow to the back of the head wasn't helping matters any. Even with his vision causing him to see about one and a half of everything instead of double he couldn't lose sight of the mountain of a man Fred Thompson was even if he wanted to.

Fred's vile visage, to Tanner's best guess, stared right back at him on the other side of the vehicle.

Out of the corner of his eye Tanner saw that his trunk had been knocked open in the chaos and everything had been dumped onto the ground. The guns, knives, hatchets and even a few explosive devices were strewn across the dirt. He also saw a dark, wet patch of soil a few feet away from his weapons.

Drawing another flare from his suit, Tanner looked at Fred whose face continued its silent gaze. Fred leaned forward and let out that inhuman bellow roar to life again, shaking the trees and ground Tanner stood on.

"Come on bitch!" Tanner screamed as he sparked the flare and held it firm in his hand. The fire burned hot.

Fred responded by reaching under the vehicle and tipped it up. Veins popped from the man's neck as his fingers penetrated the steel roof of Tanner's Impala and with an impressive, inhuman strength Fred raised the vehicle off the ground and over his head. His face twisted and screamed in a sick torture from a body pushed far past its limits; Fred's skin was tearing and ripping as muscle bulged free from flesh and blood sprayed in a fine, blackened mist all over the ground around Fred.

Tanner took one more glance at the darkened pool of soil a few feet to Fred's right that dripped from the very car held above the monster's head. Fred's skin continued to split along with the clothing he had on as the man became more blackened muscle than skin.

Tanner chucked the flare at the leaking gas tank. The flare ignited the gas that flowed from the tank and the heated dance of orange and red trailed from the side of the vehicle where the gas covered it right to the tank itself. Tanner turned on his heel and dove behind the nearest tree he could find. He covered his head and curled his body up as tight as he could to keep the tree between him and the car.

The sudden reaction to fire meeting gas in a very tight, enclosed space ensured the combustion of the gas tank that set off a chain reaction throughout the vehicle. The car exploded and sent a shockwave through the forest, shaking Tanner and the tree he hid behind. Hot, metal shrapnel seared through Fred's body, slicing into his flesh and causing black ichor to ooze, bubble, and pop from the wounds. Several chunks of skin and muscle were freed from Fred's body but the creature, now nothing but a solid mass of black muscle that shimmered in the firelight, stayed on its feet. It was not even bothered by the thick flames that burned on its head which showed no signs of dying out.

Tanner stole a peek from behind the tree and couldn't believe what he was seeing, "Holy shit!" he said, cracking a smile as a small laugh escaped from his lips. The versatility of whatever Fred Thompson had turned into impressed Tanner, but he also realized what he did to his car.

"God damn it! That was my baby!"

There was little humanity left to Fred's physical features. His flesh had either torn or burned away along with his clothing and that face had twisted into a perverted black hole. There were gleams of white, however, and when the face stopped swirling for the briefest of moments Tanner saw the dozens of pointed teeth that aligned what used to be Fred's face. It looked like a perverse, fleshy garbage disposal whirring about. The beast still carried that car high above its head but it leaned back and threw its body forward, tossing the flaming chunk of metal at Tanner and the tree he hid behind.

The car hit the tree hard enough to crack the tree nearly in half. The car fell to the ground, scraping against the bark until it nestled into the dirty ground below. Rain showered down on the vehicle and Tanner from the new hole in the top of the forest where the buckling tree had stood as a shield against the storm.

Tanner, hunkering over to avoid any shrapnel, crawled out from the forest on his knees and stood, dusting himself free from a few splashes of mud. He turned his attention to the monster that had taken over the once caring, silent giant who was Fred Thompson. The beast wasn't moving much at all. Tanner observed the changes, documenting what he was face-to-face with for future record keeping if he scraped through this encounter unscathed. He took several steps into the clearing and saw all of his weapons were scattered on the ground off to the right. The explosion had blown them all around as well. He estimated the most useful ones were fifteen feet away and the creature, with the flaming chunks of shrapnel embedded in its body, stood closer to them than Tanner did. It would be impossible for Tanner to make it to any of them for now.

"Come on, bring it you ugly son of a bitch! You can't do shit can you? Fucking hurling a man's car? That is some cowardly bullshit!" Tanner screamed, taunting the massive entity.

It didn't seem to draw any emotion out of the creature. The horrible, tortured face continued to swirl around in agony as it stood there on fire. The drizzle from the storm above was only breaking through that one concentrated flow thanks to the tree that threatened to fall over at any given moment.

Irritation washed over Tanner and he did his best to calm himself before he made any stupid, rookie mistakes. He had this. He already killed three of the possessed things and he only had one left to go. Unfortunately this one was big, strong, and possibly quick on his feet. Tanner couldn't afford to be patient for much longer and looked towards the scattered weaponry on the ground.

In a desperate gamble he drew his revolver once again and fanned the hammer three times. That was the last of his ammo inside of his revolver for now and the three were placed right inside of that whirling mass of gnashing teeth, sending the behemoth blundering a few feet backwards.

Tanner dashed to the pile on the ground and grabbed the first thing he could wrap his fingers around. It was a silver lined hatchet with a deep maroon hardwood handle. He skidded past the hatchet to begin with when he picked it up and in a mad dash he threw himself at Fred.

He brought the hatchet over his head and swung it downwards towards the disgusting creature and hit home, for the most part.

The sickening squish of flesh that the sharp end connected with was the monster's forearm. It sliced through to the bone before it stopped penetrating. Tanner panted and raised his leg to plant it in Fred's stomach while he pulled that hatchet back.

Blood sprayed from Fred's wound but that didn't stop the monster from mounting a counter attack. His healthy arm swung from the right and nearly connected with Tanner's jaw.

Tanner pulled back just in time to avoid that nasty swing the beast had and Tanner quickly spun his body around clockwise, raised the hatchet as high as he could, and with lethal intent slammed his arm down, aiming for the former man's neck and completing his dance.

Whatever the creature was it crumpled down to the ground while its dismembered head rolled into the nearby bushes. Tanner sank to his knees next to the burning body. He was dizzy from the combined drug of a concussion and the rush of adrenaline he hadn't felt in the longest time. He tried to fight it, he even tried to stand back up, but his body finally gave out and he fell to the side, slumping down next to the fiery body that continually burned thanks to the leftover gasoline and shrapnel cooking it inside and out.

30

James kicked the door shut to the bedroom he was now sharing with Kimberly. He balanced two tall glasses filled to the brim with a fizzy, orange soda, "Kimberly I have some rather bad news. Some damn odd bad news," he said and looked over his shoulder to ensure the door was shut.

Kimberly had a jean skirt on and a pink tank top covering her chest and that was it. She tilted her head and got up to take her drink away from James, giving it a sip, "What do you mean bad news? You already let it slip didn't you?" she huffed, blowing a strand of her blonde hair from her eyes.

James shook his head, his eye-line aimed right to the ground where her bare feet were, "Jimmy got hurt. I guess he injured his ankle playing around in the woods. Which is odd considering none of us are the damn outdoorsy type," he said and let it sink in for a second. "Jacque told me that the Sinfields took him into the city for some treatment and that he didn't want us to worry about him if things were going well between us."

Kimberly bit her lower lip and cast her gaze to the ground. Several locks of her blonde hair were twisted around a finger while she sipped on her drink, taking the information in.

"I know what you're thinking but . . . don't."

"James he is our friend. He's in the hospital. We should go and see him."

James took her hand away from her hair and sat down on the bed, inviting her to join him with a simple tug on her arm, "He said he would kick my ass if we came and saw him. I don't want him to feel like we pity him. What I mean is I don't think he wants his injury to ruin the vacation for the rest of us."

"Well we should at least give him a call and let him know we are thinking about him you know?"

James smiled and took his cell phone out of his pocket. He scrolled through his contact list and found Jimmy's name. Though when he touched the call sign he glanced at his signal strength and saw he had no service, "Fucking storm. I can't get a signal to save my life; nationwide coverage my left nut."

"How is that even possible?" Kimberly asked and pulled her own phone out from one of her bags. After thumbing through the options she saw that she wasn't getting a signal at all either, "Damn it. I know we had service earlier and this storm isn't that bad."

James sat his drink, half finished, down on the nearby end table and slunk back on the bed. He placed his hands behind his head, looking up at the ceiling as lightning flashed outside of the window followed by a clap of thunder. "Well going outside right now might just be out of the question. It is like a damn hurricane out there."

Kimberly turned to the window and watched the storm pick up in full force. The wind slapped against the window and the rain pounded on the roof and glass, "It is weird how this storm came out of nowhere. I guess it is kind of romantic and I don't want to miss any opportunity to use these bad boys." She said and pulled a few candles out that she had packed with her for the trip. She placed each of the glass encased, cherry and floral scented masses of wax at either end of her headboard and then next to their drinks on the end table.

James hopped off the bed and turned the lights off after she lit several of the candles. The glow presented her in a new light and it was one James had no issues with at all. He crawled next to her on the bed and looked out the window with her to the rampant downpour of rain.

"I guess it isn't too bad once you think about it. I mean it is only rain, thunder, and lighting. It mixes together pretty well," he said as one arm wrapped around her shoulders.

The pretty blonde smiled and leaned her head against his, "That wasn't too deep but I know what you mean". She jabbed his side playfully while they sat in the subtle light.

He withdrew from her from the jabbing she gave his sides and smiled, "Yeah, I guess I'm not too good at that stuff. Though do you want to stay here and watch the storm all night or did you have other plans before going to bed?"

"I was thinking about going for a swim actually. I know it isn't the best idea with this storm and all but I think it would look really cool with the way they have that space designed. All those lights dancing whenever lightning hit in different areas? It seemed really thick sort of glass as well so I wouldn't be in any danger."

"Sounds good to me, but I think I am going to bring my laptop with and look some stuff up that me and Jimmy had an interest in earlier. You know that real freaky book we found early and Jacque snatched it from us?"

Kimberly nodded, but looked confused.

"Well I figure since he is out of commission I would look some of that stuff for him. Geeky, I know, but I figure that is what he would enjoy. It would let him know we were thinking about him."

"Aw, that is such a sweet thing for you to do James. I think he would like that a lot. What as in that book anyway that perked your guys' interest so much?"

"Oh nothing too odd or strange, just some paranormal writing, that's all."

"Tell me! I mean I have been with you guys for geekier stuff than just the 'paranormal' so don't start getting all shy and awkward on me now!"

"Alright, alright, it was some sort of weird ass thing we saw in some creepy, leather bound book. It was like a ghost story or something except it wasn't about ghosts, it was more like about a man in a suit along with a bunch of freaky looking people crowded behind him. They were called 'The Bleak' or something like that. We didn't get to read too much into it before Jacque stole the book from us and claimed that it was from his personal collection that shouldn't have been down there."

"That's weird. Not on your part but on Jacque's. I don't think anyone here would have stolen it and just left it in the library. Maybe a previous group had."

"You're right. He blamed the two gay guys that were here but really it makes no sense at all. They never struck me as the thieving type and if they were then they were horrible at it since they got caught instead of making a break for it. None of us heard any arguing or commotion that night right? For criminals they sure as fuck left politely don't you think?"

"I wouldn't think too much on it," she said and wrapped her arms around him, looking out the window of her room to the storm outside. "I think it was just an unlucky week for some of us. I just hope this storm lets up before too long."

James smiled and moved away from her embrace after a moment to stretch his arms and legs out. "Well I am going to go and throw a pizza in the oven and when it is done I will bring it out to that glass place for us to have."

"Alright but we should head to bed early tonight. I want to go and see Jimmy in the morning."

"I agree. Are you okay with pepperoni?"

"Yep, and don't worry about swimming after eating. That is just an old wives' tale. I have never had a problem with cramps.

"I think you just can't stuff your face and then jump into water and start going at it like you're in a race for a gold medal." He smiled and took his leave from the room.

31

Jimmy Franklin woke with a scream. His head twisted and turned, looking around in the darkness and finding nothing. He panted several times while sweat dripped down his brow and cheeks. He felt his limbs free, they were not bound by those disgusting, burning chains and his head felt fine; it no longer felt like it was being torn apart.

A light clicked on and blinded the young college student. He groaned and heard a familiar voice, an annoyed voice.

"You have another nightmare dude?"

It belonged to James, his best friend.

Jimmy waited for his eyes to adjust to the sudden light and realized he was in the same apartment he shared with James and Kimberly. He shared a room with James and Kimberly had her own room. He spotted the comforting posters of various geek culture shocks adorning his room. Across from their beds laid a large table with various figurines and maps made for their adventures in dungeon diving. A small coffee table separated his bed from James' and he picked his glasses up and peered through them. His heart raced as he did his best to calm down.

"Damn man, you must have had something wicked going on in

your head. I haven't heard you scream like that in a long time." James said, concerned for his friend. He propped himself up on his bed and left the light on for now.

Jimmy was silent aside from several panting breaths. He jerked away when James stood from his bed, "No. No. No! This isn't right."

"You had a nightmare man. Shit like that happens you know?"

"No! You and me and Kimberly were in some fucking mansion and shit on vacation." Jimmy began, feeling his face and his body and finding nothing out of the ordinary as his breathing slowed.

James stared at him, "Yeah you need to relax man. You know what this is? It's stress of finals week getting to you. That's all."

The bedroom door opened and Kimberly stood in the opening with nothing but a pink bra and pajama pants on, "What's wrong?" She asked as a tired yawn escaped her lips.

"It's alright. Jimmy had a bogus dream again. You know how imagination works with geeks like us. It tends to go into overdrive when we go to sleep."

Kimberly crossed both of her legs and her arms at the entrance to the bedroom and leaned against the sturdy frame. Some of her blonde hair fell over her features and she blew the strands away from her eyes before smiling. "Poor guy," she began and drifted from the door to Jimmy's bed, "Don't worry about it Jimmy. I have had some bad ones in the past too. I am far too familiar with bad dreams."

"It was so real. I mean yeah that sounds stupid and clichéd but that is how it felt. I mean, in a way, I feel like I am dreaming right now guys. I mean James was going to tell you that he actually liked you more than just a friend, Kimberly."

"Well that makes sense Jimmy. We started dating a few weeks ago, you know that." Kimberly said, dragging a few fingers through Jimmy's hair.

James stood there in his boxers and laughed, "Yeah dude, you encouraged me to go for it and it worked out pretty well. Though we aren't going anywhere or abandon you. Fuck that. We got some 'Three Musketeers' shit going on right now with our little threesome." He said, his wording eliciting a laugh from Kimberly.

Jimmy's shoulders relaxed and his body lost its defensive tenseness. He slid against the back of the headboard, "That is nuts. I mean I literally felt like I have been awake for two or three days in a row. That's how vivid the dream was. It was so freaky though, I saw a family of four murdered by something fucked up, then I was caught and forced to change into something."

"Freaky."

"Yeah dude, we need to get you off the horror movies for a while until finals are done and over with."

Kimberly leaned in and hugged Jimmy tight. Her breasts pressed against his chest and closed his eyes when his chin rested on her shoulder. As he slowly opened his eyes Jacque Collo stood outside of the bedroom door and with a twisted smile the door slammed shut.

Jacque Collo sauntered around Jimmy's kennel. He let his fingers rub against the obsidian walls and over the chains that bound the thrashing male. He cackled as he watched Jimmy's face blur and shake with violent intent, "Well now look at you Jimmy! You look so much better. So much so stronger and a lot more agile than you used to be; you should really be thanking me."

Jacque reached around to the side of the stable and hit the green button on the side. The chains that bound Jimmy dropped from every piece of flesh that burned into the young man while he fought the fantasy inside. Jacque ran his hands from Jimmy's hair down to his hips, gripping his backside and giving it a hard swat, "Magnificent. You are just simply magnificent. I think you are going to outperform the Sinfields by far. The mother shows some spunk but the father, well, where the hell is that beast? Oh never mind, it is not important right now."

Jacque turned from his released pet and clamped his hand around the young man's neck, guiding him with hard, bone crushing pinches to his spine. He forced Jimmy out of that stall and turned his attention to Helena while she struggled in her stall, "I am impressed. Really I am. I surely figured you would have turned by now. I almost, almost want to release you and have you serve me with your mind still intact," the idea sent tingles through his body, "but I feel that you will be even better when fully turned. The best even."

Helena continued banging against her stall and her eyes shot daggers at the Frenchman.

"It is my nature my dear. Do you blame the wolf for eating the sheep? Do you blame the sun for setting at night?" The metaphors were wrong in more ways than one but Jacque didn't care. Anyone would have corrected him, as anyone could see that this entire situation was perfectly unnatural. That didn't matter as he escorted Jimmy to the end of the hallway, "We will find them, kill them. Do not worry about their souls, well perhaps the blonde will do. And you," he said, turning to Helena, "You will turn soon enough my dear." Jacque warned and slapped her across the face before walking away with Jimmy.

32

A violent, earth shaking crack of thunder jolted Vincent Tanner from his premature slumber. Rain splattered against his head as he tried to pick himself up from the ground and in his frantic daze spun back down onto his ass. Disoriented and with a head that was aching with the fury of a thousand drums pounding, it didn't help that his vision had him seeing double and triple of everything around him.

The only thing that was clear was hard to miss. The burning body that used to be Fred Thompson started dying out. Tanner checked himself for any injuries that the adrenaline pumping through his system masked and other than the shallow gashes in his stomach from those claws raking against him in his fight with the disgusting, vile, humanoid creatures all he had were a few scrapes and bruises.

Tanner's short term memory kicked in and his head twisted to the right, "Fucking shit!" He growled as he looked at his busted vehicle that had been tossed into the forest. Rain had put out the fire that previously engulfed his vehicle but that was the least of the car's worries at that point with how mangled and twisted the frame was.

The scraps of weapons and other arms lay on the ground around Tanner and the creature. Lightning flashed and thunder bellowed as Tanner picked up whatever he could strap to himself and holster inside of his suit jacket and pants. All-in-all he had a few knives, a couple of handguns, and one shotgun that he strapped to his back. Handgun clips, revolver wheels, and shotgun shells were poured into different pockets.

When he was situated he took the shotgun off his back and went to the body of the beast. Black blood flowed from the stump where its head used to be. Tanner nudged his foot against it several times with the barrel pointed straight where he imagined the heart would be.

Satisfied with the beast's still body Tanner holstered the shotgun on his back again and went to his vehicle. He went to the busted trunk and shook his head. Disappointed and pissed off Tanner griped the battle axe from the mangled trunk roof and ripped it free from the already loose shackles that kept it in place.

33

"Sir, Vincent Tanner cannot be reached. All calls go straight to his voicemail."

Ralph Simmons was more than agitated. His bulky, but portly, features showed signs of stress via the redness beating in his face and the veins pulsing in his neck. The pencil pusher in his office that Simmons assigned to get a hold of Tanner was not going to have a good day.

"Damn it all to hell keep trying!" He cursed at the employee who shook with every deep, bellowing word his boss spat. The gangly man in his mid-twenties almost dropped the folder he was holding but scrambled fast enough to ensure it didn't spill all over.

"Sir we can't! We did a scan of Tanner's last known location and something is interfering with cell phone and GPS signals."

Simmons looked at the man who laid the folder across the table and watched the shaken male point an unsteady finger at the reports he gathered previously, "What the fuck is this and why am I looking at it?"

"W . . . Well Sir," the employee stammered, "When you told me to keep an eye on agent Tanner's location everything was fine and dandy until this storm moved in. It is a storm, I checked the local weather of the area that he was last known to be at."

"The point, could you fucking get to it?" he growled.

Vincent's tracker swallowed hard, "I looked back at the storm activity in this region. The same kind of storm hit two weeks ago and it seems the same storm seems to coincide with Miss Kyarsgaard's timeline of missing people."

The papers in front of Simmons flew into the air when his fist slammed against the desk. He turned, grabbed his coat, and slid it on in record time, "Where the fuck was this information three weeks ago?"

34

On her way to the kitchen Jasmine stole a glance outside and shivered when she noticed it was nothing but pitch darkness. She checked a nearby clock and saw that it was only five o'clock in the afternoon, but with the weather outside it may as well have been midnight. She paused for a moment at the window again and tried to peer even further outside. She could not see the forest line any longer and the rain poured so hard that it looked like a constant waterfall drenching the windows of the home. The only relief from the endless darkness outside came in the form of lightning bolts crashing erratically in the skies above.

Another streak of lightning dotted the skies, and another, and Jasmine could see her reflection in the window.

She also saw Jacque Collo standing right behind her.

She yelped and spun around, her hand grasping her chest from being startled like that, "Mister Collo! You are a sneaky devil aren't you?"

"You know that is not the first time I've been told that today. I apologize, I was about to address you but I guess that lightning makes for some good reflection. I take pride in how clean my windows are," he smiled and closed his eyes, "Where is Mister Freason?"

Jasmine looked into Jacque's eyes and noticed they were locked on her own. She was wearing a low cut, pink tank-to and a pair of black yoga pants that showcased every curve of her body in all the right ways. She knew it attracted attention, but for her it was a comfort thing. The fact that Stan respected her faithfulness to him made it even better when she wore it. It shocked her that Jacque wasn't a typical male with his eyes locked where they were.

"Oh he went to find Ryan and Maggie in the lounge. I haven't eaten a thing since eleven this morning so I was going to go and make everyone something to eat. Probably just sandwiches for now and then we could have burgers on the . . ." She paused and puffed a breath of air from her lips to blow a hanging strand of raven hair from her eyes, ". . . rain soaked grill." She sighed.

Jacque continued his locked gaze into her pupils and nodded his agreement, pursing his lips as the weather made cooking out quite the predicament. "This is true; the rain did come in unexpectedly. The weather forecast for this region always seems to be wrong. It is a shame but," he paused and waved his hand back and forth, "never mind, never mind."

"But what?"

Jacque sighed and shook his head, "I really shouldn't. It would be a big safety issue but I understand how much you American's love your cook-outs."

Jasmine agreed with a small bounce on the balls of her feet. She followed it up with a frantic nodding, "If you could bend the rules a bit, Mister Collo that would be great! I mean I know those two college kids are probably down about their friend getting hurt so we should get them involved a bit too!" She grabbed his arm in her excitement and tugged on it, making the sleeve covering his arm jerk up and down against his flesh.

Jacque did not expect that. He stood there for a moment as she pulled his sleeve past his wrist and forearm. He noticed the sleeve exposing his flesh and so did she. The imprinted face of Jimmy Franklin faced Jasmine like a sick tattoo, swirling and shouting in a silent, tortured expression which left Jasmine breathless and dizzy.

The man's once charming grin grew sick and twisted as his hand gripped onto her arm and pulled her into his body. "Well this is quite inconvenient. I was planning for this to happen a few more hours down the line, but I do love improvisation."

Speechless and terrified Jasmine turned her body and tugged her arm as hard as she could to free herself from the iron grip Jacque had on her. As her mouth opened to scream a sharp pain exploded in the back of her head. Darkness clouded her vision as she crumpled to the ground.

"Well this vacation turned out to be a wonderful idea," Ryan groaned, sitting in the game room with Maggie occupying his lap. The television, which was nothing but static now, previously had a cop drama that kept the two of them entertained in the rainy weather.

"Knock out the television? Damn. No wonder you're irritated Ryan," Stan said as he joined them. He parked it on the arm of the couch across from where Ryan and Maggie sat, "So it's raining pretty damn hard. Shit happens. I have to say this is still relaxing for the most part. I'm just worried about where Jimmy and the Sinfields went off to."

Maggie had the remote to the television and tried to switch through the channels to no avail, "Well try not to think about them. Where is Jazz at?" The constant switching of static grated on Ryan's nerves.

"Would you stop changing the channels and just shut the damn thing off? The storm knocked the dish out, or whatever the hell they use, completely out. This sucks."

Maggie pinched his cheek, "You're so sexy when you get annoyed, you know that?"

Stan smiled and turned his head back towards the door that spilled into the hallway, "She is making us all sandwiches I guess. She wanted to make sure that you guys were hanging out here and not somewhere that we'd have to track you down." As he studied that door his eyebrows creased and his jaw clenched.

Ryan bucked Maggie off his lap, sliding her to the arm of the chair until he was on his feet. She slid down and took over his place, kicking the footrest on the recliner up to relax.

"I know that look Stan. What's bothering you?"

"I just have a really bad feeling about this place. First those two guys get kicked out for seemingly nothing, even if they broke a rule and despite the storm that family should have been back by now after dropping Jimmy off at the hospital."

Ryan gave Stan a small pat on the shoulder, "Yeah that is shitty luck, but that's all that it is Stan. Don't tell me this storm has you freaked out," Ryan said, feeling a gentle kick in the back of the leg from his wife.

Maggie rolled her eyes while lounging in the recliner, "He means that you might be reading into things a bit too much. Even though this is a terrible storm you need to try and relax and just have some fun regardless of the shitty weather."

"That's exactly what I meant," Ryan chimed in while he rubbed the back of his thigh. He turned to his wife with a squint of his eyes and a purse of his lips, "You're abusive. When we get back I'm filing for a divorce. I'll put it under spousal abuse and I'll take half your shit woman!"

Stan smiled and turned so he could slump down across the couch, "Let me know when the court date is. I would love to see you get laughed out of there Ryan. You have what? At least a hundred pounds if not more on her?"

"Emotional abuse brother; my mental state is completely shot because of this soul sucking harlot!" Ryan exaggerated and got kicked again."

"I suppose I could be your witness, Ryan, but then again Jasmine would never allow me to sleep in the same bed again if I did."

Ryan took a step to the side to ensure he was out of kicking range and scoffed, "So much for bro's before ho's."

"Maybe that would fly if you and Stan were married to whores but, lucky for you, the both of you have some classy ladies to take care of!" Maggie protested and kicked the leg rest down until it clicked into the recliner. She wasn't in a mood to attack but instead hugged her husband around her midsection.

Ryan pursed his lips, pulling away from her but then pulled her in for that hug. "I suppose you are right for once."

Stan turned his attention to the window leading into the darkness. The storm clouds were so dark they blotted out the existence of the sun and it drowned the world in a premature absence of light. He drew closer to the window and watched the rain pour. He opened his mouth and summoned hot air from the back of his throat to form some fog on the glass. His finger traced two lines, and a squiggled line. Stan looked at his made self-portrait and closed his eyes, swiping the face away.

"How long does it take to make four sandwiches anyway?" Ryan asked.

Before Stan said anything a scream echoed in the distance.

35

Oswald Matthews slammed the two oaken doors shut when he came out of the rain. He was soaked to the bone and the raincoat he wore drenched the area around him with the collected water from his short venture to his car. He snapped the buttons apart and ripped the rain slickened coat from his frame and tossed it across the railing that led from the massive lobby to the four wings of the mansion home. The rain coat protected his core from getting wet but his face, jeans, and shoes were soaked. Reaching into the back pocket of his pants he took a handkerchief out and wiped his face of most of the water that collected on it.

He was not enjoying the evening.

Ill-tempered from the weather and soaking wet from the waist down, Oswald picked up on a delicious smell wafting in from the adjacent hallway. Thunder crashed, shaking the whole house but Oswald didn't flinch and while the smell was overwhelming he reached into his other back pocket to remove his wallet.

"Ah, here we go. Don't need to fool around with you later," Oswald smiled, taking his driver's license out of a plastic protector and popped it in a deeper part of his black, leather wallet. From the same area he pulled a different I.D. out, sliding it into the spot where Oswald Matthews used to be. He slid his wallet back into his pants and left his rain coat to drip on the pristine wood.

He walked from the lobby to the hallway and then past the swinging door that led into the kitchen and saw James pulling the once frozen pizza from the oven onto the brown, cardboard section before placing it on the counter. He observed James as the young man searched for something to cut the pizza with and settled on a large, kitchen knife.

"Smells good in here; I take it that is the frozen variety of cuisine?"

James paused for a split second, a hesitation that showed more weakness in that fleeting moment than he would ever realize. James didn't turn to face Oswald, instead opting to start slicing that circle into pieces.

"Yep, I figure that since I am on vacation I would save the whole 'making a fancy feast' for when I get back home."

Oswald swung the kitchen door back and forth, playing with it, toying with it. He slapped it back one last time to have it scrape lose and open again. He placed a hand on his chin and sauntered towards James, rubbing it back and forth, "Really? Do you think your new little slut of a girlfriend is going to be impressed with what you can do outside of this place?"

"What the fuck did you just say?" James' words were seething with anger as he turned to face Oswald

He was a stranger to confrontation when it came from behind. James' reaction time was much slower than anyone who had been in an actual fight before. The split second he turned around his reflexes couldn't save him as an unexpected right fist smashed into the left side of his chin, sending the young man spinning and crashing to the floor completely knocked out from the ex-marine's one hit assault.

Oswald admired his work. He winced and shook his right hand a few times, shaking out the pain that throbbed in his knuckles before helping himself to a slice of the pizza James had just cooked. "Not bad," he muttered with a mouth full of the Italian frozen dish. Oswald scooped two more slices and placed them on one of the paper plates James had sitting out. He took one good look at the boy laid out on the floor for good measure before disappearing from the kitchen.

The harmonizing drops of rain, combined with the frequent crashing of thunder, turned the "Glass Heaven" area of the home into a symphony of multi-colored lights and sounds. The flashes of lighting, coming from different areas in the sky, illuminated the dimly lit pool and spa area of the home. Even Oswald, as he stood in the doorframe with a plate of pizza in his hand, was in awe of the dancing lights the lightning provided and the rain drops that chimed against the glass encased room. The pretty lights, however, were not the only things distracting Oswald in the room.

The other thing capturing his attention was the body floating in the pool. He could see the curve of her breasts, her thighs bobbing up and down from the water whenever she made an inch of movement, and it was addicting. He observed. He watched. He studied. She was way too good looking for her own good and it was her fault that she was so desirable. He scolded the young blonde mentally for wearing such a skimpy bikini.

"Kimberly?" Oswald called out to her with a higher pitch of tone than he normally would use.

The plate of pizza stayed in his hand as he looked to where she lay in the water. She tipped herself up, surprised by the voice that called her name. She hadn't been startled by it, and she began treading water while looking up at Oswald. "Oh hello Mister Matthews, lovely weather outside isn't it?"

Oswald placed the plate on a patio table a few feet away from the pool. "You're right about that. I haven't seen a storm like this in years. Anyway, James made a bit of a mess in the kitchen. I guess half the pizza melted through and he salvaged the rest of it. I had just walked by while he was cutting what was left and he asked if I could bring you some. He didn't want me to mention the mess; I guess he didn't want to seem irresponsible."

He took a seat on one of the patio chairs adjacent to the plate and watched Kimberly climb the ladder out of the pool and quickly wrapped a towel around her curvy features, "Well thank you Mister Matthews." She took the seat next to the plate he brought her.

"Please, call me Oswald. I think we are over titles after our little pool game and tour."

She glanced at him before scooping one of the slices up, "I know you are a gentleman Mister Matthews but we both know that we are here to relax and enjoy the week, not to make any long term friendships." She feigned a smile and bit into her meal.

Oswald's gaze narrowed and his hand gripped the arm of the patio chair tightly. "Is that so Miss Cross? Do you have any clue as to who I am? What I did for this country so little fucking cunts like you could enjoy shit like this?"

Kimberly's eyes went wide from the brutish lingo, "What the hell Mister Matthews? That was a downright horrible thing to say!" She scooted her chair out, "I think I need to be somewhere else right now."

Not a moment passed, or bolt of lightning, after her chair screeched across the tile before Oswald Matthews shot out of his seat and knocked the plastic table over, lunging at the woman's body with hands. It didn't matter how many times he played this game, his heart pumped rapidly every single time he dove on his prey. In the rapid movement Oswald reached into his pocket and pulled out a switchblade.

Kimberly turned and tried to scream for help but Oswald's body was against hers. He wrapped an arm around her neck and used his hand to cover her mouth to keep her from screaming. She hadn't seen it when he pulled it out, but the sharp edge of his knife pressed cold against the flesh of her neck.

"I'm going to teach you some respect bitch."

Oswald inhaled the scent of chlorine and faint perfume from Kimberly's neck as he held her against his body. He felt her hot tears against his index finger while he held his hand against her mouth. He squeezed her cheeks and ground the palm of his hand against her chin, forcing her head back against his shoulder so he could look down and into her eyes. It made his heart race even faster; pumped his blood even harder when he saw the fear and pleading her eyes portrayed.

He also knew she felt it in her lower back, right above her pert backside.

"Fucking little whores like you wouldn't know what respect was if it smacked you across the face half a dozen times. Then again, most women I know knew what respect meant after I was done with them."

Showing a unique dexterity with his fingers, Oswald flipped the knife from the fingers of his one hand and up to the fingers that used to grip her cheeks. He held the tip of the blade near her eye now, letting her see the glinting metal that threatened her personal safety. With his hand now free Oswald set in on feeling what he wanted to feel from her body. He gripped her bikini top and yanked the red fabric away from her breast, exposing her perky nipple erect from the cold water. Oswald looked at her crying eyes and licked his lips.

"Now don't you feel foolish? You could have avoided all of this if you would have followed me to my room instead of making some spineless coward your new boyfriend. He went down with one hit. Smacked him right across the jaw without even hurting my fist. I think I heard his jaw pop," he cackled, lowering the female to the cold tile floor.

36

Jacque Collo found the show lacking.

The Frenchman observed Oswald shuffling his lower body around while he lay across Kimberly's body. He watched Oswald fumble with the bottom of his pants and where Jacque stood the view wasn't flattering. It was boring him as he stood in the shadows inside of the doorframe of the only other entrance and exit into the beautiful, illuminated light show the glass ceiling and walls of the pool area provided. Behind him was nothing but blackness, a stark contrast to the room in front of him.

His right hand gripped on the neck of Jimmy Franklin. His fingernails dug into Jimmy's flesh while the boy tried to yank and pull away from the iron grip. Jacque had no issues holding the corrupted soul back as his arm only twitched despite Jimmy's frantic clawing at the wall to his right.

"Now this should be an interesting experiment," Jacque whispered, "That female was your friend. That other man is a homophobic rapist. I never attempted to see how much of a person's soul might linger around in their body after I have taken them. This should be an eye opener. I might have to put a little more strength when I take a soul." He smiled and then released Jimmy's neck.

From the shadows of the entryway that led down into the basement, the twisted form of Jimmy Franklin stomped across the tile in a vicious charge. The clattering of his footsteps alerted both Oswald and Kimberly; the former lifting his head to see who was interrupting his fun.

"What the hell?" Oswald shouted. He had the slower reflexes this time around as Jimmy slammed his body into the older man, sending them both crashing to the ground next to a startled Kimberly Cross.

"Jimmy?" asked a confused Kimberly as she pulled her swimsuit back into place and wrapped the towel around her body. She scrambled a few feet back at the sudden rescue.

The knife had been knocked from Oswald's grip when Jimmy tackled him. For now the ex-marine slammed his fist into Jimmy's face, following through with a twist of his body to knock Jimmy off of him. He looked over to Kimberly and saw the knife was lying right next to her, but she wasn't noticing it in the least. She was too busy staring at Jimmy's face.

When Oswald followed Kimberly's line of sight, turning to look at Jimmy who stared right back at them, Oswald and Kimberly screamed.

James' jaw was killing him. He woke up on the ground to the sound of a beeping oven. Groggy, confused, and sporting a nasty headache it took James a few seconds to remember why he was laying on the ground and why his jaw throbbed. He jumped to his feet when the moments before he was knocked unconscious flooded in, "That son of a bitch!"

James shut the oven off and eyed the kitchen knife still on the table. He gripped the handle and weighed it in his hand. Emotion ruled over logical thinking and he turned on his heel, running towards the swinging kitchen door.

When he shoved the swinging door open he almost ran head first into Stan, Maggie and Ryan. Stan jumped back with the other two and James shifted on his foot, twisting around, and despite his best efforts to stay on his feet, ended up tripping over his own feet. He slammed into the other side of the hallway but kept himself up on his knees. The knife in his hand worried the group of three.

"James? Why in the hell are you running around with a kitchen knife? I swear to God if you are the reason we heard some woman screaming I'm going to kick your ass." Ryan said, crossing his arms.

James, groaning and grunting as he pushed himself up to his feet, breathed hard from the adrenaline coursing through his veins. "Fucking Oswald Matthews sucker punched me while I was making a pizza. I think he's got Kimberly. The dude is a fucking psycho!"

"Where is she?" Ryan asked, looking to his wife with his brows furrowing.

James tried to catch his breath but he forced himself onward, "That 'Glass Heaven' pool room."

Stan narrowed his eyes, "Wait! Did you see Jasmine in the kitchen? Did she walk off with some sandwiches a while ago?"

James turned, but kept moving, "No, I've been in there probably twenty minutes at least and no one but Oswald came in." He swung the door open that led to the hallway that led to the pool area, "Come on!"

Before Ryan could say anything Maggie went after James. She turned and beckoned them to come after her and Stan, as conflicted as he was about Jasmine, couldn't find it in him to move after the other three.

Ryan Gripped Stan by the shirt and pulled him along, "Come on Stan, I know what's going on in your mind but if Kimberly is in danger right now we gotta go help. I'm worried about Jazz too, and Maggie has to be freaking out but one thing at time Stan."

Stan's jaw clenched but he let Ryan pull him along.

James burst into the pool area first. Thunder and lightning blanketed the sky, and the glass house, in constant light. The storm outside, unrelenting still, pelted the ceiling and glass walls, shaking them with every deafening crash of thunder. It masked the sounds of the pool house, including Kimberly's screams. The scene was chaotic, with a multitude of bright colors flashing against the tile, mixing around to create a surreal, psychedelic nightmare for those in the room. James, without thinking, lunged towards Kimberly but realized, as his feet pounded against the tile, that she was screaming because of the two individuals rolling around and fighting on the ground next to her. Blue, yellow, green, and other hues of light beamed over the two fighting males, making it hard to make out who was who at that point.

James had to squint but when he did he made out Oswald as the person on the bottom. It didn't stay that way for long when Oswald twisted to the side and rolled on top of the person assaulting him. Gripping the unknown attacker by the shirt, James watched Oswald start delivering those hard, right handed blows into the person's face. Though the unknown savior had Oswald's shirt wrapped in its own fist, and trading blows back and forth.

James, who stood there slack-jawed at the scene, snapped back to reality and his mind set on what was important, "Kimberly!"

Kimberly Cross couldn't move. She was in shock. Her eyes were wide and her entire body was trembling as she stood just a few feet away. She was looking at Jimmy, but it wasn't Jimmy. The thing under Oswald Matthews had Jimmy's clothes. It had Jimmy's hair and it had his height, but it wasn't Jimmy. The face wasn't there at all. It was nothing. She heard a voice calling her name, but it was so distant. She looked over her shoulder, took a step away from the fight, and her foot slipped on the wet tile after she got out of the pool. Gravity took its toll and she toppled into the water.

James dropped the knife on the tile and dove into the water fully clothed. He struggled in the water but put one arm after another to get to Kimberly. He kept his eyes open and he saw her just floating in the water along with a few spots of red that floated away from her forehead.

"Maggie, go help James get Kimberly out of the pool." Ryan instructed to his wife while he pulled Stan towards the fight.

"God damn it all somebody help me!" Oswald screamed, taking his eyes off of the thing he was beating and getting beat by. This allowed the figure to roll the two of them over again so the assailant could rain powerful shots down against Oswald's jaw. Oswald tried to block the shots and push Jimmy away by holding his arms together near his head and twisting his hips to gain momentum to flip Jimmy off of him.

Ryan gripped onto Jimmy's shoulder, not realizing who it was, and tried to pull the young man away. Much to Ryan's surprise the male swung his arm upwards, backhanding Ryan's chest and chin with enough force that sent Ryan into the air and crashing onto the patio table a good four feet away.

Stan froze.

By then James and Maggie had been pulling the unconscious Kimberly out of the pool. Maggie slid her to the cold tile and heard the crash behind her. She turned her attention away from James and Kimberly, confused and shocked at how her husband crashed through the plastic table.

"Ryan!"

Maggie's cry snapped Stan out of his frozen state. He saw Ryan rolling on the ground between the busted pieces of table and favoring his left arm. Stan watched Maggie cross over to her husband to see if she was alright, leaving James to tend to Kimberly. Stan looked to see James leaning, pressing an ear against Kimberly's lips. James shot up and started pressing up and down right below her chest.

When Ryan had interrupted the fight it allowed Oswald to overcome his adversary. He bent his legs towards Jimmy's sides and wrapped his legs up and over Jimmy's shoulders. He grunted and slammed his legs down, forcing Jimmy backwards, off of Oswald's lap, and caused Jimmy's head to bounce off the tile with a sickening smack. Oswald scrambled backwards and picked himself off the ground. Sweat poured down his busted features. His left eye was black and swollen shut, the corner of his lip split open and bled, and his jaw was swollen. He was still on his feet, however, and ready for more.

Kimberly sputtered water from her lungs as James gave her mouth-to-mouth. Through her sputtering she cried, pushing away from James who, in turn, gripped around her shoulders and pulled her close.

"Kim. Kimmy it's me! You're alright, I got you." He said, trying to calm her down as she struggled against him.

She stopped and looked up to James' face, "Jimmy?" She began hyperventilating, struggling to get her bearings and to get off the ground, "It's Jimmy! It isn't his face! He has no face James!" she cried out.

"Jimmy isn't here!" James turned to Oswald who stood on shaky knees. The person fighting Oswald stood again and lunged. Oswald shifted and ducked under the assault but the person now turned to face everyone. James couldn't believe what he was seeing.

It was just like the book he read with Jimmy before Jacque snagged it away. It was Jimmy's body, his clothes, his hair, but a blur obscured everything that could be considered a facial features. Below where Jimmy's nose would have been laid a large, black hole. An open mouth made of nightmares.

Oswald got lucky with his first dodge but the thing was too quick, too vicious. Oswald swung with a right hook and missed, resulting in an opening for the creature to tackle Oswald to the ground like a linebacker hate-sacking a quarterback clearly after the ball went air-born. Oswald crashed onto the ground and his head smacked against the ground hard enough to stain the tile under and behind his head with red.

The thing that used to be Jimmy didn't end there. With Oswald's head cracked open the ex-marine was delirious and his efforts to fight back were pitiful; he raised his arms and he patted at Jimmy's side more than hit. Jimmy, however, was done playing.

Behind the two of them Ryan groaned while Maggie screamed at him to get up. She assisted him in getting to his feet but he still wobbled back and forth, "What the fuck was that?" He reached to the back of his head and felt a few bumps but nothing wet.

"He threw you or something! He is going to kill that man I think." Maggie said, tugging at her husband's shirt. They both turned their attention to Jimmy who was on top of Oswald.

Jimmy's arms rose into the air and his fingernails elongated by an inch and narrowed, forming talons that everyone could see. Both of his hands dove down into Oswald's abdomen and he tore through fat and muscle, spraying blood everywhere as his fingers and arms dg through the man like a mole shuffling through dirt. Oswald spat blood from his mouth while his body convulsed on the ground. Jimmy ripped through his midsection and drove one hand into Oswald's body while it performed one last spasm. Jimmy's hand pushed through to Oswald's heart, piercing it with those nails.

James stood shaking. Without a word he dashed straight at Jimmy and the disemboweled Oswald.

"Jimmy stop!" he cried out. As he reached the two of them Jimmy's arm swung upwards, backhanding James like he had Ryan with even more strength. James was sent into the air and sailed at least fifteen feet to land in the pool, splashing water everywhere from the impact.

Kimberly sobbed and wished it was a nightmare. She turned and reached to James in the water, hoping he was still alive.

Stan, through all the horror, was frozen in time.

37

Jasmine's eyes fluttered several times before she rose to full consciousness. The back of her head throbbed and she saw nothing but blackness around her. She felt no fabric against her eyes, temples, or around her head so she knew she wasn't blindfolded. She tried to cry out but found out quickly that there was something in her mouth. It wasn't a piece of cloth, it tasted rubbery. Her imagination feared the worse when her mind registered the leather strap grinding against her cheek and around her head. She also couldn't move her arms or legs either and she knew then she was bound to something.

For a very irrational moment she feared that she had been blinded. The fear that she would no longer see disappeared when light poured into the room as a door screamed on its hinges. The overhead ceiling lamp, clicking on, provided a much better light for her to see after the initial bright blindness wore off.

She screamed through the gag the best she could when Jacque stepped into the room wearing only a robe. The smile on his face sickened her to the core.

Just to her left she spotted numerous screens decorating the wall next to the door he entered. On one of the screens she could see the magnificent pool area.

"Ah . . . so you finally woke up my sweet, Egyptian flower?" Jacque asked as he shut the door to his rooms and locked it tight. He walked the small distance to her and knelt down next to the chair he had her bound to. He saw her eyes on the pool monitor and smiled as James went careening in the air and into the body of water.

Jasmine's eyes went wide when she focused enough to see the bloody corpse of Oswald Matthews and that ferocious hit James had taken.

"I know you are confused, I know you are scared. I assure you, however, that I am not going to harm you my dear. That is, of course, if you accept my offer to be my companion in this lonely, large home."

Jacque felt her flesh through the fabric of her yoga pants. His fingers trailed the smooth, skin-tight, cotton. Beginning at her calves, he took his time journeying to her thighsand gave them a firm squeeze, lingering his fingers just inches away from her most private of areas which elicited a muffled scream from Jasmine's gagged mouth.

He took his hand away from her thigh when she screamed, "I am so sorry my dear Jasmine. I am so rude. You know that my name is Jacque Collo and while this is true I have had many, many different names over the years,' he said as his hand went to her other limb and pulled her pant leg up just enough to expose her flesh to him. "Truthfully my favorite has been Belial. Of course if you are not one for religious talk then I cannot blame you for not knowing what that name entails. The fact of the matter is you are the lucky one, my dear, and soon you will be overjoyed when you realize I am going to spare you the fate that will befall the rest of the guests here."

He left her alone to return to his chair near all of his monitors. Jacque smiled and pointed to the monitor that had Jasmine's room number on it, "You put on quite a show," he said and parted his robes. "I enjoyed watching you prove your love to your husband."

Jasmine closed her eyes and looked away.

"Now I am going to free you. Only for a moment because you do not understand how generous I am right now. If you run, or try to fight, or even scream it will be meaningless. I would hate to have to harm you, but I can always be as patient as I always have and find someone with less fight." He stood from his chair and knelt down in front of her again, plucking the leather straps loose and freeing her arms and legs from the chair. The straps stayed on her extremities.

Kimberly did not fight back as Jacque lifted her from the chair under her arms. He did outline plenty of things for her not to do, but acting like dead weight wasn't one of them. Even as she went limp in his arms he had no issue carrying her around, however, and even though he wasn't stripping her he still transferred her body from the chair she was in to the one right in front of all the monitors. Once she was in place Jacque strapped her wrists and legs to the chair again, ensuring with a few tugs that she couldn't slip out.

"I'm a collector of souls Missus Freason. They fuel me, they make me stronger throughout the years but every once in a while I have to feed. They are a part of me, as you may have noticed when you tugged on my suit the wrong way, but I am also a part of them, collectively. Without them I would not be here. I have been taking souls since the beginning of time and humanity, hence the many names and so very, very many forms."

Before she could turn her head away from the images on the screen Jacque wrapped a leather strap around her forehead and her chin, binding it to the back of the chair that locked her head into place. To her left he rummaged through the desk drawer below all those monitors and took two large, metal clamps out. They were seven or eight inches in length and the clamp portion was positioned more towards the top than the bottom. He placed one in front of her, on her lap, and took the other to her head.

"Don't you squirm or move Jasmine. I would hate to slip," he cackled as the thin, metal bars nestled over the left side of her face. Two smaller bars were right in front of her eye, and Jacque pressed them to her eyelids, thumbing two levers on the opposite side to force her eyelids open as they locked into place. He repeated the process with the right side of her face.

Jasmine, manipulated into watching the screen, saw Oswald stand next to Jimmy in the pool area. Their faces were blurred in the camera's eye while everyone else looked normal. James had been knocked for a loop but his splashing and efforts to get out of the pool allowed Jasmine a sigh of relief. She watched Kimberly, half naked and tossing the towel away, assist James out of the pool as he did for her minutes before. James sputtered and spit on the tile ground, but otherwise seemed no worse for the wear from the initial hit.

Stan stood a few yards away from Jimmy and Oswald. She watched her husband stand there, frozen, looking right at Oswald as blood no longer spilled from him, but instead flowed into the mortal wound. Black blood inched its way up Oswald's legs, down from his chin, and into the exposed intestines and bowels of the deceased, possessed man. His body, when the blood nestled back inside, sewed itself back together and left nothing but a hole in Oswald's shirt where Jimmy had sliced and diced.

Jasmine cried. The tears springing from her eyes were not in fear for herself, but rather Stan, Maggie and Ryan, her family. Through her bounds she struggled, wishing inside that this was all an elaborate, cruel joke. She felt Jacque's hands around her breasts, squeezing now while she had to watch those horrible images on the screen. She shifted in her seat, rocking back and forth to remove his hands but it was a futile attempt. She felt ill.

Sensing her resistance Jacque removed his hands from her chest to trail his fingertips against her neck, forcing goose bumps to bubble from her flesh. He maneuvered them against her earlobes before brushing them through her lovely locks of hair in a comforting way, like a father would try to stroke his daughter's hair to calm her down.

"I love to watch Jasmine. I love to watch you humans live their fickle little lives. You'll come to like watching as well, you'll know it soon enough. This vessel is old and withering. I think that yours is rather appealing."

38

Stan stood in silence as the twisted, wretched, non-faces of Oswald
Matthews and Jimmy Franklin stared at him. Neither of them moved but
Stan felt as if their attention was on everyone in the pool hall. He could not
tell with those faces whirling back and forth, creating a surreal dance of the
unnatural on what used to be their facial features.

Time felt sluggish for Stan. A familiar, burning feeling gathered
in his chest, reminding him that he had not let a single breath out since he
had frozen himself in place. As he exhaled the largest breath of air he ever
breathed everything started running in real time.

The creature that used to be Oswald kicked the remaining
intestines that had separated from his body out of the way and rushed
straight at Stan and Jimmy followed.

"Stan! The knife! Fucking grab the knife!" Ryan said.

The sudden shouting and noise confused Stan but he looked down
at his feet. In the scuffle the blade Oswald brought with him to threaten
Kimberly with had slid in front of Stan. The switch blade, exposed, had
not a taint of blood on it. The fear continued to cripple Stan but he forced
himself to bend down, the gleam of multi-colored light that reflected off the

dagger blinded him slightly when he picked it up at the wrong angle.

The next thing Stan felt was a large weight crashing into his body and the subsequent hard tile his back hit when he landed on the ground. Jimmy hadn't made it to Stan's body. From under Oswald's body Stan made out a blurry figure crashing into the monster chasing after Oswald. It had come from his right, and the two sailed over the tile and into the water. Stan heard Maggie scream.

Stan tilted his head with the weight of the ex-marine crushing him. His arms were pinned against his own chest and he groaned, feeling a blunt object digging into his sternum. He tilted his head a bit more to the left and watched James gather himself from the spill he had taken in the pool. The young college lad pulled himself and Kimberly to their feet.

"Kimberly just go and get dressed or something. Just go alright?" he asked but it sounded much more like a demand as the pretty blonde did her best to understand and nod her head.

When Kimberly ran off James rushed to Stan's side. He grunted, groaned, and pulled Oswald by the shirt and yanked as hard as he could to take the man off of Stan.

Stan felt paralyzed while his hands shook. The knife was no longer clenched between his hands when Oswald was pulled off of his body. The blade could not be seen, but the handle stuck clear out of Oswald's chest, right in his heart cavity. The face that was obscured by the mysterious blur stilled, showing just the face of a horrified and deceased Mister Matthews.

"Mister Freason get up!" James growled while tugging Stan's black, blood stained shirt.

Stan snapped out of his delirious state and shook his head back and forth, his neck muscles straining as he looked behind him both ways and to the pool, "Where's Ryan? Where's my wife?" he shouted, demanding to know where his family was.

"Damn it Ryan you fucking fat piece of shit help me help you!" Maggie cried while she gripped her husband's wet hand and arm. The light from above made it that much more difficult to see what was going on underneath the waves. Stan spotted Maggie and her attempts to help her husband, but she wasn't gaining any ground and neither was Ryan.

"God damn it all woman," Ryan sputtered, flopping around like a fish out of water while in the water. Every time he pushed up he was pulled back down, "I'm trying but this son of a bitch has my God damn leg!" he shouted, "Fuck!" Pushing his wife away from grabbing him, Ryan's head went under the water once more.

Stan rubbed the pain in his sternum away. He limped over to the knife he used to kill Oswald with and yanked it free. He turned and realized a much larger knife was right beside Maggie, "Grab the knife!" Both he and James ran over to Maggie's side as she gripped the kitchen knife by the handle so tight that her veins popped from her wrist. James and Stan reached into the water, both of them reaching for Ryan underneath. They felt nothing.

A few feet out in front of them bubbles rapidly formed and a figure broke the surface of the water. Maggie screamed and reached out to stab the figure but Stan, in a surprising show of reflexes, gripped her arm before she fell into the water herself. Ryan splashed around, further away this time and as Stan yanked Maggie back James reached out further, taking Ryan's hand and pulling the larger man towards the edge of the pool.

"This son of a bitch won't let go of my fucking ankle!" Ryan sputtered as he saw the knife in Maggie's hand, "Fuck this shit." He growled and grabbed the handle of the kitchen knife in Maggie's hand and wrenched it from her grip. It was hard enough for James to pull a soaking wet, full grown man around in the water, but the slickness of Ryan's forearm proved too formidable while Jimmy pulled at him from below and Ryan was under the water for the third time in that frantic minute.

Maggie wailed when Ryan disappeared under the churning waves and lunged forward towards the edge of the pool. Stan and James had to pull her back and hold her as black blood started bubbling to the surface of the waves. It was a solid minute of waiting, watching as more and more black blood oozed throughout the pool where even the brightest flash of lightning could not cut through.

The bubbles continued forming on the surface of the black pool. Two minutes in the surface of the water broke again and the body was covered in nothing but black. It brought its arms back twice, paddling backwards as two knees came up and kicked back into the water. It reached for James and Stan again, sputtering and coughing.

"Shit! It's Ryan. That magnificent son of a bitch," James laughed and gripped Ryan's bloody shirt and under his arm while Stan wrapped his arms around Ryan's chest, hoisting him out of the water with enough unneeded force it sent the three of them crashing onto the tile behind them.

Stan groaned and wondered what had changed. That was when he saw that Ryan had a souvenir. Jimmy's hand gripped Ryan's ankle still, but that hand connected to a forearm, and the forearm connected to nothing but a broken bone. Black blood poured from the hacked off limb and splattered around as Ryan kicked his leg back and forth.

"Fuck, get it off! Get it off!" He shouted while James grimaced and Stan, feeling his stomach double over, scrambled away to save his stomach and his throat from a nasty, burning bile eruption. Ryan continued to try and kick it free, and Maggie screamed when she saw the hand crawling up Ryan's leg.

James, thinking quickly, grabbed the nasty, slippery arm as tight as he could and put his back into it. He tugged, ripped, and shook the arm as hard as he could muster. The clawed fingernails gripped into Ryan's pant leg with a vice-like hold. The sound of fabric tearing echoed throughout the pool hall several times before the hand tore free, taking half of Ryan's pant leg with it. James fell hard on his ass and flung the arm to his left, sending it for a dip in the blackened pool.

James and Stan got to their feet and helped Ryan up as well. Maggie hugged him tightly and smacked him upside the head after what he had done. "You jerk did you even think about me when you went into the water?" she cried against his chest.

"Woman you are pushing my fucking buttons," he said and rubbed his head. He turned to the other two and his eyes narrowed, "What in the fucking hell are those motherfucking things?"

"I don't know Mister McCallister. I really don't. I mean it looks like those things me and Jimmy . . ." he paused.

"Focus James!" Ryan shouted, snapping his fingers in front of the boy's face. He took them both by the shirt collar and dragged them from the side of the pool, "What the fuck are you going on about?"

Stan shook his head, "Fuck what they are we have to find Jasmine and Kimberly and get the hell out of here."

"He's right. Fuck it. Fill us in later James."

Ryan, covered in black blood from head to toe, wiped as much of it off his face and clothes with his hand before he grabbed Kimberly's towel she abandoned. He wiped his face proper but it wouldn't be the same as a four day long hot shower to get him clean. Stan watched Ryan shuddered as the black blood oozed down the towel like tar. When he lowered the towel he looked past the other three and clenched his teeth.

The other three followed Ryan's look and turned, inching away from the other door that led to their escape.

"Well isn't this a surprise?" Jacque asked as he moved across the pool hall from the hallway door that led to the kitchen and to the lobby. "Ironic that the weakest one of the bunch was a rapist ex-marine, life is kind of funny like that don't you think?" The Frenchman asked as he slowly put one foot in front of the other, sliding across the tile ground that way instead of picking his feet off of the tile. He turned his attention to the black blood permeating the pool and shook his head, "And this one here is severely wounded but he is pulling himself together quite quickly, and literally."

"Where in the hell is my wife and what is going on here Jacque?" Stan bellowed, taking a step forward towards the man.

"Whoa! This is a fun little turn of events. I did not anticipate that the cowardly psychiatrist would have so much bite in him. Don't worry, she is safe. She has to be safe after all." Jacque laughed and looked to the rest of the group, "I suggest the four of you try to run as fast as you can. The party is just getting started after all, and I have many other guests who have enjoyed their stay here so much that they could never bring themselves to leave!"

Ryan pulled Stan back and hobbled forward, "You son of a bitch," his eyes narrowed on Jacque's own, "Answer the fucking man's question."

Jacque held his hands in the air and shook his head, "I already explained what I am to someone else." He said and cross his hands in front of his waist. He untied his robes just enough so that he could shrug the silken garment off his shoulders and down his arms. He tightened the robe again when his chest was exposed. He slipped each arm out of his robe and smiled at the entire group.

Dozens, if not hundreds of faces swirled around Jacque's upper body and across his arms, faces screaming in terror, in pain, and in torture. Jimmy Franklin, the two elder Sinfields, Fred Thompson, and Oswald Matthews swirled around Jacque's chest, shouting in silence at everyone in front of them. The outline of Jacque's body could be seen, of course, but as those faces danced across his body it gave the same blurry appearance as those terrible faces. Only that robe, Jacque's head, and his hands could be seen uncensored.

"You're the bleak aren't you? The blurring or some shit. Jimmy put it all together didn't he you suck fuck?" James growled and stepped towards Jacque, "We found your book and you're nothing more than some piece of shit fucking monster aren't you? You killed them all. The Sinfield family, Fred and Clark, Jimmy . . . You killed Jimmy didn't you? You God damn monster!"

"That is cute. I assure you I am much, much more terrifying than some monster. Monsters are mindless, bloodthirsty beasts. Do I look mindless or bloodthirsty?" He asked and breathed deeply. Reaching into his chest he drew that sinister book from the very depths of his body. He slid it out and held it in his hand with no signs of blood or gore on it, just a pristine, glossy blackness that absorbed all light around it. "Now which one of you . . ."

Stan's eyes widened. The middle of Jacque's forehead burst open from something pointy, and golden with a hooked claw; a fire poker. The object was yanked backwards and Jacque lurched forward, falling onto his book as the poker pulled free, taking a large chunk of Jacque's head with it. Behind Jacque Collo stood a very dirty and very out of breath teenager that gripped the fire poker in his hand with a terrible vengeance.

The group stood in stunned silence as Mark Sinfield screamed at the top of his lungs, impaling his weapon in and out of Jacque Collo's body again and again. His shirt ripped at the sleeves and it hung loosely around his body. Dried blood coated his forehead and various parts of his limbs from scrapes and cuts. Stan looked to the boy's left leg and saw several deep gashes in the boy's calf.

"Mark!"

Mark ignored Stan's voice. He continued stabbing into Jacque, poking and prodding and hitting tile with every hard thrust through Jacque's body. He screamed until his voice turned hoarse. His arms gave out and he slumped against the poker embedded in Jacque's neck from the final stab. He sobbed.

James swallowed hard and gripped Stan's arm, "Don't let him stay near Jacque. I don't know what he is but for fucks sake that book, it steals your soul or possesses you or something like that. Let's get the hell out of here," he said and started running to the exit.

Stan understood and approached Mark slowly, "Mark, it's me Stan Freason. We need to get out of here. I think you know why."

Mark didn't move from Jacque's body, "G-Go away. I am going to stay here and keep this asshole dead." Tears continued to stream down his eyes as he kept a firm hold on his weapon.

"Mark I can't let you do that. He got Jimmy Franklin. He's in the water still alive or whatever," Stan said, turning to the water that used to be fully black with blood. It was receding from the edges and to the middle.

Mark shook his head, "No. I'm not going. My father nearly tackled me off a cliff. If I hadn't grabbed onto one of the vines growing from the side I'd be dead. Daniel . . . they tore him in parts. I found him in pieces Mister Freason," he continued sobbing, "I have no family. I know my mom was taken too. I couldn't find our van."

"Damn it Mark you are still alive. That counts for something. I am sorry about your family, I truly am but you need to live on for them. You need to pull yourself together and survive. This is a fucked situation but your mother, your father, and your brother wouldn't want you to sacrifice yourself for this bullshit." Stan tried to get through to him. He reached for the fire poker and gripped it under Mark's trembling hands. "I'm scared shitless Mark, but they die with a blow to the heart. I killed Oswald Matthews that way after he was turned. We could use your help Mark."

Mark stood there without saying a word. His chest inhaled and exhaled a few long, labored breaths before he jerked the fire poker out of Jacque's neck. "Alright, I'll go. If we come across my mother though, let me take care of her. If I die, I die. I don't care." He gave one last hard thrust into Jacque's head before running off with Stan.

Moments after Stan and Mark left the "Glass Heaven" pool room Jacque's head slowly twisted around, his head sealed back together, and he did not look happy. His head completed a full, slow rotation before he pushed himself to his knees and climbed to his feet. He brushed his hand against his shoulders, dusting off, and turned to where the group ran. Jimmy sprung from the pool and landed next to Jacque and other than being soaking wet he had both of his arms intact.

"It seems like they do not want to play nice."

Kimberly Cross piled together everything that she and James brought together on the trip. Wallets, clothes, laptops; they all got shoved into one single suitcase to the best of her ability.

She changed into a pair of blue jeans and a red blouse to cover her chest but she didn't button it up just yet. She slung the suitcase over her shoulder and vacated the room without a second thought of whether or not she forgot something inside.

She nearly ran headfirst into James and everyone else when she exited the room. She noticed someone else with them and almost cried with joy. "Oh my God Mark you're alive!" She squealed and tossed the suitcase to Jimmy. She wrapped her arms around the dirty, bloodied teen, shoving her barely covered chest in his face. She squeezed him tight and kissed him on his dirty head.

James gripped her by her forearm and yanked her away from the boy, "We can celebrate later. We need to get the fuck out of here."

The silhouette of Jimmy Franklin appeared at the other end of the hallway and Kimberly Cross shared the same sentiment James did.

39

Jasmine wiggled and fought with her left fist so much against those bindings that, despite the irritation from her flesh rubbing raw against the leather, she started to slowly slip from her bonds. She did her best to distract herself from the throbbing pain by biting down on her tongue while inching her wrist back and forth, sliding free from the leather strap.

She bit down on her tongue hard when her left arm jerked back and signified her freedom. Without hesitating she worked on freeing her other hand and then her head, plucking those damn metal clamps from her eyelids so she could take a well deserved blink. Her vision blurred from the inability to moisten her eyes but that didn't stop her from reaching down and ripping the bindings from her ankles. Once freed she rubbed her aching wrist and stood up, gripping the chair she was bound to by the back. She screamed and spun the chair around, hollering as she smashed several monitors she had to watch.

After her burst of rage she panted hard. She rushed to the door and reached for the first lock, but looked out the peep-hole and froze. Jacque Collo stood on the other side of the door and did not look happy. He dug into his pockets, searching for his keys.

Jasmine trembled and backed away from the door as one by one each lock clicked open. She looked around the room for a weapon or anything that she could just to defend herself. The only other thing other than the chair she had used to break the monitors, which now lay in broken splinters after she smashed it, Jasmine spotted a strange pair of statues in the form of snakes.

She grasped at the statue's neck and noticed it did not budge at all. She growled as she tugged on it several more times. Frustrated and frightened, Jasmine huffed and smacked the snake statue right on top of the head with her palm and when the snake's head sunk into the statue it did more than surprise her, it answered her prayers.

She turned a little bit to the right when the walls before her split open and revealed a dimly lit elevator. The sliding, metal bars offered Jasmine a ride to salvation. She dashed into the elevator just as Jacque unlocked the doorknob leading into his room. She punched the only button in the elevator several time, listening as the gears turned.

Jacque threw the door open, growling from the events that he did not anticipate happening earlier. When he saw the splintered chair and the woman in the elevator, he lost it. "You fucking whore!" he screamed at her with his body bare from the waist up. He lunged at the closing doors, unable to stop them as they slammed shut.

Jasmine, on the verge of hyperventilating, stood still in the elevator as it went down. She rode it for at least thirty seconds until the cage ground to a halt. When the doors opened they revealed a brightly lit hallway, but the floors, walls, and even the ceiling reflected nothing but black. Although the floors and walls reflected black it shined bright enough to reflect Jasmine's image back at her four different ways; a black hall of mirrors.

She pushed the gate open and exited the elevator. It didn't take her but two steps out of the elevator for it to shut again and begin its slow climb to Jacque's room. Finding no alternative for escape she pushed forward, stepping through the hallway and into the unknown. Small steps led to outright running when she knew the elevator would only take a minute to get back down there. She ran as fast as she could until the hallway spilled into another room.

She skidded to a halt when she found the stable room. Swallowing hard with sweat running down her brow, Jasmine took a few steps into the unknown area.

"Hello?" she called out just louder than a whisper.

She saw nothing as she passed the first two stalls but the walls were stained in a dirty red. Various chains hung from the ceiling in each stall and her eyes followed all of them. Four sets of chains swayed a few inches but there was one set, way at the end that thrashed back forth more than the others. Jasmine tiptoed up to the first four stalls that hinted movement and peeked around the corner of one of them while trying to stay in the middle of the path.

The chains rattled and struck out at Jasmine when she tried to get a glimpse of who was inside of the stable. She screamed and fell to her knees but realized that, with how heavily chained the creature was inside the stable, that it could not reach her. She did not take her chances, however, and kept low to the ground, looking at the monsters around her. She crawled on the ground to the next two stables and saw the exact same thing.

They looked like skinned animals. Dried, black blood covered every inch of their body which only comprised of muscles and bone. They had no eyes to speak of, but their heads followed her every movement as she crawled around the ground. They writhed against the chains that bound them and growled like hungry wolves eyeing its prey. Several long, sharp bones protruded from the ends of their fingers which curved a little bit downward the longer the bone went on. Their muscles strained and tore in a frenzy as Jasmine crawled past them.

When she came to the last stable she expected to see the worst of them from the initial thrashing. She peeked over the small gate that separated the room from the hallway and Jasmine gasped. The figure in the last room hung suspended in mid-air by chains. The scent of burning flesh assaulted Jasmine's nose but the person in those chains stared at Jasmine with one human eye. Her fiery red hair covered the other side of her face, yet it did not hide the transformation she was going through. She cried out in muffled screams while she hung there, screaming through a leather gag placed inside of her mouth.

"Helena?" Jasmine questioned as the woman hung there, "Is that you?"

The redhead's one eye opened wide and she writhed against those torturous binds which held her. Screaming and nodding her head up and down, Helena shifted her attention to the side of the stable. She nudged her head towards the side and Jasmine followed her gaze.

Three buttons sat on the side of the stable. One dark blue, another a lighter blue and the third was a red button. Jasmine stood up and looked over at Helena again, "Does one of these unlock the chains or something?" She asked, and then heard the ding at the end of the hallway in the distance. "Oh fuck!" Her finger went to the dark blue button.

"N-No!" Helena screamed through the gag, trying to form the

words to stop Jasmine.

Jasmine halted and didn't know what the blue button did but instead she went to the light blue one. Helena shook her head and screamed again.

"Well fucking there is only one left!" Jasmine screamed and hit the red button.

She heard a click and afterwards the chains that held Helena in that mid-air position popped from her wrists and ankles at the same time. The redhead fell onto the floor of the stable with a thud and groaned. Her body burned, her wrists and ankles showed no signs of scaring but she had a hard time climbing to her feet. Jasmine threw the gate open and rushed in, pulling Helena to her feet. She wrapped the redhead's arm around her shoulders and helped Helena out of the stables.

"Daddy is very fucking angry!"

Jasmine clenched her teeth as Jacque's voice echoed from the hallway behind them. She could see his silhouette from the various lights that lit the hallway but could not make him out completely. She shifted with Helena under her arm and started pushing the redhead along, helping her gain her footing as more feeling came back to her extremities. She could not afford to be shy at that point, considering Helena's nude state, but she had to consider the woman's well being in the cold and rain later on. "We need to get moving Helena come on!" Jasmine coached as she helped the injured, and what mattered most to Jasmine, conscious woman into the hallway in front of them.

A few moments later Helena went from limping to walking and then to straight out running, allowing Jasmine to have her shoulders back. She followed Helena quickly while the redhead took the lead in the twisting hallways. Jasmine turned and bounced off several, sudden walls while they ran while Helena navigated the twisting corridors without missing a beat.

From behind them, far in the distance, the sounds of chains and shrieks echoed through the hallways they ran through. Jasmine panted and followed Helena as fast as she could with a newfound rush of adrenaline.

"I really hope you know your way out of here."

40

The raging storm continued its pounding of the east coast getaway. Thunder rolled and lightning streaked the skies every few moments while the rain continued its relentless downpour. The trees surrounding the vacation home swayed with violent force as the wind whipped around them. Thunder crashed as the twin doors to the mansion home burst open, allowing the rain and the wind to roll through the residence.

Stan and the others ignored the weather as they ran outside with Jimmy hot on their heels. They were soaked the moment they opened the door from the constant waterfall the storm produced. The ground almost watered over with how much rain the dirt and grass absorbed and there were even patches throughout the yard where the ground flooded. As the group rounded the corner to get to the vehicles James slipped and his body went horizontal before hitting the ground hard. Shaking the impact off, James scrambled to his feet without slowing the group down.

"God damn it!" Ryan groaned, placing his hands on top of his soaked head.

The vehicles that were left all had their tires slashed.

One of the doors they came from swung back after their exit. The body of Jimmy Franklin ignored opening anything and opted to just burst through that large, wooden door and sent debris flying everywhere as he sailed over the stairs and landed on the ground. He slid on the wet pavement and turned his attention to the group.

"Get to the gate!" Ryan shouted through the rain and thunder when he saw that Jimmy joined them outside, "Fucking figures these things don't melt in the rain."

As four of them ran off Stan stood there and watched Jimmy turn his attention to the fleeing group. "I have to find Jasmine!" he cried out, gaining Jimmy's attention from the shouting.

Ryan and James slid to a stop in the wet grass. James had to wave his arms around to keep his balance from the sudden stop. Maggie and Kimberly continued their run to the gate. "Stan would you fucking use your head?" Ryan yelled through a crack of thunder, "We need to get help first!"

Stan shook his head, "Distract him! There has to be a weapon in one of those cars!"

Ryan almost screamed at Stan again but James beat him to the punch, "We don't have any in ours! Trust me on that. Look in that fucking asshole Oswald's vehicle! The prick probably had a gun shoved up his ass for all we know."

"James!"

James turned his attention to Mark who flung the poker at James. It landed in the ground next to his feet and James picked up the long, iron weapon with a sharp point and started waving it at his possessed friend, "Jimmy! Hey Jimmy, come and get me."

Jimmy's head tilted away from Stan and twisted in the rain. He looked at James sideways with that ever blurring and twisting face.

Stan took the opportunity James gave him to peer into every car that wasn't Ryan's truck. There were only two other vehicles in the lot and one was a beat up station wagon, the other was a black Jeep. Stan found nothing but an ice scraper in the station wagon and when he turned around to open the Jeep his disappointment grew. The Jeep was locked.

Stan grabbed the ice scraper from James' vehicle and pounded on Oswald's windows. He slammed the pointed edge against the glass several times before he heard the first crack, a splinter, and then an entire shattering of the window in those three hits. He made sure to avoid any broken glass still attached to the window frame as he unlocked the passenger side door and then the rest of the doors. He dove into the backseat and dug through all the bags and finding nothing in them.

He switched his attention to the trunk equivalent of the Jeep and saw a small latch attached to the bed of the back of the Jeep. He pulled it upwards to reveal a tire iron and a spare. It wasn't much, but he gripped the tire iron tight. Stan crawled out of the Jeep through the back and slid out.

James gripped the handle of the fire poker tightly and held his other arm behind his back. It was force of habit, a muscle memory reflex whenever he fenced. He feigned and poked, shifted and sliced. His heart beat a million miles a minute as he kept Jimmy at bay. The urge to survive fought against practice and technique. James moved in forward and backward movements, keeping on an imaginary mat while he distracted Jimmy from the rest of the group. He held his own.

Maggie and Kimberly tugged on the gate that lay in the distance. They screamed and pulled on the large, iron barricade and could not get it to budge.

James held Jimmy back a few moments more before his front foot hit a slick patch. His balance faltered and Jimmy took advantage. The possessed man tackled James onto the ground, sending the fire poker flying as James' back crashed against the wet grass and puddles of water. Ryan and Mark responded quick by running up and kicking Jimmy as hard as they could. When that didn't faze Jimmy, who was punching James several times in the face during this, Mark and Ryan reached down, grabbing Jimmy by the arms and hauled him off James' body.

They pushed Jimmy back just as Stan came running in with the tire iron. Stan slammed the weapon into the small of Jimmy's back, hoping to at just cripple the boy. It did nothing but anger the beast as Jimmy swung his arm back hard, hitting Stan in the sternum and sending him reeling a few feet back. The tire iron landed with a squish in the grass.

His face, still locked in that silent scream, turned its attention to Stan who continued to stumble backwards after the hard hit to his chest. The creature bore down on him and gripped Stan by the throat, lifting him off the ground with ease.

Ryan rushed to the tire iron Stan dropped and scooped it up. He gripped it tight and swung for the fences, or in this case, Jimmy's head. He slammed the iron against the base of Jimmy's skull, doing enough damage to make Jimmy drop Stan to turn his attention to his third attacker by swinging his body and arm around, slashing out at Ryan with elongated finger nails sharp as daggers. Ryan ducked the slash and swung upwards, hitting Jimmy across the chin with the weapon.

Kimberly and Maggie rushed to help Mark help James to his feet. James felt dizzy from the few blows Jimmy gave him, "The gate?"

Maggie shook her head, "It's not working. The power must have been cut."

Stan coughed and wheezed while Jimmy concentrated on Ryan. He continued slashing at Ryan, who had to use the tire iron to deflect some of the blows aimed at his arms and chest. "Jesus Christ! Come on Stan, man the fuck up buddy!" Ryan encouraged as he blocked another slash.

Stumbling and slipping on the wet grass, it took Stan a moment or two to gather a decent enough stride and with a grunt he shoved Jimmy forward as hard as he could.

Ryan took advantage. He pulled back and swung the tire iron as hard as he could right into Jimmy's non-existent nose. The crack dwarfed the thunder that shook the clouds and Jimmy's head snapped back. Ryan repeated the motion two more times as Jimmy's body crumpled to the ground, much to the ranting and raving of Kimberly, who was held back by James. Ryan tried to catch his breath after the deed was done. He watched, horrified as Jimmy's blurred, twisted face finally halted. Ryan was looking at just a boy, a young man possessed by something he couldn't explain.

"Son of a fucking bitch!" Ryan screamed as the rain pouring down masked the true emotions he was feeling, evident in his eyes. It was loud and forceful enough that veins popped from his neck and his face reddened. He backed away from the lifeless body and with a shaky hand dropped the weapon onto the ground.

James held Kimberly as she sobbed. The immediate threat was taken care of so he started pulling her back towards the house. He bent over to pick the tire iron from the ground for protection. Jacque was dead but there was no telling if he got to Jasmine the same way he got Jimmy.

Ryan collected himself and had overheard Maggie when she said the gate was a no go, "Stan and Mark, you two know how to change a tire right? We should have at least three spare tires and that is a hell of a lot better than four flat ones. I'm going to go inside and look for Jasmine."

"Alright," Stan said and looked at Mark, "Take the fire poker. I don't think Jacque is human. I mean he can't be. We saw what the fuck he was."

Maggie approached her husband's side and hugged his arm tight, "I'm going with you. Don't tell me no because I don't want to hear it. Who knows what Jacque might still have in there?"

James swallowed hard and kissed Kimberly as the rain poured on the both of them. He hugged her tightly as his own tears flowed silently, "I'm going with them. You help Stan and Mark change out the tires. Keep an eye on their back and your own okay?"

Kimberly simply nodded.

Stan knew his way around a tire iron and he also knew they could get the job done faster with two of them working on the car. "James, keys." He said, holding out his hand. He caught the keys sent flying his way and the constant, cold rainfall started affecting him. He sneezed on the way to the vehicles and he felt miserable thanks to the hit he took earlier.

"We'll find her Stan, just get those tires fixed." Ryan said as he led James and Maggie back into the establishment, leaving Stan, Mark and Kimberly out in the rain.

41

Through the dark and very reflective hallways Jasmine and Helena ran as fast as they could. Grunts and screams chased after them along with the horrible sound of nails scraping down the side of those obsidian walls, grating against them like a rake on a chalkboard. Jasmine had no clue where they were going at several twists and turns but Helena reached back and gripped Jasmine's forearm when she began falling back. She pulled Jasmine hard to the right and a short distance later down the barely lit hallway she and Helena smacked against a large, iron-plated door. Helena gripped the handle and heaved, yanking the door several times until it slid open enough so she and Jasmine could fit through.

When they both slipped through to the other side they each held onto the handle and pulled together, sliding that door close with several hard pulls while the shouting, grunting, and scraping grew closer. The door slammed shut on one final yank and steel thudded, vibrating their hands against the iron bar they held. Helena looked to her left and cried out, gripping a steel beam and sliding it through the handle as Jasmine let go. On the other side those slashing, ear splitting cuts into the iron persisted for a few seconds and then dissipated. They were safe.

Jasmine waited with bated breath when it appeared nothing was on the other side of the door. She sighed and turned around to put her back against the iron door and slid down it until she sat with her knees to her chest. She took several hard, deep breaths to calm herself as Helena looked around the room they were in.

"Not shy about your body at least," Jasmine laughed while her body shook after the encounter.

Helena narrowed one eye at her, the only good one she had at that point, and shook her head, clapping her hands and pointing her thumbs up, "Up!" She gurgled out.

A single light hung motionless in the room they were in. As Jasmine rose she saw that the entire room was covered in the same black, reflective surface like the hallways she and Helena ran through. The surface was cold to the touch and as smooth as polished glass. It covered the floor, the four walls, and the ceiling but in the middle stood a singular podium. Jasmine approached the four foot pillar and noticed that it had been disturbed recently. A rectangular line of dust occupied the middle of the podium and nothing else. There was only one other door, a wooden one, on the opposite end that spilled light from underneath the frame.

Helena gripped Jasmine's hand again and tugged her towards the wooden door, "Is this the way out?" Jasmine asked, following without resisting.

The redhead pulled the wooden door open and they spilled out into the black hallway. It was a little more lit and Jasmine could see that there was a storage room left open on the opposite side of the hallway and there was a right corner they could turn about halfway between each end of the hallway. Helena took the right.

"Is this the way out?" Jasmine asked again, still shaking.

The hallway they turned into was much more devoid of light. She nodded and pointed in front of her, "Th . . . There!" She motioned to the stairs in front of her and rushed to them. Halfway up the creaking steps she paused and turned to Jasmine, "V-Vin . . . Tan?"

Jasmine's blank look turned into one of revelation, "Oh Vincent? Yeah he left hours ago to chase down a van that had a family in it. I think they were at least, or well they were turned into those things maybe." She frowned.

Helena pushed the door at the top of the stairs open with her shoulder. Her expressionless facial features didn't change in the least, but her eye closed and her throat bobbed while she swallowed hard. A faint light poured through the opening and Jasmine, standing behind Helena, recognized the area.

"Son of a bitch; I knew Fred and Clark weren't thieves," Jasmine said, "This is the library!"

Four dim chandeliers provided some light, but the majority of what illuminated the library came from the raging storm outside. Helena, caring nothing for the damage she caused, ripped a crimson curtain from one of the large library windows and wrapped it around her body to give a little bit of modesty to her condition. She tucked the remaining amount of curtain down the front of the makeshift dress and left her arms and legs bare so she could move them easier.

"Oh come on we don't need to worry about your body! We need to get you out of here," Jasmine scolded.

Helena shook her head. All she could do was muffle out sounds now and she scampered up the stairs to the book shelves and grabbed the blackest book she could find. She whimpered and cried as her twisted lips sealed shut.

"What in the world are you doing?"

Helena slammed the black book down on the nearest table, pointed at Jasmine and then directed her finger back at the black book. She shook her head back and forth and put her hand on the book and then made a circular motion around her face. She then repeated the process again.

Jasmine put her hand against her forehead and her eyes narrowed, "Hand-book face?"

Helena let out a muffled scream. She placed the book against her covered chest, and waved her hand in front of her face. She did the process again but placed the book against Jasmine's chest and waved her hand in front of her own face, pointing at Jasmine.

"So if I touch some book I end up like what you're becoming? I take it Jacque has the book we need to avoid?"

Helena nodded and put the book back on the table. She brushed a few strands of her red hair behind her ear and scanned the room. Finding nothing of what she needed she pointed to the book again and curled her fists together, bringing them down towards the book but stopping before she touched it. She made the motions several times before looking to see if Jasmine understood.

Jasmine took a moment before putting it together, "So if we

can't touch it, we have to stab the book or something like that? So what is happening to you is tied to the book and the book is tied to Jacque?"

Helena squealed and clapped her hands, nodding as hard and fast as she could.

"Well that sounds easy enough! Just get the book from Jacque without touching it and stab it with absolutely no stabbing items."

From the open door that led down the stairs into the strange hallways a loud crash startled both of the women. Jasmine pointed towards the exit of the library, and as their legs pumped for the exit they skidded to a halt as the large, library doors were kicked wide open.

42

It took Stan and Mark longer than anticipated to replace just two of the tires on Ryan's truck. The rain struck them both in the face and while Mark was stoic in his work, Stan's body shivered and his teeth rattled. On top of that he had a few uncontrollable bouts of wheezing and feeling lightheaded. His head ached every time Kimberly jumped and screamed with every bolt of lightning and crash of thunder. She was piled inside the ass end of the truck, looking out the window of the hatchback to make sure nothing surprised Stan or Mark while they worked.

Kimberly did spot something between the flashes of lightning. The rain made it hard to see what it exactly was but it looked like a man. With the storm obscuring her vision the only option she had was to pound against the window and scream. The figure ran at Stan who was working on the last tire and Kimberly screamed even louder, pointing behind Stan.

Stan didn't hesitate. He yanked the tire iron away from the rim and spun around, swinging it as hard as he could.

"Whoa!" The figure shouted as he skid to stop and leaned backwards to avoid the tire iron, slipping against the slick pavement but he stabilized himself before he fell.

Stan was about to swing again but stopped. His eyes widened and his jaw dropped along with the tire iron, "Vincent!"

"Fucking hell slugger, watch where you're swinging that thing," Tanner said. His features were drenched in water and black blood. Even some of his clothing was torn but he was packing heat on his back, his hips, and even on his chest. Several weapons hung from his body, most notably he had huge, double bladed axe in his hands. "I get back from God knows how many miles of straight running, chop about a dozen foot holes in a tree, monkey my happy ass up and over that fucking wall and I nearly get taken out by a tire iron. Fuck me." He said smiling.

Mark picked up the dropped tire iron and gritted his teeth, "How do we know he's not with that fucking asshole?" The young teen asked with his grip tightening on the iron.

Tanner took one look at Mark and the condition the boy was in and didn't need much else, "I'm sorry about your family Mark."

Stan gripped Tanner's shirt and pulled him by it a little, "Please tell me you have some sort of idea what the hell is going on here. Jasmine is missing and Jimmy is dead, and Mark said his father and brother are dead as well. On top of that I think Jacque is a God damn monster!"

"Just focus and listen to my voice Stan," Tanner began, yanking Stan's hands from his shirt, "Listen to me and you'll make it out of this alive. These things have a weak point in the head and in the heart. The heart will be easier to take out than the head because I've only got a shotgun left and a few bullets and I am going to need them." He said. Tanner placed his hands on Stan's shoulder and got eye to eye with the psychiatrist, "Jacque Collo should be the same way. They are possessed by something Stan."

Mark shook his head, "If Jacque is alive then he isn't like the rest. I shoved a fire poker through his head. I also put my foot through Clark Thompson's head. He had no jaw." Mark shivered.

Tanner narrowed his eyes at Mark and his chest rose and fell softly, "Alright, I'll keep that in mind if Jacque is still alive in there. I knew that slimy bastard was hiding something."

Stan pointed to the house, "Ryan, Maggie and James are back inside looking for Jasmine. I think that book Jacque had with him has some sort of way of possessing people, like you said, or it's a fast acting infection, a parasite. If they get inside your body you turn. I saw it happen to Oswald." Stan eyed the weapons Tanner had, "You had all of that with you? Where is your car?"

"Destroyed. Fred Thompson did a huge number on it. This is what is left of what I had in my trunk," he said and reached behind him with both hands. He pulled out two daggers shining with silver emblems around the handles, "Keep Kimberly in the car but keep these on you." He said, handing one to Stan and one to Mark. "Remember that they can only be killed—"

Kimberly beat against the window and screamed again.

Tanner turned his head in time to see a blurred face, and a low swinging jaw, crash into him. The thing took him off the ground in a hard tackle that had him grunting when he hit muddy grass a few feet away from the driveway. He felt the shape of the shotgun on his back dig into his spine and muscles and the breathlessness of the wind getting knocked out of him. The force of the body slam had the two of them skidding across the wet grass and mud and despite the blow Tanner took to his back he used the momentum of their sliding bodies to curl his knees under his assailant, kick his lower body up, and somersault the both of them around so that he was on top and his attacker was on the bottom. He gripped around its wrists and looked down, noticing the auburn strands of hair caked with mud.

"Mom!"

Tanner took his attention from the woman and saw Stan holding Mark by the arms, pulling back to keep the boy from running in. Mark twisted and turned before he slipped one arm free and turned his body around. He slammed the palm of his hand into Stan's chest, right near his heart. The blow sent Stan against the car, gasping for air. Mark didn't stick around long enough to watch Stan fall to the ground after the hit.

Tanner growled and held Stacy down as hard as he could. She tried to bite at his arms, but with her lower jaw hanging lifelessly it would be impossible for her to achieve that goal. Tanner shifted his body down her own for now, putting a knee into her sternum, "Mark the dagger!"

Mark shook his head at Tanner and slid to a stop a few feet away from them, "Get off her!"

"Damn it Mark this isn't your mother anymore!"

The teen nodded his head and cleared his throat, "I know that! She's my mother and she is my responsibility." He cried out.

"Oh God damn it Mark now is not the time for some misguided fucking honor or some shit! That's now how this business works!" Tanner yelled and raised upwards on one knee, getting a little bit of distance between her and his body and then brought is knee crashing down on her sternum. He felt nothing crack.

"Go after the others Mister Tanner!" Mark said. Gripping the dagger tight he took careful steps towards the two on the ground. The rain, still relentless in its downpour, only made the mud and grass slicker.

Tanner looked past Mark. Stan was motionless on the ground.

"Shit! Mark, give me the fucking dagger! I don't know what you did to Stan but he isn't looking too fucking good right now."

Mark turned his attention back to Stan and didn't know why he was lying like that, "I didn't even hit him that hard!"

Stacy Sinfield, or what used to be Mark's mother, raised her head up and clacked her jaw against her upper row of teeth. Tanner growled and shoved the woman down as hard as he could by her wrists. Thanks to the rain and the muddy ground her skin was just as slick as his, and with a twist and a yank she weaseled her right wrist away from his hand and buried her fist into Tanner's chest, knocking him off her body.

Tanner twisted his body around so he didn't land on his shotgun again but he still landed hard on his side a few feet away from Stacy. He groaned as his right side skid across the wet grass and slid into a pile of mud and water. The ground was flooding around the entire home. Tanner spit out a few chunks of mud and grass from his lips and quickly turned to stand.

Mark froze. The dagger was clenched in his hand but before he could use it on his mother she had been faster than he was. Her hand gripped around his own, crushing the boy's wrist with a sickening crunch. Mark screamed in pain and relinquished the dagger. Stacy pulled her free hand back and shoved it forward, aiming for Mark's soft chest. Her hand met Mark's own. He caught it just before it connected with his chest. It stung his hand and cracked a few metacarpals. Mark did his best to squeeze his mother's hand.

Mark grimaced as his mother squeezed his wrist and hand as hard as she could. The carpals, radius and ulna in his right wrist and hand were dust and his left hand was coming close to sharing the same fate. In a flash of lightning the pressure in his wrist was gone. He opened his mouth to scream, but someone else's cry echoed around him.

Stacy's hand was still attached to Mark's wrist, but her arm was sliced clean from her shoulder.

Kimberly Cross was done playing the victim. She panted hard

while rain washed over her body and the battle axe, which was now buried halfway in the ground between Mark and Stacy, had taken everything out of her to raise it up and bring down. It had cut clean through Stacy's left shoulder and her left foot, spraying black blood everywhere. Kimberly didn't even close her eyes as the black blood sprayed across her features. Her eyes narrowed and she screamed again, her face twisting in anger but despite her best efforts that axe was buried in the sticky mud, adding more weight to it and it became too much for Kimberly to brandish.

It gave Tanner enough time to step up behind Stacy Sinfield. From her chest burst a silver dagger, the last one he had that he gathered from the car. He twisted the blade and put his hand over her face, wrenching her body away from Mark and throwing her onto the ground away from the three of them. Her body rolled across the wet grass and mud until she came to a stop with her face and stomach facing the ground.

"You alright Mark?" Tanner shouted through the rain as Mark favored his wrist and his hand. His right hand rolled around without control and his wrist swelled and darkened. "Hell you'll be fine boy," he turned to Kimberly who refused to let go of the axe, "Kimberly! Focus! Get Mark into the car, I need to figure out what's wrong with Stan." He snapped his fingers several times in front of her face to get her attention. His chest ached from Stacy's hit.

Kimberly finally let go of that axe and stumbled backwards. She looked at her hands and then wiped her face, seeing the black blood on her hands now, "Oh God I'm infected!" she screamed before Tanner slapped her across the face.

"That isn't how it works woman. Look at me? I'm covered in this nasty shit too but I'm perfectly fucking fine."

Kimberly cried again, but it was much softer and more controlled.

Tanner ran over towards Stan and slid onto the ground. He pulled the man away from the vehicle and pressed his ear against Stan's mouth and chest. He didn't feel or hear anything. Tanner knelt next to Stan and began CPR.

43

Ryan caught himself in mid-swing after he kicked the doors to the library open and gripped James' wrist to prevent him from attacking as well, "Jazzy! Holy fuck me Jazzy we nearly caved your head in woman." Ryan said. He quickly picked his sister-in-law up by the waist and hugged her tight. Maggie came in behind him and hugged Jasmine as well after he set the woman down.

James, however, gripped his tire iron even harder when he spotted Helena. "Who is she?" he asked.

Jasmine shook her head and put herself between the redhead and the others, "Her name is Helena. That gentleman Vincent Tanner is looking for her. I don't know what is going on but I am so happy to see you guys are alive." She said. Sniffing away a few tears she looked over her shoulder, "We gotta get out of here. Jacque was right behind us."

Ryan shook his head, "No, Mark Sinfield is still alive. He put this fire poker through Jacque's head. After what I have seen tonight I'm not going to put him on trial for killing the prick."

"He isn't dead Ryan! He captured me and put me in his bedroom. He's been watching us this whole trip, he's got cameras and monitors and whatever he has been doing to people here he is going to try and do it to us. I saw what Mark did on the monitors. After you ran he got back up and unleashed four more of those monsters."

Ryan furrowed his eyebrows and looked away, "They aren't that hard to kill."

"Those things in the basement weren't like Jimmy and Oswald. They were skinless and had like, muscles bulging and claws as long as my finger I think. They looked like they were turned inside out and they were violent Ryan. They were monsters."

James had his eyes on Helena and the curtain she had wrapped around her body, "So what is wrong with her? I can still see part of her face and she isn't trying to kill us."

Helena rolled her one good eye and shook her head. She waved her arms in front of her a few times and waved her hands to shoo them from the library.

"I think she wants us to get out of here and I agree fully. I think the only way we can save her is if we destroy that book Jacque has with him. She acted out that much I think. The book is what turns you into, well, that." Jasmine pointed to Helena.

The doorway leading into the basement splintered away from the frame with two of those creatures following the destroyed doorway. Their muscled, but gangly bodies piled into the library. They emitted an ear piercing wail as their claws scraped down the walls of the library. The black blood that should have been inside of their bodies flowed around the muscles and bones of the creatures that blocked the way Jasmine and Helena escaped from. They stood there hunched and breathing deep.

"Okay we should probably get the hell out of here now," Ryan said as he turned and crossed into the doorframe.

The rest of the group kept an eye on those motionless beasts until they heard a gurgling groan from behind. Jasmine and Maggie turned their attention from the monsters and to the entrance of the library.

Ryan stumbled backwards from the doorframe, clutching his throat with his free hand. Crimson sprayed from in between his fingers and the fire poker held in his hand dropped to the ground with a resounding clank. The sound echoed in everyone's ears while they watched in stunned silence as he fell backwards onto the tile. The shadows from the darkened hallway produced a twisted hand with blood covered claws. An arm followed the hand and then the rest of Ryan's assailant stepped through. It was the same twisted creature that blocked the exit to the storage room and pens down below. The muscular, blood caked creature extended a split tongue from between its jaws and slid it slowly against the claws that slashed Ryan's throat, savoring the taste with a twisted, vile grin. Sharp rows of incisors made up the creatures mouth, now exposed as it licked itself for its reward.

Maggie screamed.

Jacque Collo relished the scream. The pure agony made him shiver as he walked down the library hallway. It pierced his ears and shook him to his very core. The scream is what he enjoyed the most; the hopes and dreams of a soul crushed in a moment. The energy from a scream almost fed him. The smell of blood and the taste of despair lifted his spirits when they were down from Jasmine's crafty escape. He looked at the doorframe that led into the library and saw the amount of red that dripped down it. Drawing a finger down that doorframe he tasted it, groaning loud in the darkness at the simple pleasure. He wanted it all to himself.

He peered over the shoulder of the Bleak in front of him and witnessed James, Jasmine and Maggie gripping at Ryan's shoulders and arms to pull him away from the new threat. He knew the scream was Maggie's at that point. The victim was her husband after all. The Frenchman pushed through the darkness and into the library, followed by the final, evolved Bleak.

"Well this is just such a shame. I really thought you all might actually escape," he said. He turned his attention to Jasmine and his smile grew wide, "Especially you Jasmine, you cheeky thing, and to think I had those bindings tight enough on your wrists and ankles to keep you from squirming. Well fool me once, shame on you, fool me twice, well you know how it goes." Jacque danced around the Bleak in front of him, gliding across the floor like he was sliding on ice.

Maggie and Jasmine, ignoring Jacque, yanked Ryan across the floor the best that they could towards the nearby window in the library. There were no bars on the windows and Jasmine canted her head at the window. James picked up on what she was thinking and grabbed the nearest chair he could find. With a grunt and heave he raised the chair above his head and bashed it into the window, shattering the glass into several jagged pieces. He ran the back of the chair over the bottom and sides of the window to clear any remaining glass from it. The fierce and violent weather outside sprayed in through the exit James created.

"Hey! That is private property you just shattered. You are going to pay for that window, young man." Jacque howled, snapping his fingers at his minions to attack the group.

James set the chair aside and reached down to help Maggie and Jasmine with Ryan. They pulled him to the window and tried to lift him up to the frame. Jasmine and James watched as Ryan's hand fell from his throat and his chest no longer rose. His body felt heavier. He was gone. As the Bleak walked towards the remainder of the group James grabbed Jasmine around the waist and pulled her towards the window away from Ryan. Maggie, however, stayed next to her husband.

"Maggie he's gone" Jasmine cried out. Her eyes blurred with tears as she watched her sister kneel by Ryan's side.

Maggie wrapped her arms around him and pulled him close to her body as tight as she could. She rocked back and forth while she held him and she brushed his hair slowly. "I'm not letting them take him Jasmine. They can't have him!" She screamed.

Jasmine tried pulling away from James but he held onto her tight, pulling and tugging her towards the window as well to try and get her to escape while they could. He could not take his eyes off of Ryan and Maggie and his teeth clenched. His chest hurt inside and his stomach somersaulted over and over since he could not do a thing for Ryan and the pain it caused Maggie because of it and the fact he hoped Kimberly was safe.

Helena had nothing but empathy for Maggie McCallister. The redhead had to duck under a table when the four Bleak and Jacque entered the library and the upside to the sorrow, guilt and pain that shot through her meant she was still in reality. This was not her happy place. Screaming did nothing, as the only sound to escape her non-existent lips was silence. In her state the only thing she could do was provide a distraction. As the Bleak formed a semi-circle around the three who were still alive she pulled every ounce of willpower she had left and pressed her hands against the table she resided under.

Another crack of thunder disguised her efforts until she barreled into the beasts. She crashed into them, using the table as a battering ram, and when she pushed the table away from her body she stumbled backwards.

Her efforts were rewarded with Jacque gripping her by the back of her hair and yanking her body into his "That was very, very foolish," he growled. He relinquished her hair for only a moment to wrap his arm around her upper body; his other cradled that terrible book. "Grab the black haired woman. She is mine," he snapped at his minions while Helena struggled. "Make the other two suffer for their lack of respect for me and my property!"

"Jasmine would you get the fuck out of here?" James shouted. He continued his efforts to pull her to the window to get her out of there and to the vehicle but she resisted every step of the way.

The Bleak descended upon them again. Maggie, being between them and the target of their master, tried to shield Ryan from them and their wicked claws but they were far too quick and vicious. Three of them grabbed at Maggie's hair, arms and her leg, yanking her from Ryan with no effort at all. They wrenched her arms back and broke them with their strength, forcing a scream to escape her lips once again. She fought back with her free leg, however, raising it up to clipthe jaw of the third Bleak holding her other leg.

"Let me go!" Jasmine screamed. She twisted her body back and forth and finally stomped on James' foot, causing him to wince in pain and let her go from around her waist. She wiggled her arm free from his hold and shoved him into the wall next to the library window. As she ran to her sister the fourth Bleak seized her by the arm and pulled her away from the group of three assaulting her sister.

Jasmine's eyes widened as the two that had a firm grasp on Maggie's arms and head, along with the one swiping at her kicking leg, raised the woman into the air and then wrenched her back down towards the table Helena had used to push them away. They drove Maggie's midsection through one of the legs of the table, impaling her. Maggie spit up several large, thick strands of blood from her mouth as the last few seconds of her life passed through her eyes. She turned her head back towards her husband before her arms and legs laid still.

Jasmine's eyes rolled into the back of her head as a sound went off that she thought was thunder, but was much more sharp and sudden, right before her world went dark.

44

Tanner tossed his head back when Stan sat up in a rush. The four of them heard the screams coming from inside the building and Stan caught the last few seconds of them when he rose from his unconscious state. He rubbed his chest and groaned and the memory of Mark hitting him came flooding back quick. The rain still poured and the grounds in front of the mansion were flooding over. There were only a few patches of grass in the large front yard that was visible.

"What the hell was that?" Stan panted.

Tanner shook his head, "I don't know I was too busy saving your ass. I put Mark in a time-out by getting the rest of the tires on the vehicle. We should be up and running. I still can't believe a teenager knocked you out." He stood up in the pouring rain and gripped Stan's hand, helping him off the wet ground. Tanner pointed with his thumb to Kimberly who was rubbing her face over and over, along with the front of her body and arms to try and clean the black blood off. "Kimberly here kicked some ass as well. I don't think she's up for an encore though." He said as he wandered towards the battle axe in the ground.

"I'm sorry Mister Freason; I didn't mean to hit you that hard." Mark said as he finished with that third tire. Having no spare fourth three was better than nothing.

"Don't feel bad. You kind of hit my weak spot," he said and turned a worried glance to Tanner, "We need to get inside."

Tanner gripped the axe and nodded his head, "I do. You don't. Stay here with the car and if anything comes to destroy it, kill it dead. If I come back kill me dead as well and get the hell out of here." He left no one time to argue as he ran off and into the mansion.

That didn't sit well with Stan. He looked back to Mark who favored his right wrist and Kimberly who looked more than disheveled from what she had done to the possessed Stacy Sinfield. "Kimberly, get in the back and hunker down. Try and keep an eye out for anyone. Mark, are you alright?"

Mark nodded but his wrist was swollen to the size of a baseball by now, "I can drive I think. My right hand hurts; I think that . . . thing crushed it." He said and bit his lower lip as his eyes welled.

Kimberly scurried into the back of the truck again, taking shelter from the rain and Mark parked himself in the driver's seat. He didn't need to adjust the seating to feel comfortable in the vehicle.

Stan gripped the tire iron Mark used and held it close. He turned and ran towards the home.

45

The Bleak that held the fainted Jasmine in its grasp crumpled to the ground a few moments after Jasmine had passed out. The previous bang caught everyone's attention and the exit wound in the back of the Bleak's head was large enough to ensure that the brain matter inside had been turned to mush.

Jacque spun around with Helena's hair still gripped in his fingers and laughed as he watched Vincent Tanner enter through the library doorway. Tanner had a rather large axe in one hand and he kicked the empty revolver cartridge from his gun. He swung the axe into the doorframe, opting to stuff a fully loaded wheel clip into his custom made revolver.

"Well isn't this just a glorious surprise?"Jacque squealed with glee as he held Helena tight, forcing her head down enough to bend her at the waist and keep her looking at the ground.

"James! Catch and aim for their head." Tanner called out as he kicked the hatchet in his belt buckle into the air and gripped it, throwing it into the window frame next to James.

The handle of the hatchet shook back and forth from the sudden stop when the head embedded into the wood. James lunged for the axe and the Bleak nearest to him dove for the college boy. As it reached for James its body jerked violently to the right, spilling against the open window with buckshot embedded in its internal organs. As James gripped the hatchet and pulled it from the wall another Bleak descended upon him. He swung the hatchet up as quickly as he could right as one of those clawed nails swiped towards his face. The hatchet sliced clean through the wrist of the Bleak that attacked him, and James ducked under the dismembered hand and subsequent arm that followed. James dodged the spray of black blood that came with his attack and stumbled a few feet back.

The creature Tanner shot to give James some breathing room turned around to face Tanner. The shotgun blow had torn a hole in upper chest portion of the creature. On any other person it would look like it had collapsed a lung but the Bleak showed no signs of slowing down. It leaped at Tanner as the man reloaded the shotgun with the last two shells he had on him.

Tanner cocked the shotgun back into position and jumped back a few times to avoid the slashing claws of the Bleak, "So you ugly fucks do have some emotion!" He jabbed the barrels of the shotgun forward, butting the front of the gun against the front of the Bleak's head and in doing so knocked it off balance. "Is that all you got?" Tanner taunted as he put the shotgun against the creature's chest and pulled the triggers.

Buckshot from the shotgun shells, and also blood and gore from

what used to be inside the creature, peppered the library walls and stalls and the books that occupied those spaces. He smiled and then turned his attention to where he dropped the first Bleak, expecting to see Jasmine laying there on the ground unconscious still.

"Shit."

"Tanner! The head isn't working!" James screamed as he had no weapon in his hands. The Bleak attacking him had a hatchet drilled into its skull, past the brain, and was gaining ground on James. When those claws got a hold of James the Bleak sent the young man flying across the library with a strength Tanner only saw in the deceased Fred Thompson. James landed with a thud and rolled several feet before coming to a stop.

Tanner now starred down the last three Bleak and Jacque himself, who now held Jasmine in his arms. Tanner narrowed his eyes on Jacque's face, which had a sick grin spreading across it, and watched Jacque shift to his left and stepped to the side. He revealed the fourth body that was behind him.

Helena starred back at Tanner; her face blurred all over with a black hole where her mouth should be opened in a silent scream.

"You two must know each other. I know that look Mister Tanner and looks never lie . . ." he paused, licking his pale, cracking lips as he held his arms around the unconscious Jasmine, ". . .but I do."

Tanner switched the shotgun over to his left hand and dropped his left arm down. He reached into his waistband and pulled out his customized forty-five Colt and fired it.

The shot penetrated Jacque's head. It went right between his eyes and out the back, splattering black blood and brain tissues across the desk behind him. Jacque looked shocked for a moment. He raised his hand to the hole in his head, pushing his fingers into the empty space. He withdrew his finger, examining it inches from his eyes. He smiled.

Helena stood still as the last remaining Blink began their assault.

Tanner unloaded the other four shots of his Colt into the three attacking Bleak. He nailed two of them in the chest, a shot in each heart and they went down like a rock. With the third he hadn't been quick enough to draw on. The hole in the creature's head continued to leak black blood as it charged and leaped into the air.

"Get down!"

Tanner didn't look back. He dove backwards, his colt drawn in the air. As he fell back he saw the blade of that large, battle axe swing across his vision. He pulled his arm down as soon as he saw that blade and watched as the axe connected with the sternum of the creature.

James' arms strained with veins popping out as it took every ounce of strength inside of him to dig the axe in harder and slam the Bleak into the ground. Black blood splattered everywhere as the Bleak lashed out with its deadly claws. James brought the axe back down again and again, chopping through the creature's stomach several times, severing the spinal cord before the axe came down one last time through the Bleak's chest. The heart was split in two.

"Well isn't this just an exciting turn of events? My hat is off to the both of you for being so well versed in surviving," Jacque huffed as James ripped the large, blood covered axe from the dead monster's body. "Though Mister Tanner, my boy, can you kill this one?" he asked as he nudged his head towards the stationary Helena.

Tanner rose to his feet and narrowed his eyes at Jacque, gripping his colt tightly. He licked his lips and pointed the gun at Jacque's head again, "Let her go! Whatever the fuck you've done to her I want it stopped now." He said as he centered his weapon square at Jacque's chest. He hesitated to fire when Jacque drew Jasmine's body in front of his heart, that book he held in his other hand stopped inches before her chest.

"Hey now, let's not be so demanding Mister Tanner. Get him." Jacque laughed as Helena moved.

"James you have to finish this. You have to kill Jacque. Aim for his fucking heart!" Tanner shouted before he tossed his gun aside and took Helena's tackle head on.

Helena's arms wrapped around Tanner's waist and she pivoted her hips to the right, turning them both before she drove forward and picked him up, driving them both into another table in the library. Tanner groaned as his back hit the table but didn't go through it. The wood cracked, but did not break even with Helena straddling Tanner's waist from her initial attack. Her fist rose and fell, aiming for Tanner's face but found only table. That was enough for the table to split in two and sent the two of them tumbling to the ground.

James' hands ached against the battle axe. The veins in his forearms pulsated while sweat poured down his face and from under his arms. "You're a fucking monster, you know that? James panted as he raised the axe with both hands. "Let her go and fight me, or are you too busy hiding behind her like you do with your little fucking creatures?"

"Let me take a moment and wipe a tear from my eye, Mister Newberry."

James curled his upper lip and took a step forward.

"Let my wife go you son of a bitch!"

A very wet, and very angry, Stan Freason stood in the doorway of the library. He clutched the dagger Tanner gave him tight in his hand. His eyes drifted for the faintest of moments to Ryan and Maggie McCallister and his heart sank to a level he never thought possible. His rain soaked clothes and hair caused his skin to goose bump and his hairs to stand on end, yet his violent shaking wasn't due to the cold, or fear. He gripped the dagger tighter in his fist and all sane thought went out the window after he saw that his brother and sister in-law had been murdered.

He saw that book held so close to his wife's chest and charged. He raised the dagger in the air as he went for the kill. He observed the bullet hole in Jacque's head and knew the heart had to be what took Jacque out for good.

"Cute," Jacque muttered as Stan came at him.

Jasmine stirred from her fainting spell long enough to watch as Jacque shoved his arm forward and pushed that obsidian covered book against Stan's chest.

46

Stan grunted when the book touched his chest and when his eyes met with Jacque he saw the same shit-eating, ear-to-ear smile Jacque had when they first met. Stan, however, tilted his head to the side when he felt nothing, absolutely nothing. He still felt the cold handle of the dagger in his raised hand, still felt the cold rain dripping down his body, and the book only caused a slight discomfort against his chest compared to the number Mark did on him outside.

Jacque's broad grin disappeared over the course of a few moments when he continued pushing the book against Stan's chest and got nothing out of it. "Well this is new," his cracked lips puckered closed and his eyes narrowed.

Stan had enough. He yanked the book straight from Jacque's grasp.

In the Frenchman's genuine surprise, Jasmine bent her head forward and threw it back as hard as she could against Jacque's chin. It was a hard enough blow to daze the Egyptian beauty but Jacque still held her tight, "Stan you have to destroy the book somehow, stab it or something!" she cried out and tried to wiggle from Jacque's grasp.

Stan backed away from Jacque, stumbling several feet away from the man before he turned on his heel and ran to the nearest table that wasn't broken or turned over from the fight going on inside of the library. "Fuck you Jacque. Fuck you, this God damn house, and fuck this God damn book!"

Jacque flung Jasmine from his grasp and onto the floor. He chased Stan as fast as he could and discarded the robe from his body to reveal the naked flesh that contained all of those souls he had consumed throughout the ages. The faces swirled and all came to a head on the man's chest and stomach, screaming at Stan and cheering him on with silent, overjoyed faces for a change. Jacque's body froze with his hand inches from Stan's face.

"What? No! You listen to me! You do not control me, I own you all!" Jacque cried out as the faces turned inwards. Faces were no longer visible, but the back of their heads were seen. They were pushing against Jacque. The face of Jimmy Franklin and Fred Thompson rolled over Jacque's neck and began gnashing their teeth, poking holes in Jacque's flesh and turning his neck into a strainer for that black blood to leak out.

Stan swallowed hard and flipped the obsidian book open. He closed his eyes, turned away from Jacque, and stabbed into the milky white pages.

The silver blade pierced through the pages of Jacque's beloved book. Stan opened his eyes and saw that the book contained nothing more than a collection of names. A collection of souls and faces kept forever bound in servitude to Jacque Collo. "Owned by Belial" followed every name that Stan could see but the names disappeared under thick, black pus. Stan turned his head to see a gaping hole in Jacque's side. From him the same black pus oozed. Stan did what any normal human being would do in his situation.

He stabbed again and again.

The book and pages were nothing but gashes of black pus after Stan finished with the last knife insertion. When the final knife blow struck into the book a shockwave of energy burst from the book that rippled through the room. The blast knocked Stan, Jacque, and Jasmine into the air and onto the ground several feet away from the book's final throes.

Jacque Collo slowly sat up and his jaw gaped open, "You have no idea what you have done!" He said and then screamed. One by one, and in rapid movement, the faces on his body churned around his flesh and pulled away from his skin. The black, inky faces pulled from his body, the book as well, and morphed into small red lights that danced around in the library before they poured out of the busted out library window.

Vincent Tanner groaned as he did his best to hold Helena at bay. His cheek swelled from a few hits he took while trying to keep her held away from him but he was growing weak. He held her wrists tightly as her nails grew, scraping against his cheek and his neck as she bore down on him. A faint, red glow from one of those red, dancing lights outlined Helena's form before it pushed against her back, right into her spinal cord. The light shot through her body and the blurred face that never uttered a sound let out an earth-shattering scream that shattered every window in the house and dazed Tanner like a flash-bang grenade.

Helena's body slumped against Tanner's. He heard nothing but bells and he kept his grip tight on Helena's wrists. After a few moments passed he shifted his body and turned her onto her back to get a look at her for the first time in over a month.

Her features had stilled.

"Helena? Helena!" He cried out to her and released her wrists. He placed his ear on her chest, hoping for anything.

Meanwhile Jacque Collo convulsed on the floor. The obsidian, his book, lay on the table covered in black ooze. A moment later it exploded into a black and blue flame that immediately consumed the very dagger that had destroyed it. The flame twisted and danced, rising higher and higher until the tip of the flames licked the ceiling of the mansion home and set the ceiling ablaze. The flames from the book descended and vanished, leaving the top of the table singed and covered in ashes. The wind from the broken windows quickly swept the ashes away, but the ceiling was still on fire.

Jacque's body shivered and expanded and then contracted several times. His naked flesh shriveled and sank against his bones. His already gaunt-like features to his face sunk in even more and his eyes withdrew into his skull, leaving his eye sockets showing nothing but dank darkness. His ribcage showed through his skin and the rest of his body outlined in that constricting flesh that continued to shrink. It tore soon enough, skin giving way to muscles and bone. What hair he had left on his scalp fell from his flesh as he lay there on the ground shaking and rocking back and forth. He had no skin on his body any longer and his bones and muscles convulsed. From his mouth came an eruption of black blood that sprayed towards the flames on the ceiling before it came raining back down on his deformed body.

"You fool! You fucking idiots!" he cried out, but those throws and pain and anguish formed into laughter. "You have no clue the hell you just brought upon yourselves!"

Jasmine was the first to get back to her feet. She rushed to Stan's side as he lay on the ground near the broken windows and his forehead had a nasty gash across it.

"Stan!" she cried, shaking him and slapping him a few times. "Come on baby wake up, I know you're alive so get your ass in gear!" Frustrated beyond reason she did the one thing she was told never to do. She raised her shirt above his chest and looked at the scar that taunted her. With a deep breath she slammed the side of her fist down right in the middle of his physical marring.

Stan's eyes shot open again for the second time that night and he gasped for air. The rush from her hit sent him scrambling to his feet and shuffling back and forth, "Fuck! Fuck! Ouch! Fuck!" He shook back and forth while on his feet until he felt that rush die down. He looked at his wife and blinked, "Jazzy?"

"He's getting back up guys," James growled a Jacque sat straight up without using his arms. His body, still convulsing, bloated in his arms and legs but he still had that sick smile on his eyeless, and skinless, face.

James wasn't willing to wait around. He gripped the battle axe tight and swung for Jacque's head. The sharpened, stained metal edge sliced halfway through Jacque's neck before it came to a halt. James growled and yanked the blade free and swung again. He penetrated Jacque's chest this time around and no blood, or any muscle, went flying. The axe sunk in and stopped halfway through. Something obstructed the blade from sinking through to Jacque's heart. The blockage didn't deter James as he brought the axe back and swung it towards Jacque's chest one more time.

Jacque's hand grabbed the handle of the axe and twisted his wrist. In that one movement Jacque broke the axe in two, causing the blade to fall in between Jacque's spread legs. Jacque kept a grip on the broken, splintered half that James still held and starred at James with those empty eyes. Jacque's hand and wrist twitched, and with it tossed James and the stick he held onto into the air and across the library. James' body tumbled next to Jasmine and Stan.

"None of you are leaving the premises alive! I am going to devour ever last God damn drop of your flesh! I am fucking Belial and I am starving!" The last of Jacque's, or the demon Belial's, human disguise started to fade away.

"Figures, your first investigation and it happens to be a demon. You know how to pick'em," Tanner growled and kissed Helena on the corner of her mouth. "Come on Helena, not like this, not when I almost had you back."

Tanner grimaced and groaned when he felt a sharp pain exploded in his side near his ribcage. He looked down to see a fist retreating.

"Took you long enough," the redhead under him said, pushing him off her body with a smile. "We can do the tender kissy kiss thing later, I think I just got my soul back and I'm feeling pretty good about it." She shuddered as she thought about Belial, "We have work to do baby, I have seen the inside of that ugly son of a bitch and we need more than what we got to kill him." She stood up and held the red curtain around her body with it tied just right to ensure she wasn't showing anything off. "Everybody run!" she called out to the other three. She grabbed Tanner's wrist and pulled him towards the exit of the library, stepping over the broken tables and the bloody corpses of the Bleak that were strewn about.

The fire licking the ceiling traveled down the walls. The flames that dropped from above set the book rows set the entire room ablaze. Small balls of fire licked at Stan's heels while he and Jasmine pulled James to his feet.

"Fuck this . . ." James said groaning, rubbing his head as he saw the library burning up around them. He stood next to the shattered window ". . . the window," he pointed as the fire roared to life. He saw a chair nearby, one that hadn't been knocked over or smashed in the fight, and grabbed it for them to use to get out of the busted window. The fire consumed everything faster and faster the longer it lived. When James set the chair down on the ground he took the lead, placing a foot on the chair and leaping to the windowsill and scraped a bit more of the broken glass from the frame with his shoulder. He shifted sideways and held his hand out to Jasmine.

Jasmine took his hand and climbed onto the chair. She took the place of James who jumped out the window moments after she joined him in the window. She looked back; extending her hand to her husband and saw him crouched next to Ryan's lifeless body.

"Stan, come on!"

"Ryan has the keys to his truck. I have to get them."

"I'm sure Tanner is capable of hotwiring the damn thing!"

Ryan's body was only a few feet from the window as it was and

Stan hurried through the pockets of his best friend and brother by marriage. Stan clenched his teeth, fighting back tears that caught in the corner of his eyes, "I'm sorry. I'm so God damn sorry." His teeth chattered and his stomach turned and doubled. He closed his eyes to blink away the wetness and the images of Jason Jacobs flooded his mind. All of Stan's pain, all the doubts he had about himself came rushing back in an instant. He swallowed hard as his fingers found Ryan's keys. He stood up and tossed them to Jasmine who let them the sail out the window for James to pick up.

"Stan what are you doing? We have to go now!" Jasmine cried.

He shook his head, "Not this time Jasmine. Maggie and Ryan are dead because of me, because we had to take this damned vacation due to the fact I was so down on myself and depressed. I didn't stop blaming myself until it was too late and this entire time I have just been running. I am not going to run away from this. I'm not going to let this ugly mother fucker win." He said and bent over, gripped Ryan by his arms and slowly pulled him over to Maggie. "They deserve to be together for eternity and not in the hands of that sick monster."

"This isn't your fault Stan! This is a nightmare and not just yours so come on and let's run!" Jasmine cried again, tears bursting from her eyes as she stood there on the windowsill. Her nails dug into the wooden frame. The wood above her started creaking and cracking from the fire that disintegrated everything it touched. She opened her mouth again to scream at Stan but arms wrapped around her waist and yanked her from the window frame right as it collapsed. She and James tumbled onto the ground as the side of the building covered the window in debris and flame. Jasmine screamed.

Stan worried about Jasmine, but trusted she was alright outside in the rain. He turned his attention to the demon Belial as it stood up. The flesh was flayed from every inch of his frame and those two sunken black holes where its eyes used to be glared at Stan Freason as the psychiatrist stood his ground. Belial took one hand and gripped onto his throat as fire burned around him and Stan. The fire covered over half of the library now, from the back to the middle and Belial appeared less than worried as he wiped that gash in his disgusting throat away, flinging black blood across the room.

"I am most curious why my book did nothing to you. You, of all people, should have easily crumbled into a fantasy. Your dream life where you could be as happy as you can imagine, where you could have everything you want in life and take it all in for yourself. Why did it not work?" Belial asked, convulsing in rapid jerks. His body expanded a little bit.

Stan shrugged his shoulders and cleared his throat as he stood a few yards away, "I'm not good at biology but I know how the mind works. You're an infection. Your magic, or whatever the hell it is, it must affect the heart first and then spreads from there. You create an illusion, you create hallucinations. I don't even think you harvest souls. I think somehow that book is a collective consciousness and when it died, every single parasite died with it, but you are still nothing but a fucking insect in that regard. The stronger the resistance the less your infection can spread." Stan trembled, but pulled his shirt down by the collar. He exposed a five inch scar that ran between his pectoral muscles to his belly button. "When you have no biological heart your disease cannot spread. All artificial for me and you can thank a former patient of mine for that."

The demon Belial reached up and slapped his hand down on his muscle and bone knee. He shook his head with a smile on his face, "You humans. Such crafty little creatures and you do not even realize it," his body expanded in a rapid pulse once more, "You really should have run."

His body twisted left and right in a violent seizure. His stomach bloated and sank in again while Belial laughed, shaking the foundation under Stan's feet with every bellowing roar. He extended his arms and spread his legs as the rest of his body followed his stomach. Contracting and releasing for several convulsions Belial's body exploded in a hurricane of blood, bone, and muscle. The bursting body sent a wave of energy out just as the book did and it knocked Stan backwards near the exit door of the library. Stan skidded to a stop and looked up as black blood and innards rained down around the library and on top of him. He turned his head away, protecting his eyes and his glasses from getting messy. When the shower ended he turned his attention back to Belial and his jaw dropped.

The illusion was shed and the vacation was over. The demon Belial's true form nearly touched the burning roof of the ceiling and it was hunched over to avoid such a singe. Its bloated body expanded at least ten feet across. Streaks of black and purple etched over its green flesh like terrible scars and several different kinds of sores littered its body. Black pus oozed from dozens of boils that decorated its disgusting flesh, peppering across its stomach and arms most of all. The creature had no head, but as it kept its fat body bent over to avoid the fire Stan saw why. On each side of Belial's massive shoulders sat two bloodshot eyes and between them was a large, black hole. At first glance it looked to be eight feet in diameter. The monster grunted once and a bright, green light appeared inside of that black hole, illuminating the beast's maw.

Stan's eyes widened when the green light deep inside of Belial's "throat" showcased row after row of teeth that circled into the body of the monster. As Stan looked into the mouth of the monster he saw that the black space between the teeth in each row grew smaller and smaller the deeper it went into Belial's mouth and throat, it was like looking down into a tornado of teeth. Stan breathed a sigh of relief; however, as he saw that the beast really had no way to chew.

From Belial's back three prehensile tentacles pushed forth and slapped around the burning library. The sticky tendrils acted like a frog's tongue as they slapped against a few pieces of furniture and yanked it from the ground. The green tendrils wrapped around the wood tightly, crushing the pieces of chairs and tables around its length before the pieces were thrown into Belial's gaping maw. When the wood hit against the teeth Stan's eyes widened. The teeth rotated against the "jaws" that held them in place, whirring about like a demonic garbage disposal. The furniture shred like pieces of paper against those grinding teeth and nothing was left to waste.

"Jesus Christ . . ."

Stan slowly stood to his feet and his gaze traveled to Belial's legs. Eight legs, built like a hairless tarantula, sprouted from the roly-poly waistline. Four legs on each side allowed Belial to keep his balance without difficulty, and the immense weight of the demon crushed the tiles underneath him. The boards and foundation held him, however, as he finished his transformation. He raised one of those thick, green legs and slammed it down on the ground, shaking the ground around him and roared so loud that the sheer force of his scream and breath knocked Stan back a few more feet towards the library exit as he tried to get up once more.

"It's feeding time!" It roared as several of those sticky, thick tendrils shot out, seeking Stan Freason as he pulled himself to his feet.

47

Tanner and Helena burst from the front door of the mansion and out into the cold, relentless rain. By this time the entire front yard was flooded with oversaturation and the paved road and subsequent parking lot had an inch or two of rain covering it. Helena, still barefoot, shivered next to Tanner, "Give me your shoes!"

Tanner, perking an eyebrow and narrowing his eyes at her, pointed towards the hatchback which would provide cover from the rain, "I'll buy you a pair if we make it out of this alive."

"Jerk."

"Cry about me being a jerk or sexist when we get home alright?" He said, taking her hand and began jogging towards the truck. She kept up with his pace and the back of the hatch opened up.

"Where is James?" Kimberly shouted through the rain and thunder. She dropped the back of the truck and Helena dove in, "Who the hell are you?"

"A very relieved woman, I'm sorry for your loss. My name is Helena. I guess I got lucky with everything that has happened." She shivered and curled into a ball in the back of the truck. She grabbed whatever she could to cover her body from the freezing cold rain that splattered her bare skin. The curtain wrapped around her body wasn't helping.

Kimberly gripped the dagger tighter, "You mean, were you one of them?" Her lower lip trembled.

The driver's side door opened and Mark, nursing his swollen wrist, climbed into the backseat of the truck so Tanner could slide in, "She was Kimberly. Stan destroyed the book but we aren't dealing with just some sick old man. Jimmy is gone, so is your family Mark but I assure you they are in a better place now thanks to Mister Freason." Tanner said. He swiped his hand across his forehead and flung a good amount of water across the seats. He shifted to the side and bent sideways, reaching under the steering wheel and ripped the plastic compartment protecting several different colored wires off and tossed it out the window.

"Tanner, which one was James?"

Tanner clenched his teeth as he dug through all the wires that were there, "The college boy Helena, he is fine Helena. They should be right behind us. Ryan and Maggie didn't make it," Tanner swallowed hard.

Kimberly shrunk into the corner of the hatchback. She closed her eyes and buried her head in her knees, "We're all going to die aren't we?"

Helena scooted her wet body over to Kimberly and put an arm around the frightened girl, "We've survived this far, we just have to keep it up but you have to focus on that. We are dealing with a demon. One named Belial. We are going to run Kimberly; we are not going to fight okay?"

Tanner sliced through a few of the wires and began scraping them together. Each time the car would sputter and die, "I know you're not a piece of shit truck, come on!" He growled.

"Mister Tanner!"

Everyone looked to the back of the truck and back to the house. James and Jasmine ran towards the vehicle as quick as they could. Helena reached over and dropped the hatchback again and James dove in, sliding against the plastic lining and slammed his shoulder against the back of the truck, groaning but looking no worse for the wear aside from a few new cuts and bruises.

"Hey babe," he groaned.

Jasmine went around the truck and got into the passenger side and tossed the keys into Tanner's lap. "Stan stayed behind. We have to wait for him. I'm not leaving here without him!"She slammed the door and rubbed her arms free of as much water as she could. She looked back and watched the flames from the library survive the pounding rain that fell upon it. The fire grew larger as she watched, tears brimming her eyes.

"He stayed back? God damn that man." Tanner growled. He twisted the wires together he tried to spark and pushed the key into the ignition.

The five of them froze when Belial's roar echoed from the library and shook the truck they were in.

"Oh that is not good," Helena groaned, "Tanner, we have to get the hell out of here."

"How do we do that? The metal gate would turn this truck into shredded metal wheat," James protested.

Tanner shook his head, "Then we pull the truck up to the wall, climb over and run as fast as we can."

"Well we can only hope he's slow," Helena added.

Tanner turned the key and the engine roared to life. He was glad the wires didn't lose their connection after he twisted them together. He gunned the accelerator a few times to get the engine revved and turned on the heat to counteract the cold rain that covered them all in various degrees. "What did you learn your first day of training Helena? Never count on anything being slower than you."

"It was wishful—" Helena's shriek cut her off when Tanner threw the truck into reverse and gunned it hard, whipping around the flooding parking lot. She wasn't the only one tossed around in the truck either; no one else expected the sudden take off. He whipped the tail end of the truck around and squealed the tires against the wet pavement. Once the tires caught traction they seared through the few inches of rain collecting on the pavement.

The truck fishtailed to the right and left for a few moments until it shot straight forward. Tanner put as much pressure on the pedal as he could. Jasmine, who looked more than distressed with her silent tears running down her face, looked at the burning mansion as the fire spread over the main entrance and licked across the top of those two massive, oak doors that they first entered a few days back. She clutched her hand to her chest and continued to stare at those doors, even as Tanner turned the vehicle sharply to the left, sending everyone in the back sliding to the right of the vehicle and Jasmine pressed hard against the glass as the rain poured down. With her forehead pressed against the glass she wailed.

Unnatural flames engulfed the vacation home completely as the truck careened down the path. James and Helena popped open the top of the hatchback and looked to the front of the burning building. Helena squinted through the rain and watched, for a split second, the flames parted in the middle of the building. Through the rain she could barely make out something coming through and leaping from the steps onto the wet ground.

"Tanner! Hit the brakes!"

Tanner obliged, slamming and skidding on the wet pavement when he locked the wheels. He looked out the rearview mirror and saw the figure as well.

"Don't stop! Keep going!" Stan Freason screamed at the truck. A moment later the front of the mansion exploded, raining down fiery debris and shrapnel around Stan as he ran as hard as he could without looking back. The blaze from the vacation home illuminated the surrounding area and the monster that burst forth.

Belial roared, shaking the very foundation and ground around it while the flames licked at its slimy skin. Tendrils shot towards Stan as he ran and the sticky extremities only licked the flooding pavement where Stan's feet were a moment ago. Belial's fat hand grabbed one of the burning oak doors and ripped it from the frame. He swung his arm sideways and threw the burning door towards Stan and the vehicle.

"Get down!" James and Helena screamed.

Stan dove to the side into the flooded grass and mud and the burning projectile almost hit him in the head. The door-turned-missile had a new target and Stan looked up just to see Tanner accelerate, spin out on the wet pavement, and turn the vehicle slightly to the right so that the door slammed against the metal, back end driver's side of the truck. The force of the blow sent the truck spinning as the door shattered into splinters and sizzled in the flooded ground.

"Jasmine!" Stan screamed. He pushed himself out of the mud and water as the spinning vehicle was forced off the flooded pavement and into the water filled dirt and grass. Stan saw movement inside of the vehicle and the door did nothing but set the truck into a spin. The rain continued to pour as the wheels on the truck spun, but went nowhere. The muddy ground provided no traction, and as the tires spun the ground only devoured the rubber faster.

"Fuck, alright everyone out." Tanner shouted from inside the vehicle. He opened his door, nearly kicking it off. The truck faced Belial and the headlights illuminated Stan and the beast that stood less than thirty feet away. Jasmine popped out of the passenger side and Stan ran to her. He grabbed her in a hug and kissed her hard on the lips.

Belial took several large steps towards the out-of-commission truck, "See what you have done Stan Freason? You all could have had the happiest existence inside of me, but now you will just have to feed me the old fashioned way!" Two of those tendrils struck towards the group and the truck.

Jasmine drove Stan forward and the two of them fell into the muddy ground and grass a few feet away from the truck. Tanner also jumped out of the way and looked to the back of the truck, "Get the hell out!" he shouted at Helena and James who were pushing hard against the bottom portion of the hatchback. It had been clamped shut by the impact of the flaming door.

"It's stuck!" Helena screamed. The top was wide open, however, and she gripped James by the collar and shoved him towards that opening, "Tumble James."

James understood and dove out of the top half of the truck. He landed on the ground hard and rolled away from the truck as Helena followed. The tentacles slapped against the front of their escape vehicle and shattered the two lights that illuminated the area. Belial pulled back and the truck started pulling out of the deep sinkhole it was stuck in.

James regained his senses after the fall and looked around. He saw Tanner and Helena, who picked herself up much faster than he did, standing in front of Jasmine and Stan. Mark opened the passenger door with a hard kick as well, and nearly slipped and fell on the ground. He couldn't see Kimberly.

"Kimberly!"

He skidded to the back of the truck and saw her curled up in the back still. Other than her entire body shivering and her head shaking back and forth she refused to move, "I can't do it anymore James. I can't," she sobbed.

James gripped the bottom steel of the hatchback and tugged on it roughly. Stan and Tanner joined him when they saw what was happening.

Tanner growled and yanked as hard as he could before giving up and just diving halfway into the back to grab at her leg, "Kimberly, focus on me and just come on!"

Tanner reached out for Kimberly's hand when she looked at him and the sickening, sucking sound of the tires filled the three men's ears. Tanner fell from the backend as the truck pulled free from the ground. Belial tugged so hard on the front end of the truck that it picked it off the ground and sent it towards the monster's churning and grinding maw.

48

James glued his eyes onto Kimberly's tear streaked face as the truck went towards Belial. Tanner and Stan took off running and James froze. He couldn't comprehend what was going on. It was too confusing. They had survived up until that moment and she was now going to die in a more violent way than he could ever imagine.

What confused him more was the sudden flash of light that appeared from behind them all. It was fast, it looked like a shooting star, and it hit directly against Belial's body. When it impacted against the demon it exploded, sending a shockwave through the air that knocked Stan and Tanner backwards into the water covered ground and deafened everyone in the area. The truck dropped. It landed closer to the demon and rolled several times until it stopped upside down.

James' eyes squinted when a bright light illuminated the area around Belial and the house that was lit aflame. A high pitched screech filled the air before several more bolts of light fired into the body of Belial, knocking the immolated beast back a few feet. James followed the lights and looked up to the sky. The ringing in his ears from the blast prevented him from making out the sounds of the helicopter in the sky. The beating wings were muffled but the whirring of the machine gun underneath it was unmistakable.

James turned his attention away from the savior in the sky to the upturned vehicle facing Belial. He dug his feet into the ground and sprung from it, dashing to the vehicle while his feet and legs burned, sticking deep in that mud with every hard step he took towards Kimberly.

Another earth-shaking blast came from behind Jasmine, Mark and Helena. The iron gates that prevented their exit blew open and fell useless to the ground in twisted metal. From the smoke a set of headlights appeared and Helena pushed past Jasmine and Mark, waving her arms high in the air back and forth. The massive, camouflaged colored humvee blasted through the wrecked gate and slammed on the breaks, skidding and screeching to a halt on the flooded pavement. From the top a man popped out with a camouflaged helmet on his head and fatigues. He pointed an automatic rifled at Helena, "Hands in the air and identify yourself," he shouted.

"S.I.N agent Helena Kyarsgaard and these are civilians. Agent Tanner is with a few others up ahead on the path," she turned and nudged her head towards the three men running to the upturned vehicle. "Tell your superiors we are dealing with a Class S demon and infection. He calls himself Belial." The soldier lowered his weapon and she breathed a sigh of relief.

Helena pulled Jasmine and Mark into the grass so that the humvee could move closer in. Behind it several more armored vehicles entered the premises and broke off onto the muddy grass. They fared a bit better in the sticky, flooded mess but even then a few of the trucks got stuck in the ground. Wheels spun but nothing but mud kicked up but five well armed vehicles sat spread out on the front lawn of the mansion.

The last vehicle to pull in was much different. The Cadillac, black as night, stopped outside of the gates. It flashed its brights at the two women and Mark. The back passenger door opened and a rotund, bulky man stepped out puffing on a cigar. He was dressed in a black business suit and growled when the rain immediately snuffed his cigar.

"I don't give a shit. Give them cover fire now! Do not let up on that motherfucker until it stops breathing, and even then make sure it's in five thousand pieces!"

"Mister Simmons!" Helena squealed, dragging Mark and Jasmine with her through the grass and water. Her make-shift dress, caked in mud and gore, didn't curb her confidence as she approached her boss at the gate, "Mister Simmons, Tanner is still up there with three civilians. One might need immediate medical attention. She was in the back of the truck that fuckrod tried to devour." She explained and nodded to Mark, "The boy needs medical attention as well, he has a fucked up wrist."

Simmons glanced over Mark and Jasmine and gave a strong nod of his head, "The medical team is on their way. We are going to hold him at this juncture if we can. I did not believe we would need this much firepower. Get these two civilians into the streets behind us, for some reason this area is the only spot that seems flooded. It is wet back there but not enough that you're swimming in it." He turned his attention back towards the field where the helicopter and humvees continued their relentless assault on Belial. "Congratulations Agent Kyarsgaard, your first outing produced the location of a class S demon. That is one hell of a first assignment. After you're done with them there is an extra outfit and guns in the trunk. Are you alright to fight?"

"Sir, for the past two weeks I've been pretty much violated in more ways than a person can imagine. I want to rip the heart out of that demon more than anyone here," Helena said.

In front of them, where flames engulfed most of the mansion, Belial coughed through the cloud of smoke and ash from the helicopter's assault. The demon howled, clearing its eyes the best it could with its hands and looked to the sky. The eyes on its shoulders narrowed and several tentacles shot out at the annoying hunk of metal. The pilot banked to the right and surged forward while the side gunmen peppered the beast with machine gun rounds. Despite the helicopter coming right for it, Belial was too slow to get a good hit or stick on it.

With Belial distracted Tanner and Stan slid to the upside down truck and Tanner turned, pushing James back, "Kid let us handle this. You and I both know you aren't in a good frame of mind and you'll get in the way. Don't take it as an insult kid; I just don't want to lose you as well if things get hairy up here." Tanner said and coughed as the ash and the smoke created a fog around them. He ducked down and looked inside of the vehicle.

"Just get her out of there. I'll keep on the lookout," James offered.

"Good man," Tanner grunted. He shoved himself inside of the small opening and narrowed his eyes. The flames around the home provided a little light but he also heard no whimpering or screaming. He cleared the smoke a bit and grit his teeth. Kimberly was crumpled on the roof of the hatchback. Tanner saw a lot of blood and her right leg twisted backwards. He followed the path and saw a bloody bone pushing out through her shin. The blood flowed free from that wound and her blonde hair was also matted in crimson. "Son of a bitch, Stan, pullme out!" he said as he gently wrapped his hands around Kimberly's underarms and pulled while scooting back.

Stan took hold of Tanner's pant legs and did as the man asked. He drug Tanner out into the wet grass and Tanner pulled Kimberly out of the vehicle. James saw the damage to her shin and her head, closed his eyes, and looked away. Tanner, ignoring James, put his head to her chest, a hand to her mouth, and shut out everything around them. A few seconds later he scooped Kimberly up and turned away from the truck.

"Stan, James, get your asses in front of me and get the medical team's attention. She's alive but barely," he growled. Another crack of thunder masked the sound of their feet stomping against the watery pavement. Behind them Belial roared again and Tanner turned his head for a quick glance, "Shit."

"I will devour every last ounce of your flesh for this!" Belial shouted, wrapping a thick, sticky tendril around the very truck that Kimberly had once been in. With a heave he launched it into the air, whipping it at the chopper that sprayed shots into its fatty, slimy flesh. A full size truck provided a much harder challenge for the helicopter to swerve away from. As it banked to avoid the oncoming projectile the truck was just too large to dodge. The beaten pick-up crashed into the tail end of the helicopter, busting off the rear propeller and sent the air-born vehicle into a tailspin. The front of the chopper hit the ground first and its nose dug into the wet grass and mud. The propeller spun into the ground and broke off into lethal chunks of steel, slicing the ground to bits and spraying sharp debris in different directions. Two large hunks of metal from the propeller buried into Belial's body but the demon paid no attention to the shrapnel inside of him. He gripped the pieces in his form and pulled the jagged metal shards out, holding both of them in his hands as impromptu weapons.

One of the broken off pieces of propeller seared the ground right behind Stan, James, and Tanner, kicking mud and water onto the three men while Tanner carried Kimberly in his arms. The three looked at one another before double timing it behind the semi-circle of humvees that stood between them and Belial now.

"James, Stan, take her," Tanner barked. He handed Kimberly's limp body to James and turned his attention back to the humvees, "Aim for the heart! So far every fucking thing's weakness has been the heart!" He watched Belial take those two chunks of steel out of his body and groaned, "And now he has weapons, great, just fucking wonderful."

Several well dressed, black suit and tie types poured out of the humvees after they got in position. A young female, brunette, waved at Tanner and threw him a military issued M4A1 assault rifle. Tanner didn't object and caught the weapon, checked the safety, and pressed it tight to his shoulder. He spun around and squeezed the trigger. A short burst of three bullets peppered one of Belial's stray tentacles and left it hanging by a thread.

The creature roared in annoyance.

The entire group of agents lit the scenery with gunfire. Muzzle flashes illuminated the area around them but Belial brought the two propellers across its body and blocked as many shots as it could with its makeshift weapons. Belial took a step towards the agents on the left side of the semi-circle of gunfire before its right side jerked violently backwards. The blade in its right hand shattered an instant before Belial's right arm split from its shoulder. A moment later the speed of sound caught up with the action and everyone leaped a foot in the air after the jarring boom of gunfire reached them.

Tanner turned around to see what caused such a massive hit to the creature and saw the source of the massive shot. Ralph Simmons sat on top of his Cadillac perched behind a Barrett M107 sniper rifle. Only half of Ralph's pudgy face peeked out from behind the scope of the five foot long weapon. The front end of the rifle sat propped on twin legs while Ralph burdened the backend weight against his shoulder along with the grip he had on the handle. He waved to Tanner and pointed to his head. A large, noise canceling set of headphones covered Simmons' ears and Tanner realized what Ralph was signaling.

"Cover your ears!"

Tanner covered his ears, ringing as they were, and the other agents that saw him do so followed suit. Everyone's heard bells at that point, but the second shot from that fifty caliber rifle proved less pain with a bit of blocking.

Belial howled in pain after its arm had been blown off from the close proximity of the powerful gun. It turned its body around as the second blast went through him. The pain of the bullet shredding through him came first, and then that explosive roar followed. A small spurt of black blood shot from the front of Belial's body but a huge amount of flesh and blood exploded out of his back along with that fearsome round. Belial's two large, shoulder eyeballs blinked a few times before the creature's legs gave out and the creature plopped onto the ground, sitting upright but slumping forward while those eyes rolled into the back of its shoulders.

The crowd stood silent after Belial slumped down. Fingers were on triggers through that whole semi-circle for a minute, waiting for any signs that the creature was still alive. Blood continued to fall from the ripped stump of its right arm and the holes that riddled its body dripped the thick substance as well. A few agents touched their ears and approached the downed behemoth.

"Keep your distance! That shot looked clean but keep on your guard." Tanner shouted as the agents approached the downed demon.

Helena slung her red hair back into a ponytail as she approached Simmons from behind. She changed into her own black suit and decorated her feet with a pair of sleek, black dress shoes, "A little warning before you use that thing boss. I'm still hearing bells and I was back fifty feet." She said, thumbing back at the medical vehicle that set up camp.

"Are the civilians accounted for?"

"Yes sir. Mark Sinfield has a shattered wrist and will need surgery on it as soon as possible. Kimberly Cross suffered a very nasty broken leg and a concussion. She is stable but she will not be in any shape to be debriefed when the time comes. The rest of them have a few bumps and bruises but right now they will live."

"Excellent. Miss Kyarsgaard you have my apologies for not issuing help sooner. I never imagined I would see Belial come across our radar."

"I'll make sure to tell Tanner you said that."

"I would appreciate it if you didn't."

Helena smiled and turned her attention towards the four agents that crept towards Belial. There were two agents on each side of the demon's body with guns drawn. They made slow, careful steps around the massive body of the beast to look at its back to see the damage it had done. Its legs twitched here and there, but it was not enough movement to warrant a retreat. The four agents were still on the defensive, however, when they rounded the large body of the beast.

A large chunk of Belial's back vanished with the exit of the large bullet. The spinal cord of the beast, along with the inner workings of the monster was on full display to the four agents.

"Sir it was a direct hit. I see the demon's heart and half of it is gone. You blew it in two sir," the agent reported and lowered his weapon.

The heart throbbed once.

49

Cheers echoed throughout the stormy night upon the confirmation that Belial's heart had been decimated by the giant caliber bullet that pierced its chest. The agents clapped and Vincent Tanner breathed a sigh of relief. The thunder and lightning continued to rain across the sky in its erratic pattern and the only way they could see through the thick rain was due to the burning mansion behind them.

Tanner stood halfway between the beast and his boss. He tapped his foot on the ground a few times and noticed that the flooded ground split open a little bit. He turned his attention to the pavement and noticed the cracks in the cement as well.

"I don't think this ground is going to be stable for much longer," he called out to the agents still surrounding Belial.

Tanner growled as his shoes stuck in the muddy ground and he had to force his legs into the air comically to escape the sucking muck with each footstep he took until he stood upon the pavement on the other side of the crack. He scraped his shoes on the pavement and shivered in the rain now that his adrenaline had worn off. His heart stilled to a normal pace and the four agents that surrounded Belial began their retreat.

A moment later a scream pierced the storm. Tanner's head shot up and he watched as one of the agents, a female with her brunette hair tied into a ponytail, was flung into the air by one of Belial's tentacles. Tanner couldn't do a thing as she fell into the large maw and nothing but a shower of red shot out from that grinding mouth. Belial stood tall in an instant and every wound that once decorated his body started sealing shut. The monstrosity roared again with full vigor, shaking the foundation it stood on.

"Did you really think a tiny bullet would kill me? You arrogant, prideful scum," Belial roared as he started his charge.

"Open fire, kill it with extreme prejudice," Simmons growled.

The ground shook with every thunderous step Belial made towards the three retreating agents. One by one each agent became a victim to the lashing tentacles that fed each agent into that grinding death maw where blood was the only thing that could escape. With each stomp on the ground Belial made, however, increased the size of the large crack formed in the land and Tanner followed both of the lines until the end.

"Simmons, Helena, blast the ground," Tanner shouted as he started his own retreat with the other agents that had to abandon the stuck vehicles.

Belial continued his charge but another powerful fifty caliber round blasted the creature right in the maw, sending it stumbling back a few feet. Simmons reloaded and continued to assault the creature with round after powerful round, "In the trunk agent Kyarsgaard. I don't pack light in the least."

Helena rushed to her boss' trunk and fumbled with the lock a few times before finally releasing the latch, "Holy shit!"

Simmons packed himself to the brim with high powered weaponry. The massive grenade launcher attached to the hood of his Cadillac drew her attention first but she also noticed a few blocks of standard dynamite. Good old fashioned dynamite. "Christ boss, I'm going to start referring to you as Yosemite Sam from now on. Dynamite? Really?"

Another ear piercing shot rang throughout the night sky, "Always pack for a rainy day agent. Remember that."

Helena piled some dynamite under her arm and took the grenade launcher from the trunk. It was empty, of course, but she found the large explosive rounds in a container next to the dynamite. One by one she popped the rounds in and slammed the cylinder shut. She didn't bother shutting the trunk of Simmons' Cadillac and rushed out to meet Tanner who had four other agents following behind him.

"I'm pretty sure the fuse is waterproof. Can't fish with a wet fuse you know?"

Tanner snatched the five sticks of dynamite from Helena and surveyed the space from the edge of the land facing south, and the edge of the land facing north. Belial was almost to that line. Tanner distributed the dynamite out to the remaining agents and turned towards Belial.

"Drive him back!"

Tanner and the agents spread out just as Helena launched the first explosive shell Belial's way. The armed tip slapped against Belial's belly and exploded into shrapnel and flames. Belial roared and stumbled backwards several yards with his massive legs stabbing into the ground to keep him from wobbling too much.

The ground cracked further.

The agents and Tanner spread out as far from each other as they could and buried the dynamite into the ground. Each agent kept an eye on Belial as three more rounds exploded against its chubby body. The ground was wet, cracking, and sticky. That made for the perfect placeholder for each stick of dynamite. Tanner knelt in the middle and watched Belial try and fight forward, "Light'em up!" He cried out to the other four agents.

Each stick of dynamite lit with some effort. The waterproof fuses burned quickly as the four of them retreated back as fast as they could.

Helena had two shots left in the six round grenade launcher and she pulled the trigger again, lobbing another shell at Belial. The demon reacted fast to the fifth shell launched and wrapped a sickly tentacle around the edge of the round before it hit its body. The tentacle reared back to throw it straight back at Helena. Before it let go, however, another clap of gunfire rang through the night and struck the grenade, exploding it against Belial's tentacle and near its maw.

The blast knocked the beast onto its side. Belial roared again from the blast and its legs waved in the air to try and regain its balance. It had to use its arm to push itself back to a sitting position. By now chunks of flesh and bone slid and dangled from the front of its body and its side. The grenade rounds damaged the beast but couldn't finish the job. As those sticks of dynamite fizzled further down, however, Tanner could only hope this would buy them some time.

The first blast came from the southernmost stick of dynamite to the south. The explosion rocked the ground everyone stood on like an earthquake and the first stick to the north went off and did the same. Dirt, grass, water, and mud kicked into the air and formed a huge crater in the land. Each stick had blown enough land up on the two sides that the last three explosions did more than Tanner expected. As Belial stomped its large body down on the ground again the other three sticks exploded almost at the same time. Belial, who was far enough from the blast to not pay it any attention, bellowed when it realized what Tanner had done.

The manor that sat on the edge of the cliff continued burning and crumbling to the ground. The edge of the cliff, standing strong for centuries, started to collapse. Tanner took his revolver out and ensured he had a few shots left as the dynamite forced the rest of the crack in the ground to split and break apart. The land Belial was on began falling.

"No! You think a little fall is going to hurt me?" The demon shouted at Tanner as its legs dug deep and charged while the land split and cracked. The demon ran uphill at this point while the edge it stood on collapsed. It huffed and growled, both eyes on Tanner who had the revolver pointing right at him.

Tanner squeezed the trigger and blew one of the eyeballs which sat on Belial's shoulder out, "Not at all. I expect the jagged rocks below to do more than hurt you."

Belial roared once more when its eye was damaged by that bullet. The creature stood its ground, however, and continued charging up that falling path.

"Your soul is mine Vincent Tanner!" It screamed as its final tentacle whipped itself at Tanner. The agent shifted his arm to the left and fired again; taking out Belial's other eye. The tentacle went wide, sailing over Tanner's head from the second shot that blinded Belial permanently.

The creature roared and stumbled on the shaking ground. It swung with wild abandon to try and grab onto anything it could with that last tentacle but found nothing. The rest of the ground split away from the mainland and took Belial with it. Tanner stood at the edge of the cracked cliff and peered over while Belial bellowed. The screaming stopped in an instant and Tanner peered over to see what caused the sudden stop. The constant rain and darkness from the night didn't help him see anything at all, but as the lightning flashed he spotted Belial.

Tanner could see the heart of the beast pulsating around a blunt edge of a rock formation below. The rest of Belial's body split in several places from the spiked pit of rocks and water below. Waves crashed into

Belial's body as the demon did its best to use one arm to scrape the heart back into its body. The black heart of the beast was just out of reach, however, along with several other organs that dripped from the rocky deathtrap. Belial arched once to try and obtain his heart and just could not reach it. The beast laid back and the massive arm dropped into the ocean. The lifeless body stilled completely but that black heart continued to beat.

50

"Demons never die, do they?" Stan Freason asked as everyone involved aside from Kimberly Cross and Mark Sinfield sat underneath an emergency tent which was set up just inside of the gate. The storm died down and much to Stan's surprise the sun wasn't shining. "I mean you said that the heart needed to be contained. Does that mean that Belial is still alive?"

"Why hasn't the sun come out? I mean we beat him right? And he was causing all this trouble with the weather so why is it still so dark?" James asked before Tanner could reply to Stan.

The agent of S.I.N rubbed his head, "For one it's around one o'clock in the morning I think, secondly we are not sure if Belial is dead or not. For all intents and purposes it's dead. The body hasn't moved and our team is extracting that heart from the rocks as we speak. I believe the heart needs a host. I think that book was an extension of the demon itself and the real parasite is that black heart. The plan is to keep the heart separated in half and ensure it can never join together again. I think buried in opposite oceans would be the best bet and if he is alive in that heart then he will be imprisoned for a very, very long time."

James Newberry shivered under the warming blanket everyone in the tent had been provided with to fight the freezing cold they had been subjected to, "Not good enough for that freak. Kimberly is going to be alright, right?"

Tanner nodded, "We have the best medical field team taking care of her right now. She's suffered a broken leg and a pretty nasty concussion but it could have been a lot worse." He shifted his attention to Helena and patted her knee, "You're handling this all really well. Actually you all are."

Helena shrugged as she sat in her own chair, curled up in her blanket, "This was my first assignment Vincent. If I didn't see this through and got all erratic it wouldn't reflect too well on my record. I'm a wreck right now Tanner but we sort of have other people to worry about," she pointed at Jasmine, Stan and James.

James dismissed the thought with a wave of his hand, "I'm fine. Mentally scarred for life but I'm fine."

Jasmine shivered a bit under the blanket and clung to Stan's side. She didn't say a word.

"I'm sorry for your losses. All of yours," Tanner said, "I empathize with you entirely and I am sorry I wasn't honest with you all to begin with. Though if I was to tell you all that I was an investigator of the supernatural right off the bat I don't think that would have helped either." His eyes drifted between the three of them, but came to rest on Stan's chest, "In spite of that I think we need to know how you weren't affected by Belial's book."

Before Stan could answer Jasmine placed her hand on his chest, "He has an artificial heart. A temporary replacement from an attack he suffered a few months ago. It's why we came on this vacation." She spoke just above a whisper. She also wasn't looking at anyone at the moment, just staring down at the ground.

Tanner thought about that fact for a few moments, "I'm not one to believe in fate, or destiny, or any of that but without you Stan we might all be dead now. All of you showed impressive bravery today in a situation that any normal person would have gone insane from. I can't make what happen just disappear but know that both Helena and I are grateful for how courageous you all have been. You're a special group of people."

The flap of the large emergency tent spread and Ralph Simmons stepped through. With a signature cigar in his mouth, taking several puffs at that, he turned his attention square on Tanner. "You're right about that Tanner; we have a special group of survivors on our hands. In fact I have to admit this situation could have been much, much worse."

Stan turned his attention to the portly man and sighed, "Mister

Simmons we have been through a lot. We lost family and friends in this insanity. I mean Christ that boy Mark lost his entire family."

"And I assure you, Mister Freason, he will be taken care of for a very long time. This is not the first time a child has become an orphan because of an event like this. He will not be issued a padded cell either. We are a very well funded company and we help take care of victims of tragedies like this."

Tanner rolled his eyes and sat back in his chair, "I have to admit for a bureaucrat you actually showed some stones out there boss. Going to actually start doing field work again?"

Simmons shook his head, "This was a matter of pride agent Tanner. You are welcome for the bail out as well, considering you broke every rule in our books to come out here."

"You did take your sweet time."

"You know how bureaucratic bullshit works Tanner. Not all of us can enjoy the freedom of telling our bosses to shove it while we play the maverick."

Stan shook his head, "Sorry to interrupt but what about the organization itself? I am thinking that 'Fantasia Getaways' isn't what it seems, is it?"

Simmons puffed on his cigar again, "You'd be right about that Mister Freason. We have several agents descending on the headquarters as we speak. Chances are it is lesser demons working for Belial. In any case we aren't expecting much resistance. Rumors have already spread that you were unaffected by Belial's magic. I find that highly interesting."

Tanner butted in, "He's got a fake heart Simmons. He's apparently waiting for a transplant. Belial's magic, or whatever he was using, seems to only affect biological hearts for the point of infection. That being the case, since Stan assisted in the destruction of a class S demon I think we could find him a new heart, correct? Didn't we have an experimental heart that was waiting for a new home?" he grinned.

Simmons' eyes shot daggers at Tanner.

Helena sighed and rubbed her head, "Sir this group has been through a lot. I know how Tanner is but he believed in me and what I tried to accomplish here. It was supposed to be a simple search of missing people and it wound up to be far higher than my pay grade. We have five civilians whose lives are not going to be the same after this. You know how well we compensate for their cooperation."

Ralph Simmons took another drag from his cigar and knocked a few ashes to the ground. He stood with one foot forward and placed a hand on his hip. His hand holding his cigar rubbed his chin while he looked over the three survivors and his two agents. It was his turn to grin.

"You know what Helena you are absolutely right. You always were our best desk jockey until your promotion," he began and stroked his chin again; "You're all earning a promotion after this. That is, of course, if the Freasons and Mister Newberry would accept a job offer from us."

Stan and Jasmine's jaws both dropped and James looked up from the ground, bruised and a little worse for the wear than the other two.

"Excuse me?" James asked.

"Tanner has filled you in on who we are, right? We belong to an organization that hunts everything that goes bump in the night. We are the Supernatural Investigation and Neutralization agency, or syndicate, whichever you prefer. S.I.N for short," Simmons said. He continued to stand in his contemplative stance and looked Stan and Jasmine over, "We could use a mind like yours and the courage your wife has Mister Freason. You figured out Belial's magic before anyone else and according to Tanner you had your suspicions all along. That kind of gut feeling isn't something you train for. You're born with it." He turned to James, "I heard that you and your friend Jimmy were well versed in the supernatural from a mythological point of view James. I would be honored to have you as one of our researchers."

Stan's eyes were as wide and his jaw still slack. He composed himself a moment later, "Are you insane? We lost two people very dear to us and you want us in this line of work? You're crazy!"

Jasmine leaned up and kissed her husband on the cheek, "Let's do it Stan."

Everyone in the tent was silent. Stan turned to his wife slowly and looked at her with that same shocked look, "Jasmine what are you talking about? We can't do this."

"I lost my sister and brother-in-law Stan. I know I sound crazy right now, and I think I am but we both have been through too much trauma to just ignore what happened to us tonight. We know things other people shouldn't know and that is going to keep us both tossing and turning all night long after we leave this place. We are going to be in constant fear of wondering what else is out there and I know Maggie and Ryan wouldn't want that for us and if the situation was different you know we wouldn't want them to feel like victims their whole lives. This is an opportunity to start a new life together and I have never seen you so alive than what you did confronting that demon. I don't want to see that spark die because this Belial freak is going to be the new Jason Jacobs."

James looked at the flabbergasted Stan and nodded his head, "She makes a lot of sense," he turned to Ralph, "I'm in if Kimberly pulls through alright. If there are more things like that in the world I want to be prepared for it. I don't know how Kimberly will feel about it but I think I could talk her into moving to wherever you want us, all expenses paid of course. I'm a poor college student after all."

Stan weighed his options. He narrowed his eyes and looked towards the ground and went through the motions in his head. "I don't want to be a victim any more. I sure as hell don't want any more nightmares," he rationalized and sighed, picking his head back up from its downward position. "If we come on then I want trained. I want to be physically capable of handling anything that comes at me."

Ralph grinned, "Sounds like a deal to me. Tanner will be more than happy with his new position as a captain."

"Captain?" Stan asked.

Tanner's jaw dropped at that announcement, "Oh no, no, no, no, no. I am not a team player Simmons and you know that! I mean hell I barely trained Helena and look at the trouble she got into; which, by the way, wasn't necessarily my fault to begin with but the fact remains I do not run team operations."

"Well to be honest Tanner this promotion isn't a reward, but rather a punishment for breaking the rules. I know what came of it, but still the rules were broken. It will be your duty, when we all get back to headquarters, to train these civilians. They will be your team and I am quite eager to see how you handle it when someone breaks the rules." Simmons laughed.

Helena nudged Tanner's side, "Its one hell of a raise Tanner. Besides I'm sure after discovering a rather powerful demon that Mister Simmons will be more than happy to promote me to supervisor underneath you. I think that is fair right?"

"You're pushing it Helena," Simmons said, "But you guys worked well together and deserve some recognition. We will hold a funeral service for those involved and the agents we lost. Try and get some sleep tonight and do your best to relax in the next few days. As for the three of you it is going to be a wild, terrifying world you're going to be exposed to, but even I would never have any other life if given the chance."

Tanner stood up and winced. Without the adrenaline rushing through his body the cuts to his side throbbed. He stood before the three survivors and extended his hand, "Welcome to S.I.N."